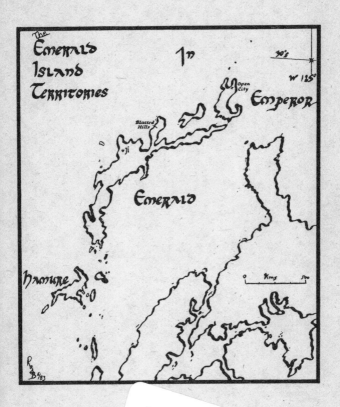

The
Emerald
Island
Territories

Emperor

Open City

Blasted Hills

Ji

Emerald

Hamure

0   Kms   50

W 125°

D1415165

the blue tiles to the farthest stall and closed the door behind her. From a pouch in her notebook she took a cotton first-aid pad to replace the sodden one she removed.

The water splashed as Ellia dropped the used pad into the toilet and tripped the flush. As the rumbling wash of water began, Ellia turned to leave, but then froze with her hand on the door latch. The water was not going down! She groaned.

Suddenly somebody booted open the restroom door. Ellia's heart skipped a beat when she heard the painfully disharmonic humming of Personnel Master Hanssan. Most of the minors hated him because he administered the grading tests at the beginning of the cycle, but Ellia disliked him because he pried into people's backgrounds, making her his number one mystery.

As the man took a nearby stall, Ellia watched the water rise. She prayed silently, but it didn't help. The water spilled over until a huge puddle had spread across the tiles. No boy would passively accept such an affront to his dignity; Ellia swore loudly for effect.

Hanssan chuckled. Moments later, she heard a stall door open and close. Hanssan hummed as he washed and dried. Pausing in his tune long enough to chuckle again, he finally booted open the restroom door and departed.

Ellia sighed and bowed her head against the stall door, vainly hoping that her new headache would go away. Quickly, she stooped and fished the wet pad from the toilet. Wrinkling her nose, she unlatched the door and exited without looking up.

"So, Minor *Elthen*," a voice greeted her. Ellia jumped as her heart tried to fly from her chest. In a flash she had the used pad behind her. "Evening," the personnel master finished personably.

"E-evening, Master Hanssan," she stuttered, her legs shaking.

The gawky young man smiled and nodded. His black

hair was shoulder length, marking his origin in one of the continental colonies. "Had a *minor* problem there, did you, Elthen?"

Ellia did not smile at his quip. Barely able to speak, she nodded.

The man lost his merry expression. "What is that you have behind your back, Minor?"

"What?"

"Clean out your ears, boy. I asked you what you are hiding behind your back like a scared little rooster? Contraband perhaps?"

"N-no. No, Master Hanssan."

"Then what is it?"

Ellia swallowed hard.

"I asked you what it is! Do you wish me to take it from you?"

"You really wouldn't want to do that, Master."

"Well, show the thing then!"

Her hands shaking, she presented the dripping pad. Hanssan's eyes widened.

"You're bleeding, Minor!"

"It's a sore," Ellia blurted, feeling on the verge of tears. "On my last cattle drive I became tangled in my throw rope, and it burnt my side. Th—the sore's healing now."

"Blind priests, boy! Personal modesty is no reason to risk an infection. If I could only knock some intelligence into you minors! It's to the doctor, *now*."

"Master?"

"What now?"

"Can I get rid of this, please?"

"Yes, yes." He gestured. "Get rid of it. How someone so smart could act so stupid, I don't know." Ellia entered another stall and flushed away the evidence, that time with no problem. She began to perspire. She had managed to dodge the medical examination at the beginning of the ritual cycle; this was the fifth time she had run away from home, and as was inevitable, she had been caught again.

One

Forgive me Kantilphanes, but the Codex of
the Unification *is not honored everywhere. I
cannot hold my tongue. Protect me.*

Ellia's favorite study hall was on the third floor of the
shrine's main secular building. From there she gazed
through a black laquered window frame to the square
below. Cool air wafted in as she stared out and occasionally cringed.

In the square, a boy tied to a creosoted post received
lashes from the master administrator. Repeatedly the
electric whip cracked, but the lash left no welts. The
boy's cries were painful to Ellia. Jan was barely twelve
years old, yet he deserved his punishment; he had stu-
pidly stampeded twenty-six head of cattle off a cliff
and killed his horse at the same time.

The whip snapped. Ellia twitched sympathetically
as the boy screamed again. The punishment was brutal,
and though watching was optional, many viewed the
spectacle that cold, gray evening.

If they ever caught her, Ellia wondered, could she
expect any better treatment?

She attempted to return to her textbooks, but the boy's screams distracted her. She felt ill. Shutting her book, she replaced it on a dusty shelf. She had never done anything more risky than running away to enroll at the Stone Coast shrine, but only there could a boy obtain military training. The required labor was at least as exciting as could be found anywhere: cattle husbandry, usually from horseback. Not all could handle such tough work—Jan was an obvious example—but to Ellia it was fun.

She slid her chair under the table, ignoring its squeak and the continuing whimper from outside. She wished the pains in her sides and back would just go away. Taking her notebook in hand, the girl adjusted her black uniform and left the study hall. In the corridor she nodded to several boys whose names she knew. Suddenly feeling nauseated, she detoured to a restroom. She opened the door with a masculine kick of her boot, wishing she were male in more than just outward appearance.

At a washbasin, she splashed cold water across her face. Cheeks tingling, she stared at her image in the mirror above the sinks. She had almond-shaped eyes with irises of a rare, dark green; her mahogany hair had been cut to a boyish four-centimeter length and dyed black as a disguise. Even at eighteen ritual cycles, though her facial structure was perhaps too soft and her physique too light, she could still pass for a boy of twenty-one cycles. A girl of her age and build intruding into all-male territory had only one major problem, and that came once a lunar month. Ancient customs of privacy afforded to all—shrine faculty as well as the minors—gave Ellia a private sleeping cubicle and the use of a private shower. Even in the fields, persons were expected to walk some distance away before relieving themselves; custom went a long way toward allowing Ellia to preserve the secret of her femininity.

Ellia waited quietly for a few seconds. The stalls were unoccupied. Her heart beating fast, she crossed

TEST OF FAITH

The recorded music sailed up the scale, though the pulsing bass remained steady. The white-furred wolf-humanoid began to dance around Ellia, eying the girl with a manic expression.

Ellia swallowed and tried to relax.

The beat doubled, and Chriz suddenly transformed into a wild thing. Her claw knives became a silver gleam. She jumped in front of Ellia, landing spread-legged, then struck. Then, twirling, she danced off.

Ellia felt the right side of her face give way. Skin separated along parallel gashes just below her eye. Drops of liquid spattered on the plastic apron over her lap as pain engulfed her.

"*Djo*, Hunter!" Chriz cried.

THE GIRL FROM THE EMERALINE ISLAND

Robert S. Blum

A Del Rey Book

BALLANTINE BOOKS • **NEW YORK**

A Del Rey Book
Published by Ballantine Books

Library of Congress Catalog Card Number: 83-91265

ISBN 0-345-30847-6

Manufactured in the United States of America

First Edition: May 1984

Cover art by Linda Benson

To Mom (of course)—
and for all the Ellia's in this world.

Acknowledgments

Many people over many years made my career as an author possible. I must thank Carole Lax and Jerry Yefsky for being my biggest fans. Thanks to Sam Lax for all his generous support. Thank you Michele for being one of my first readers and for being a friend. Thank you, Mrs. Schlesinger, at Fairfax High, for all your encouragement—I told you I would become a writer. Thank you, Prof. Eisenstein, for writing "Go on" on the first chapter of this story. Thanks also to Deborah Paine, who taught me that I could write and how to make my writing enjoyable to read. And finally I must thank Ashley, Owen, and Shelly, who have all worked their tails off in my behalf.

Or maybe not! Smiling momentarily, she returned to stand near the personnel master.

"Where is the sore?" he asked.

"On my left side, just under my belt."

"Must be painful."

"It is," Ellia grumped and kicked open the wooden door to the corridor. She hit it hard enough that it banged against the wall. Hanssan gave her a puzzled look but kept his distance. At the end of the hallway, they descended a staircase to the first floor where Ellia turned away from the building's exit and proceeded down another corridor. The infirmary was outside, in the priests' quarters behind the temple.

"Where are you going?" the personnel master asked, glaring at her. Next to the granite statues of the old warlords who watched over the hall with terrible eyes, Hanssan appeared harmless.

Hefting her notebook, Ellia faced him. "Do you mind if I get rid of these? My cubicle is just down the hall."

She could see a flush of anger color Hanssan's swarthy features, but he said, waving her on, "Yes, yes, go ahead."

Ellia spun neatly on her heels, and her bootfalls clattered across brown tiles as she turned into her cubicle maze. Breathing rapidly, she tore open her privacy screen and threw her notebook on the bunk within. She hated to leave; none of her previous lodgings had been half this comfortable. But gray woolen blankets, electric lamps, and books were minor luxuries to trade for her freedom—or to prevent the indignity of discovery. She opened the closet door and grabbed her warmest jacket, then fastened a knifebelt around her waist.

At the entrance to her cubicle she stopped briefly and silently said farewell. Another dogday, just ten plain, uneventful days, and this run would have lasted two ritual cycles. No use being sentimental, Ellia thought, and shut the privacy curtain.

Ignoring the scent of jasmine incense from an occupied cubicle, Ellia approached the window. The balance mechanism in the sash had centuries on her, but one good heave brought it open. She had just moments before Hanssan would realize she had disappeared; she had better be gone when he began searching for her.

She landed in the bushes outside the secular building. Keeping between the ornamental greenery and the brick wall, she followed a dirt path around the side of the building. Soon, through branches covered with fragrant pink flowers, she saw the square she had viewed earlier. The spectators had left a few minutes before, when the main event, having passed out, had been removed. Only the old black flogging pole remained.

Glancing once more at the pole, she left the bushes and crossed the dusty square. As she strode through the shrine grounds, she passed others in black uniforms. Near the temple she passed a priest clothed in emerald green robes, but the old man merely eyed the jeweled knife at Ellia's waist and shook his gray head. Ellia entered the stable where the pleasantly familiar smells of hay and horse droppings made her smile. A couple of horses snorted as she entered. Her luck held: none of the stable hands were around. As usual, the door to the tack room stood ajar. Ellia grabbed reins, bridle, and blanket, then selected a light messenger saddle which was little more than a piece of leather to pad the horse's spine. She picked out the best gelding, offered him a handful of oats, and saddled him up. Sounds came from behind her; quickly she gave a last jerk to tighten the cinch, then mounted.

"You, Minor," the stable master's gravelly voice called from the far end of the stable. Half-blind, the old man probably couldn't even see her. "What are you doing there? Huh?"

Turning the restless animal, she replied, "I'm stealing a horse."

"A horse? Huh? Well, if it begins to rain, bring the animal back, you hear? No broken bones. Hear me?"

Ellia smiled and called back, "I hear!" She reined the horse out.

Across the green, in front of the granite walls of the temple, Hanssan was yelling something to a priest. He stopped mid-gesture when he spotted Ellia. "Elthen!"

She pressed the horse into a gallop. Hanssan ran a few steps after her, but the red dust kicked up behind her left him coughing.

Riding felt good: the air on her face and in her hair, the sound of hooves pounding in her ears, the rhythm of the animal between her legs. She guided the horse through the huge southern gates. Centuries ago during the reign of the warlords, the shrine had been the major stronghold of the Great Chi. The granite rubble of the western wall demonstrated the power modern weapons held over the past, but then only the physical artifacts of society had really changed, as Ellia well knew—a woman's place then was a woman's place still. She brought the horse around the eastern wall, following the paved asphalt road that branched off through the forest toward the north.

She wondered how irritated she had left Personnel Master Hanssan. Having seen her riding out, the man would be even more furious: not twenty ritual cycles before, there had still been one place on the Emerald Island that put men to death for horse stealing.

Her best chance of escape was to catch the north-bound train that would pass along the coast just after dusk. She might make it. She urged the black to keep up his gallop.

Pine trees gave way to nearly bare deciduous fare trees as the land sloped toward the coast. The sunset soon painted the cloudy sky mauve; distant thunder rumbled as Ellia left the forest. Her mount began to balk. Impatiently she walked him so he could cool off. She scanned the road behind, but found no indication of pursuit.

The darkness grew quickly, as if a blanket had been

tossed over the world. Phantom images began to co-
alesce amongst the trees; twice Ellia was almost
spooked enough to go on before her horse was ready.
She led the horse for almost twice the five-minute margin she had allowed herself, then checked between his
forelegs and found the skin only slightly warm.

Ellia remounted and rode into a recently harvested
grain field. The horse liked this trotting pace better and
whinnied; his good spirits battled the lonely feeling that
often followed Ellia. She had always been separate
because of her ambitions. At the shrines she could
befriend the boys, but only with caution. She defined
loneliness as one of the conditions necessary to bet-
tering her life.

The evening winds wafted salt air her way. Suddenly looking behind her, Ellia saw the orange glow
of torches. Squinting, she counted three sources—a
minimum of three masters were following her, probably more.

"King of the Dron!" she swore, using a provincial
curse as she urged her mount on. She counted her
advantages: a relatively cool horse, a definite destination, a good kilometer lead. Not much, she knew.
Swallowing hard, she began to pray.

Long minutes passed, and still her pursuers trailed
her through the dark. She must be leaving a trail a child
could follow. Already the fields had given way to weedy
heath and pastures that sloped down to a flat, dark
horizon which could only be the sea. The railroad tracks
had to be nearby.

In the distance the single lamp of the lead locomotive appeared suddenly, having pierced a wall of
fog. "You won't have to keep up this pace long," she
assured the horse, patting him on the neck. Pulling on
the reins, she guided the gelding to her right. As if he
really understood that the end to his exercise lay ahead,
the horse lengthened his gait to as close to a gallop as
was possible on unsure ground. Over her shoulder,

Ellia saw that in a special saddle behind each torch-bearer sat a chee, a type of spotted coursing cat. Chee were domesticated hunting animals—was Hanssan *that* determined to catch her? Ellia felt perspiration cool on her neck. She appeared to have sufficient lead to flag down the train, board it, and have it rolling again before her pursuers could stop her. Let it be, she prayed.

Only when she could hear the roar of the locomotive's engines, did she abruptly remember that she wore a black uniform and rode on a black horse. Even her hair and the saddle were black. And she had nothing to make a fire. Standing on the tracks would be fool-hardy, she knew. Swearing, she realized she would have to pace the train and try to catch the engineer's attention. The horse's hooves scrunched on the ballast of the tracks as the huge diesel roared closer.

The dirt access road beside the three metal rails appeared smooth. The torchmen were gaining: they were only two-thirds of a kilometer back now. Ellia kept the horse cantering in the direction the train traveled.

"Don't worry, whatever your name is," she assured the suddenly skittish horse as the diesel approached. "It won't hurt you. No, boy. You'll just have to race it a short distance. You can do that, right, boy?" Although she patted her mount gently, it shied and pawed the gravel. Ellia's heart pounded.

The train thundered up to meet the horse and its rider. As the headlamp flashed across them, Ellia heeled the horse in the ribs. Neighing loudly, the gelding balked, then broke into a frenzied gallop down the access road. First one diesel engine passed, then another, pulling a long line of boxcars and tankers. Two silvery passenger cars followed the engines.

"Hey! Anybody!" she cried against the roar of the engines and the clatter of metal wheels. Waving one arm and shouting, she tried to attract someone's attention, anyone's. Finally she pawed for her knife belt, aimed, and threw it hilt first, striking the engineer's left-hand windshield.

"Halt!" a voice barked somewhere ahead of her. Ellia's mount immediately slowed. A lone horse and rider—torchless and without a chee—blocked the road. The man wore a black uniform.

Ellia's horse reared in fright, and Ellia held on for dear life.

"Minor Elthen, surrender yourself!" She recognized Hanssan as he maneuvered closer.

"Rot!" she yelled, savagely kicking her mount. The animal reared—and Ellia was thrown.

She landed on the gravel just centimeters from the shrieking wheels of the speeding train. Drenched in cold sweat, she scrambled to her feet when the train had passed and crossed the tracks into darkness, clawing her way through the saltbrush.

"No minor is going to get away with stealing my horse!" a man yelled over the diminishing racket of the train. "Release the cats!"

Ellia stifled a scream. Throat afire and breath ragged, she ran through the brush.

Suddenly her boot found a large root in a thicket and she tripped. Then she froze when a massive jaw full of sharp teeth clamped snugly around her throat.

Just how well-trained are these cats, anyway? Ellia wondered. Then she fainted.

"Minor Elthen, wake up!" a young voice demanded.

Warm sunlight streamed in on Ellia's face, and for a moment she thought she had overslept again. But that was only wishful thinking. She found herself in a dirty corner of a punishment cell, covered haphazardly with hay. Her uniform had been confiscated, replaced by a colorless smock and britches.

They knew she was a girl.

"What is wanted of me?" she asked the neatly dressed boy with Karta Coast red hair.

The guard blinked, looked at his companion, then shrugged and faced Ellia. "Minor—" he started. He cleared his throat. "Elthen, your presence is required."

"About what?"

"You stole Master Administrator Mikitsu's horse." The two guards led the frightened girl from her cell into the early morning sunshine. The brisk air, which fluttered the hem of her smock, invigorated the girl.

Ellia stopped breathing, though, when they dragged her to the square. Only when they bound her hands to the creosoted post did she actually begin to believe what was happening. It was impossible that they should whip a girl.

She strained her neck about, shivering, and caught sight of the master administrator standing before the reviewing chair. He held the silver electric whip. Only the guards and two other masters were present. Though Elthen had proved to be a girl, the master administrator was obviously going to have his satisfaction. The minor population appeared to be prohibited, for the sake of propriety, from witnessing the event. Ellia closed her eyes and tried to regulate her breathing in preparation for the inevitable.

The man left her shivering in the dawn cold a full minute, her hands stretched high above her head. Then she heard bootfalls approaching, and her heart beat wildly. The sound stopped behind her, and she tensed. In one savage swipe, the master ripped her smock to bare her backside, and Ellia bit her tongue to keep from crying out. She flinched when she heard the buzz swarm to life behind her. She had only a moment to recall Jan's punishment a day earlier before she heard the whistle and felt the crack of searing pain against her back.

She clenched her teeth and remained silent.

Again, fire splashed against her back. Her muscles screamed and twitched against the electric attack. Ellia clenched her teeth so hard her head shook. Again the snap. How could it hurt more each time?

She refused to scream, refused to whimper. She _would not_ give the master administrator his satisfaction.

Again a monstrous crack. Her legs gave way. Ellia hung by her bound wrists. Time dilated, stretched toward tomorrow. Suddenly the pain became so intense, so fiery, that her mind disassociated from the wrong inflicted on her body. She tried to number the lashes, but after every third, she lost count.

Ellia fainted after nineteen lashes, none of which left visible scars. She had not whimpered even once.

Ellia had made a fool of the master administrator.

Nowhere in the _Codex of the Unification_ or by right of tradition did the master administrator have jurisdiction over a girl; that right belonged to her husband, father, or brother, generally in that order. And in the end, the man had done nothing but make Ellia look brave, a martyr to his efficient, often cruel, policies.

Ellia awoke face down on a pile of hay. A pillow, which had no place in a punishment cell, lay under her head. The movement of her head jolted bruised muscles and static–burned skin.

"Morning."

"Uh!" Ellia started at the unexpected voice, then levered herself around to face a young man in a black uniform. Though one couldn't tell by his babyish face, Ellia knew he was twenty-two cycles old, more than old enough to have taken the Test. Some boys were more reluctant than others: fewer than fifty percent passed the Test, and the rest died. "Sorry, Wren. I am a bit out of sorts today."

"I realize that," he said, cracking a smile. Bending down, he placed a white jar next to her. "A salve for your back. It'll ease the inflammation a bit. You'd find a real whipping would have healed quicker, even if it would have left exterior scars."

"Thanks."

"So you are a girl?" He chuckled. "I would never have guessed."

Ellia chuckled also, then looked significantly toward the stone door that stood ajar.

Wren shook his head. "No, I can't let you go. You should realize that."

"I wouldn't get very far right now, would I?"

Wren nodded. Suddenly he sighed loudly. Facing the wall, he said, "Half of the minors saw what happened this morning. I am sorry, Elthen. Mikitsu made a fool of himself."

"At least someone had the decency to get me a new smock," Ellia said when the boy's voice faltered. He turned to face her.

"It hurts, I bet."

"Blind priests, does it! Aren't you going to get in trouble visiting me?"

"Me, in trouble? No. No one said anything about visiting you, but I had better leave so you can apply the salve. That stuff may stink, but it's made from mapleweed and it works. So put it on, all right?"

He left, locking the door behind him. And so it went. Many visited her, some out of guilt, not a few out of curiosity. Though she was being punished, she had blankets, decent food, a lamp—even books, something no male would normally think to give a woman as Emeraline women were not taught to read.

Late the first day a master visited her to obtain the name of a male relative. She provided a name but refused to tell him anything else except which shrine-school the male relative attended. When the master departed, the anger visible on his face warned Ellia that the master administrator intended to try to get back at her through her family—the one thing she feared most. But they had no means to force the information from her. She had always retained her anonymity; this time would be no different.

*   *   *

After three days, a pair of master guards woke Ellia an hour before dawn. They handed her an emerald-green robe like the ones given girls during the celebrations recognizing their tenth ritual cycle. Then, with one minor at each side, she exited into the brisk early twilight. In the square stood an open carriage, bearing the Stone Coast megalith emblem on its side. A pair of grand northern prancers steamed and snorted in their impatience to be off. At the reins sat Personnel Master Hanssan in a black leather dress jacket and tricorn hat.

"Morning," he said affably as one of the guards gave Ellia a hand up into the carriage. The vehicle tipped twice more as the two guards boarded behind her. Wrapping the inadequate robe tightly around her shoulders, Ellia returned Hanssan's greeting while her teeth began to chatter.

"I trust you slept well," he returned. He clicked his tongue and snapped the reins to set the team going. Hanssan was usually more direct, and Ellia disliked and mistrusted the sudden change in the man's methods.

Hanssan reined the horses down the southern access to the shrine, setting the animals at an easy trot. They rode silently as the western sky brightened above the line of mountains; the only real company Ellia had was her thoughts, the rattle-bump of the carriage, and the grinding of the wheels on the gravel road. Ellia shivered in her seat. She settled back to wait.

The sun rose and warmed her skin. Finally the carriage left the coastal forest and rolled onto the paved main road of Nagasan, a small cannery town important enough to merit a depot on the east-coast rail line. Traffic swarmed all around them, men pushing huge wagons filled high with canned fish, bullock carts filled with farm-fresh greens and driven by men carrying prods to keep their gray animals plodding along, and many others on foot running this way and that on errands. The northerner freight would arrive in a short time, Ellia discovered when the carriage halted at the depot.

Without a word, one of the guards helped her jump down from the carriage. Her bright green girl's robes contrasted with the brown and blue work clothes worn by the locals, and Ellia suddenly felt self-conscious. That she appeared to be a boy being treated as a girl caused many people to stare. Ellia ignored them, telling herself it mattered little what others thought—black-haired Elthen, who had been publicly humiliated, would soon cease to exist, as had Tellsu, Hiroshat, Nguzachi, and Bellsan before him.

Silently she sat on a hard bench beside Hanssan and the guards. For many long minutes, Ellia could only worry, fidget in her uncomfortable seat, and watch the blue waves breaking on the beach, visible between two buildings across the pair of tri-rails. Soon Ellia had trouble keeping her eyes open.

A sudden train whistle startled Ellia out of her seat, and she cried out. The guards grabbed her.

"Where do you think you are going?" Hanssan asked the breathless girl as she was forced back onto the bench. His smile at her discomfort made Ellia bristle. Hanssan chuckled and shook his head.

She replied after she felt the flush leave her face. "Nowhere. Just stretching my legs and being bored senseless, which you doubtless intended me to be." Her outburst attracted the stares of some passers-by.

"My intentions are none of your business, Elthen. Continue being bored and spare our ears, please."

Ellia ignored him and gazed down the tracks. After five more piercing whistles, a shiny silver diesel rounded the bend. Accompanied by the sounds of screeching metal and whirring engines, the train rumbled to a stop.

None of Ellia's escorts approached the train. She sighed loudly and resigned herself to watching the activity about her. Boxcar doors were rolled open to receive a dozen crates stacked for loading. Five palomino mares clopped down a ramp from a livestock car. But the two silver passenger cars most interested Ellia. A conductor helped a few farmers step down. One had a pale wife who seemed intimidated by all the big machines and loud noises about her. The sight made Ellia ill. She had seen too many such women.

A mahogany-haired youth, wearing blue farm pants and a flannel shirt, stepped out next. He looked about, saw the three black uniforms and the green-robed girl, then marched emotionlessly toward them. As Hanssan stood to greet him, the boy's dark green eyes narrowed, and he scowled.

"I am here to escort this girl back to her proper home," he announced with barely disguised irritation. Ellia stared at her bare feet on the wood floor of the train platform in an effort to control her emotions. The train whistle sounded the departure warning.

Taking some papers from his pocket, Hanssan asked, "Are you Nguza Dekellsy?"

"I am not! That worthless cousin of mine, he'll pay for this! No, I am not. He's out searching for this useless slip of a girl as he is half the time," the boy said, roughly taking Ellia's arm. The girl jerked free and fell. Everyone ignored her as she righted herself.

"Oh." Hanssan seemed confused. He examined his papers again. "But it says here the Stone Coast runner found your cousin."

"Well, he didn't."

"Oh? Oh, very well. You *are* related to this girl, aren't you?"

"Thankfully not. Not within third cousins at least."

"What? How do you expect me to release her to you?"

"This is how." The boy fished out a thrice-folded paper from his breast pocket. The careless manner in which he handed over the sheet demonstrated his contempt for military personnel.

"Ah, Adra Chi. That's your name? This looks valid—signature, seal, and all. I guess I could release her to you. No need to keep an expensive freeloader on our land until a close relative can be discovered."

"Smart decision."

Hanssan adjusted his tricorn hat and stared at the boy, who refused to be cowed. The master blinked and asked, "M'administrator Mikitsu of the Stone Coast shrine requests, though, that you confirm the family or clan name of this girl. It is Dekellsy, is it not?"

"I doubt it. Nguza is related to her through his mother."

"It figures. If you don't know her name, could you at least tell me where you are taking her?"

"To the Dekellsy landhold."

"Which is where?"

"Don't you think you are overstepping your authority, sir?" the boy returned smoothly.

"I—Marvelous!" Hanssan gestured briefly at one of Ellia's guards, but though Ellia tensed for trouble, Hanssan only had the young man sign a paper from Mikitsu. Hanssan pocketed the document, then turned to Ellia just as the train whistle sounded the second warning. Already the train was beginning to move.

"You are to go with Adra Chi, Elthen, do you understand? And let me warn you. Should I see you disguised as a boy again, the fact that you are a girl shan't be discovered until some bones have been broken. I hope you realize accidents do happen." He smiled menacingly.

"Rot," Ellia drawled venomously. Her escort caught her left wrist and dragged her toward the last passenger car. Ellia glanced back. She nearly tripped when she saw one of her guards point her out to a stranger who then began to run after the train. So neither Hanssan nor Mikitsu had any intention of giving up. Ellia ran beside her companion, and together they caught the railing at the rear steps to the passenger car.

"Somebody's following us!" Ellia cried. She slipped on the stair and grabbed the railing.

"What!"

Ellia did not reply. The man, breathing hard, his brown hair blowing in the wind, had reached the steps. Ellia flailed out behind her with one fist, then slipped again as the diesel locomotive passed through a rail switch and accelerated unevenly. She fell backwards.

Twisting to keep her balance, she caught the man in the stomach with her foot. He hit the tracks rolling. Ellia landed on her tail upon the edge of the lowest step, cutting her hanging right foot on a railroad tie.

"Ellia!" She was jerked back onto the steps. "Of all the fool things, El!"

Ellia hugged the boy to keep from falling and gazed down the tracks. All she saw of the man she had thrown from the train were his legs. "Kantilphanes!" she cried and buried her face against her escort's flannel shirt. She had not meant to kill the man! Her freedom was not worth that.

"He's moving, he's all right!" the boy said a moment later. She had only time for a confirming glance and a sigh before she was tugged, limping, inside the car and led to a private compartment.

"Oh, Sang!" Ellia cried. She embraced him tightly, then began to cry.

"You crazy girl!" Sang patted Ellia on her back. She allowed herself to be gently pushed into a cushioned seat. As she continued to cry, he tended the gash on her foot with wound sealant from a first-aid kit. When Ellia finally looked up at him with red eyes, he said, "Father is not going to believe this one, my crazy sister."

She laughed. "Want to bet?"

"The Stone Coast yet! *Both* cycles you were gone, or just this last one?"

"Both."

"Ha! You have more courage than I have, El. I figure, when the gods put you together, they told San,

the Oldone, 'We want curls on this one, curly hair.'
Curls. But San is the god with bad ears. Instead, with
one stroke of his chisel he made you one of the girls."

"That's not at all funny!" Ellia cried out, unable to
keep a straight face. They broke into laughter. Assured
finally that his twin was all right, Sang unpacked one
change of his own clothes and a pair of shoes. He
turned around while she dressed.

"Tell me, how did you get caught?" he asked as she
finished buttoning her shirt. Ellia snorted, then sunk
back into her thoughts for a moment.

"Kantilphanes knows, it's not pretty," she began.

Two

The train stopped for the twins about two hours later, leaving them off in a wide valley. The Caran Mountains, snow-capped peaks all, stood between the Stone Coast and the valley. Mighty volcanic Ji could be made out in the far distance. Nearby, the Caran River, muddy and swollen from the recent rain, chewed a swath through newly green pastureland. After they walked two kilometers from the little shack standing sentry on the tri-rails, Ellia and Sang were offered a ride by a local farmer leading a weathered bullock cart.

Eventually they came to familiar farmlands and again had to walk. As they followed a dirt track between recently mowed rye fields, Sang lost his cheerfulness. Ellia noticed, but she remained silent until she made out the thatched roofs of the cooperative.

"Is something wrong?" she asked tentatively.

"There is." He pitched a rock down the road. "I've

been trying to think of a good way to tell you, ever since I heard the call for Nguza. You should have come home at the end of the last ritual cycle, you really should have."

Ellia shivered. "What happened?"

"Fan was rather upset about it—you, that is. Father was worried. What you do always worries him."

Ellia walked a few paces ahead of him, then turned so she could look into his green eyes. "What happened?" she asked again. Her brother looked older, not quite the same boy who had convinced his scared twin sister to run away with him, dressing her in boy's clothes for the first time, eight ritual cycles ago when their mother had died. He had given her the courage to rescue Terra, a girl adopted into the co-op, while providing her first chance to be mistaken for a shrine-school boy; he had given her a taste for adventure. When he kept his lips pursed for too long, Ellia screamed, "What is it?"

"Rand left for the Test—" Rand was their second eldest brother.

"And never returned," Ellia finished, closing her eyes. Sang confirmed her conclusion by his silence—another boy lost to whatever inhabited the Blasted Hills. All males on the island traveled there once in their lives. Those who survived became adults and never revealed the horrors they had found. What hurt Ellia more than her brother's death was that one inescapable fact about herself; she was female. She could only play at the game of being a boy, play as a child would, never to face the cruel probabilities of the Test. Males paid for their privileges. Ellia cheated.

Her brother Rand, as was usual for a brother, had paid little attention to his sister—Sang's friendship was very much an exception. Rand had been someone who did farm chores, ate heartily at the dinner table, and often listened with interest to the stories Father spun before the hearth. Ellia remembered him as a tall boy who liked threadbare overalls and said little. She searched inwardly for a void, but found none. That hurt most.

"There is something else," Sang said.

Ellia saw a brown-haired toddler playing with marbles on the porch of her father's house. The child suddenly froze and stared in the twins' direction. Then, yellow sarong flying, the little girl shot into the open door. "Our eldest brother, Tagii, is married."

"I missed that too, huh? I am not returning to the same family, am I?"

"No, you're not," Sang replied.

Ellia detected the smell of cooking fish in the air and saw chickens busily scratching for grain outside the community barn. Lost in her thoughts, the sound of her stepmother's voice took her by surprise.

"Ellia!" the low-pitched, singer's voice cried. "Is that you?"

Fan stood on the porch, her tall, thin form draped in an emerald-green sarong, her overrobe sleeves rolled above the elbows for kitchen work. Long, black hair lay in disarray over her shoulders; clearly she had been toiling since dawn. The toddler came up beside her, taking hold of her mother's hand and staring at the stranger with scared, almond-shaped eyes.

Her free hand on her waist, Fan said venomously, "You would have done us all a favor by staying away." Ellia halted just in the shadow of the long porch, but before she could reply, Fan continued. "Not one word, not a single word as to whether you were alive or dead! Nearly *two* ritual cycles, girl! Two! And not one word! And now you have the audacity to return?"

"Mama," the toddler interrupted, tugging at her mother's clothes. "Who is that?"

"Your sister, I think," Fan replied in disgust, examining her stepdaughter's appearance.

"I'm sorry." Ellia felt small and cold when she finally got it out.

"Sorry?" Fan drawled sarcastically. "Oh! She's so sorry! Did you know your second brother is dead?"

"Yes." Ellia glanced momentarily at Sang who stood in the sun, looking across the golden fields of rye stubble.

"Yes? Then you realize you missed your brother's funeral? Such a thing is inexcusable for an unmarried sister—disgraceful. And have you any idea what you did to your father? He lost his second son and at the same time feared he had lost his eldest daughter, too. I wonder sometimes: are you a girl or a stone?"

A stone? Ellia stepped up onto the porch, blinking away tears. "I said I'm sorry. What do you want me to do?"

"'Sorry' won't work this time, my daughter. You'll have to answer to your father when he returns from the south. You hurt him this time, Ellia, and you've hurt him sorely."

Mention of her father brought more tears. "I can't mend the past!" Ellia cried. "Do you think I want to hurt anybody? I can live only one lifetime, and I would like to at least enjoy it a little. Tie me up and I'll die!"

The muscles in Fan's cheeks relaxed, and her black eyes softened a measure. "Is being a woman being tied up?"

"Yes. Unless you've been on both sides of the lake, you can't say which view is more lovely."

Fan just shook her head. She turned to Sang. "Son, all the other boys who've returned are in the barn preparing thatch for the Vounder house. Go help them, will you?"

"Yes, Mother." Ellia heard her brother shuffle off to her right. Unable to meet her stepmother's eyes, she stared at the woman's bare feet. The toddler—she had not been named when Ellia had departed—looked up and tentatively smiled. Fan put both hands on Ellia's shoulders.

"You're right, I can't understand you, if that's what

you mean. But I understand you are a girl who has misbehaved badly. The question is, what do you expect me to do? Look at me, Ellia. You hurt both me and your father."

Ellia could say nothing, nor look up.

"I don't know what to do, and I don't have enough time to worry about it either. The Vounder house is being rethatched, seed for the next planting is being bagged, and the tax collectors arrive in a dogday and I haven't been able to sit down with Tagii yet to figure who owes what. And on top of that, I've volunteered a fish stew and potatoes for the feast tonight. But first things first, a bath for you. You smell like—" Fan went silent and paled. "Are you a woman yet?" Fan asked. Ellia nodded, and Fan abruptly released her. "And I have to cook in this house! I don't suppose you took the time to get the purifications the first time, did you?"

"Yes, as a matter of fact, I did. I got purifications for eating unclean meat. It's a similar uncleanliness, and the ritual is identical. I'm not stupid."

Fan narrowed her eyes. "Well, at least you inherited one thing from my cousin," she said. Taking Ellia by the shoulder, she led her to the bath house, a little building in the tiny courtyard the house itself enclosed. Fan placed her stepdaughter in a stove-heated barrel of water, then left the girl to soak languidly in citrusy fragrant, steamy water until the last traces of the male world dissolved away.

"Mama asks if you are coming out." The door opened just enough to let in a draft.

"Yes, soon," Ellia replied, startled. "Shut the door."

Ellia felt too heavy to budge, but she forced herself from the bath. Quickly she toweled herself off, then wrapped on the gray sarong and overrobes left for her. Finally ready to face the world, she stepped outside to find the toddler digging with a stick in the black courtyard soil beside the cherry tree.

"Hi," Ellia said.

The yellow-robed tot looked up. "Hi," she said. "I'm sorry for scaring you, Ellia. Mama told me to tell you what she told me to tell you. She did! Are you a boy?"

Ellia knelt on one knee beside the little girl. "No, I'm a girl."

"Oh, good! Everyone else has a sister and now I do too, don't I?"

"Yes." Ellia sighed. "What's your name? You were just mouse-sized the last time I saw you."

"Shana." The toddler giggled. "I'm almost four years old."

"Four ritual cycles is more like it, isn't it?"

"Uhh, uh-huh." Ellia stood, and Shana copied her. "Where you going, Ellia?"

"I have to put these towels away."

"Oh, I'll do that. Mama says she wants to talk to you now. You'd better go b'fore you get in trouble."

Ellia found Fan chopping vegetables in the kitchen. Even in the middle of the day with the roof panels cranked open, the room was dark. Near the cutting boards a kerosene lamp burned to light Fan's work. On a cast-iron stove sat large, shiny pots, their lids clacking without rhythm as their contents boiled.

"I thought you had drowned," Fan said.

"Shana told me you wanted me here."

"Yes. I need twenty more potatoes peeled. The peeling basin is already filled with water, the knives—"

"I know where the knives are," Ellia returned. Without a word, she angrily scratched at the potatoes for a half-hour.

"Good, put them here," Fan said when Ellia finished. Drying her hands with a towel, she inspected Ellia's new clothes. "Think of what you would look like if that sour expression froze on your face," Fan said suddenly. "A woman needs her beauty."

Ellia remained impassive.

Sighing loudly, Fan scraped the chopped carrots and greens, along with Ellia's potatoes, into a pot. "Did you have to cut your hair so short?"

"It makes me look like a boy."

"Yes, it does. I teach you how to make yourself beautiful, and what do you do? Black-dyed, short hair—"

"They don't let girls into the Stone Coast shrine."

"Stone Coast?" Fan asked, dropping her pot on the counter. "Stone Coast? Where they teach boys to fight?"

"It's paramilitary—"

"Your father and I prohibited Tagii or Sang from going there! And you went?"

"What do you want from me?"

"I honestly don't know. Here, take that box of hand bowls to the Vounder house, then bring extra benches from the sharecroppers' houses out to the tables."

Ellia headed for the door. "Anything else? You'd think the other girls could take their own benches out."

"They went to market," Shana piped up from behind her mother. Ellia's expression lightened a little.

"Besides," Fan added, "you're the second oldest girl now. Go on, and take your sister with you. I'm busy."

When the other six unmarried girls returned from the market on the bullock cart, Ellia had help in her tasks. They covered wooden tables with green checkered cloths, set out dishes, lanterns, and torch holders, and finally filled the hand bowls with citrus water. But no one talked to Ellia, not even Marsai, the eldest girl of the co-op.

Ellia heard giggles behind her back. She had never felt so out of place before. She would have to strip the black from her hair, preferably before her father returned. He had never approved of Ellia's escapades, but he did believe people ought to learn their own lessons. If she had hurt him as Fan insisted, he might have changed his mind on that. What would she do then?

An hour before dusk, the men returned from the fields. The girls rushed steaming pots of stew and soup to smoky outdoor fires. Rye and wheat loaves hot from the oven were placed in baskets next to cups of fresh sweet butter. The men of the co-op climbed to the wooden eaves of the Vounder house, where they sang the roofer's song as they kicked dragoncycle-old thatching from the roof.

> *Off with it, ox, do you hear?*
> > *Old hay, old straw, rats and scratch,*
> > > *Kick to the ground, all gray and sere.*
> *Less feed for you, old ox,*
> > *(but for me, sweet green thatch!),*
> > > *Last cycle's ghosts do not fear,*
> > > > *It's only the sun setting we'll match.*
> *Off with the gray, old ox, did you hear?*
> > *Did you hear? Use your ear, old Patch,*
> > > *Stupid old ox! Where's my beer?*

And so it went on through nine other verses, following the catalog of ten days: ox, chee, dragon, snake, horse, boar, rooster, sheep, goat, and dog. Ellia resented that the girls were not allowed to sing the song. She worked as directed with a sour expression and low spirits.

As the sun left the sky, nothing of the Vounder roof remained but a skeleton of dark beams and four stone chimneys. The men began to toss up the newly tied thatch, singing as the women arranged the tables, readying bowls and fetching water. The older girls commented on the unmarried boys, their giggles causing some on the roof to blush. Ellia stood back and watched, feeling apart from the festivities. When the thatching was completed and the men climbed up on the roof with Vounder's protector-godbox to throw salt and set the weather vane, the girls had their chance to sing, but even then Ellia felt alone.

Surrounded by the other girls, Ellia mouthed the words to the girlsong and stared at the ground. At the appropriate point in the song, the Vounder father threw the flowerbread and the girls screamed in joy, startling Ellia. The sunburst-shaped pastry flew toward her; as the girls jumped and vied to catch it, Ellia was pushed to the ground. A painful kick in the ribs brought tears to her eyes.

Fan pursed her lips and turned away from the scene. Terra, the third eldest girl who Ellia had once rescued, had caught the pastry—tradition held that the tiny girl would be the next to be married. Vounder had aimed at Ellia.

"You almost got it!" Shana cried, trying to help her sister up. Ellia dusted herself off and dried her tears before any could notice them.

"I wouldn't have wanted it anyway, Shana." Ellia sniffed and looked back at the laughing girls congratulating Terra for her catch. They escorted the winner to the place of honor at the table, the only place a girl could be served first. "Foo," Ellia added under her breath.

"You don't want it?" Shana asked, incredulous. "How are you going have baby cousins for me to play with?" she asked.

Ellia sighed and shook her head. Rather than explain that she could provide only nieces and nephews, she said, "Your eldest brother is married, Shana. Remember?"

The little girl brightened. "Oh, yes!" she cried and ran off to find her brother and his new wife, who was already pregnant.

Cousins, indeed! Ellia thought. She kicked old thatching out of the way as she headed for the tables and the light and the laughter. The boys were getting their food. Nobody paid attention as Ellia served herself a ladleful of fish stew, a mug of plum wine, a spoonful of butter, and a half-loaf of brown rye, then left the festivities to sit against the Vounder house. As the night wore on, she watched the party, lost in her thoughts.

The celebration ended with dessert pastries and more songs. Then the women began collecting their pots and dishes. The tables were cleared quicker than they had been set. Tableclothes came off and were snapped clean. Having done so much of the work earlier, Ellia decided to let the other girls do the cleaning up. She stretched out in the dark and fiddled with the thatch litter beside her.

When only the benches and torches remained, Ellia noticed someone approaching her. The silhouetted form resolved into Marsai, a large but not uncomely girl, the eldest unmarried girl of the co-op. One ritual cycle older than Ellia, Marsai had been her friend before Ellia began running away from home. "Here," Marsai said, handing Ellia a sweet, fish-filled pastry. "A flavorful apology."

Ellia smiled and took a bite. "What for?" she asked.

Marsai sighed and sat down, brushing strands of hip-length black hair from her face. "That half, the one you just bit into, is for not saying hello before and for giggling at you with the other girls."

Ellia swallowed. "Accepted. And the other half?"

"That half is an apology for what happened during the girlsong before. I really didn't mean to kick you. It was an accident, really it was."

Ellia paused a moment; her left side still hurt. But the pastry *did* taste delicious. "Accepted," she said. Marsai's eyes twinkled in the torchlight as Ellia slowly finished the pastry.

"Would you mind helping me with the benches?" Marsai asked sheepishly.

Together, they moved the benches into the barn; it

was too late to move them back to the homes they came from.

"It must all be terribly adventurous," Marsai said, breaking the silence that had fallen between them. They dropped a bench just inside the entrance to the barn where a small hanging kerosene lamp provided more shadow than light.

"Oh, it's not always adventurous, but it's always interesting," Ellia said.

"Interesting? What do you mean?" Marsai followed Ellia out for the next bench.

"Every time I return home, I realize how boring it is to be a girl."

"Oh, Ellia, really! There's the rituals, the celebrations—"

"—the drudge work—"

"—and boys. I don't know about you, but I had fun tonight. You just don't want to enjoy being a girl."

"And you don't know what you are missing." Hearing the pony whicker, Ellia said, "For example, you've probably never ridden a horse."

"A horse? You've ridden a horse?"

"For days at a time; it's fun."

"Maybe. But as a girl, you don't have to be tested to become an adult, you just become one. Which, incidentally, means you don't face a chance of dying in just a ritual cycle or two." Marsai shook her head. "I don't understand you at all, Ellia."

"You and Fan both, I guess."

"That flowerbread today was aimed at you, not Terra. Your stepmother's doing, no doubt."

"Well, in that case, I am glad someone knocked me down. There is no way I'd want to catch that. Let go of the bench."

Marsai seemed disturbed by Ellia's words. As they lugged in another bench, she asked, "You've no desire to taste a flowerbread? Terra told me it tastes like spring and makes you feel real good."

"Wine does that too, Marsai."

"I really don't understand you, then. You even walk like a boy."

"I take that as a compliment. And you walk like a girl, Marsai, from the hips." Ellia exaggerated her companion's feminine wag. The two girls giggled.

"And I take that as a compliment. At our age, you have to do something to start getting the boys interested in you. And we do have a couple of handsome ones here, or haven't you noticed?" When Ellia remained quiet, Marsai added, "Myself, I am working on becoming your sister-in-law, though Sang doesn't know it yet. He's cute."

Ellia put down the bench. "Really?" She smiled.

"Then you don't mind?" Marsai asked, sitting down on the bench.

The sound of squawking echoed from the chicken pen. Glancing into the barn, Ellia asked, "Why should I mind?" Her heart beat rapidly. The sudden lowing of the bullocks made her feel uneasy.

"Well," Marsai said, looking at the ground and fiddling with her hair. "You seem so protective of your brother sometimes."

"I'm not my brother's keeper, Marsai. And what girls chase him is his problem, not mine. If any boys were to chase me, now that would be a problem."

Marsai giggled. "Thank you," she said.

"I can't think of a person I'd rather have as a sister-in-law, though Terra, the simperer, is someone I would object to. Do you realize I haven't met Tagii's wife yet? His marriage was arranged."

"It had to be. Nobody was interested here in the co-op, and I was the prime marriage prospect."

"Yeah. Maybe I don't want to meet Tagii's wife."

"She's nice."

"I was afraid you'd say that." Ellia let out a long sigh.

Suddenly Marsai gave a strangled scream. "Look!"

Marsai pointed to a print in the dirt. The girls fell to their knees to study the mark.

"King of the Dron! It's a dog."

"Only *one*?" Marsai asked, frightened. "Just one dog?" In the barn, the chickens squawked angrily again.

"I don't know. Come on!" Ellia pulled Marsai to her feet and raced for the torches. Sending her friend to get the men and guns, Ellia turned back to the barn. She knew the vermin had to be caught and killed or they would be around for days causing trouble and bringing disease.

"Ellia! Where are you going?"

"I've got to protect the oxen and our pony! They're too valuable to be bitten and then have to be destroyed!"

"But you're a girl!"

"Blind priests! Get the men, quick!" Ellia cried. She shoved Marsai on her way, wrestled a torch from the earth, then ran back to the barn. A long-handled spade was the only sharp tool she could find—she grabbed it and tried to calm herself. She heard snuffling sounds from the northern stalls and walked carefully to where the messenger pony was stabled near the two milk cows. She inserted her torch in a holder on the wall. Every shifting shadow drew her eyes. The straw covering the floor made it difficult to see if any dogs had come this way.

"Hi, Ellia!" a little voice behind her said jubilantly. Ellia jumped. She turned away from the pony's stall, her hand over her heart. Shana stood before her, giggling.

"What are you doing here?" Ellia yelled. She could barely catch her breath.

"I brought a sweet for Kamakura," Shana returned. The pony whickered, smelling the sticky pastry in the toddler's hand. "Mama lets me bring one every night. I'm sorry if I scared you."

"Sorry!" Ellia began, then caught herself. Dogs were

rare, and it wasn't Shana's fault that they were there; unfortunately, Shana was just the right size to be a dog's prey.

"What are you doing, big sister?"

"We have problems." Ellia quickly picked up the toddler and sat her on a barrel of oats.

"Oops!" Shana dropped the pastry which stank of carrots and oatmeal. It rolled a short distance into the dark.

"I want you to stay here," Ellia instructed. Then a sudden noise made her freeze. She took a deep breath. Carefully, she turned around and found five pairs of feral eyes appraising her, reflecting the red from her torch. The leader growled deep in its throat and advanced with uncharacteristic courage. Ellia shivered and mouthed a prayer. Behind her, Shana whimpered.

Ellia inched over to where she had left her spade leaning against Kamakura's stall. The lead dog wrinkled its nose into a snarl and stepped closer. Ellia barely breathed.

She felt for the spade, keeping her eyes locked on the dogs. Another couple of decimeters... Ellia seized the spade handle. Whirling, she yelled and lunged at the lead dog.

Her foot came down on Shana's pastry; she slipped, and before she knew what had happened, she was on her back—without the spade. The dogs, who had retreated when Ellia attacked, saw her go down, and the madness of their leader renewed their courage.

Ellia had the wind knocked out of her, but not her senses. The defense courses from the Stone Coast suddenly proved practical; she used the momentum of the fall to turn it into a roll. She came up with a crack against the pony's stall and flailed out for the torch holder. She hit the torch, knocking it loose. She grabbed at it and missed. The torch fell. Ellia screamed as slavering jaws snapped at her throat.

The torch fell almost on top of her, and the lead

dog's trajectory brought it square into the flame. Snarling in pain, the animal crashed into the stall gate hard enough to knock it unconscious. It landed on Ellia's head.

She screamed, and with strength she never knew she possessed, she hurled away the flaming gray-furred beast. Scrambling to her feet, she saw the other dogs back off. The odor of burning fur and straw filled her nostrils. Taking the spade in both hands, she prepared to bring down the edge for the fatal blow.

But then, suddenly, she could not move. The dog whimpered in pain and rolled in the dust to smother the flames. A second later, it got to its feet.

Strike! her mind told her, but she was frozen. She had never killed anything before. With its one good eye, the beast sized her up and growled once more.

Then—*Crack*!

A rifle bullet smashed in one side of the animal's skull. Ellia stared as the suddenly inert body fell to the ground. Yelps filled the barn. She dropped the spade as more shots exploded. Stupefied, Ellia bent and picked up the torch, then stamped out the fire that had caught in the straw.

"What are you doing in here!" Tagii yelled. The muscles in Ellia's throat contracted. She began to shake as she looked from the bloody dog at her feet to the man with the rifle.

"Ellia saved me from the scaries!" Shana cried as Ellia stumbled past with a hand over her mouth. A moment later her stomach delivered what was left of her evening meal.

Three

*Ellia retired that night on the pillows in the common-
room; during her absence her own room had been given
to Shana. She could not sleep.* She tossed and turned
until past midnight, then finally decided to go to the
family god shelf to think and pray. Kantilphanes, her
protector god, knew she had enough to think about.

She was amazed to find His tiny cinnabar dodecahedron still sitting amongst the little jade statuettes and
soapstone idols on the shelf. Father would have dis-
carded the focus-stone if he had thought Ellia was lost
to him... No. Kantilphanes was her twin's protector
god also.

Ellia sighed and proceeded through rituals she knew
by rote. At the celebration of her tenth ritual cycle, a
priest had presented her with a calendar painted with
colorful animals, dates that a girl could read and understand. These, charted against the world's birth rit-

ual cycle, indicated her own prayer and ritual days, which assured the proper rebirth of her spirit every 270 days—the length of time it took for an infant to be born after conception. Ellia had missed some of the dates when, disguised as a boy, she had been unable to chant the girlsongs. She had to catch up, and she wished to thank her protector god for his help.

But the red dodecahedron held no answers. Eventually, she leaned forward and placed the warm stone on the shelf.

She sighed again as she lit a stick of vanilla incense. What could she do? She could stop running away, settle down, and learn to be a girl. With hair grown long and stripped to its original mahogany-red blaze, a little perfume and makeup, and another three cycles of growth—certainly she would be ravishing. She looked more like her mother with every succeeding day. She would be married and have two children by her twenty-fifth ritual cycle. That was what adults expected of her. But what did she expect of herself?

Marsai fit into the pattern, and so would Shana. Fan fit the pattern, as had Ellia's own mother. Everyone else fit the pattern, but did that mean she must? She frowned and felt tears come unexpectedly to her eyes. She sniffed and, with a pitiful laugh, wiped the corners of her eyes on her nightshirt. Even if she decided not to settle down and accept the role of a traditional woman, she could not become a boy instead. Her eyes began to burn.

Ellia recalled suddenly what her mother had said long ago, just before she died. Ellia had recently begun her tenth ritual cycle, a special occasion marking the end of a girl's religious training and her recognition by the adult world. Ellia's mother had taken her to celebrate her tenth at the same shrine where all her female ancestors had celebrated, rebuilt after devastation by a tsunami twenty-seven ritual cycles before. But Ellia's mother had been sickly ever since delivering the twins, and the stormy weather that accompanied the home-ward trek sapped the woman's remaining strength.

The girl had been called in to see her dying mother. "Ellia, I want you to promise me something," she had said. Ellia had to lean close to hear her mother's weak voice. The woman's hand tightened its grip on hers. "You've been the sun in my life. Be that true to yourself, El."

Ellia lit two incense sticks, one to comfort what part of her mother's spirit her thoughts conjured and one for Kantilphanes. She sighed and whispered a prayer-chant a priest had composed for her mother. She continued to fight away tears.

All those years Ellia's mother had been sick, cousin Fan had taken care of the children, and Ellia had not been pampered the way most daughters were. In her mother's last minutes, when she knew she was dying, it had been Ellia of all the family who she had summoned. She felt she had cheated her daughter of her childhood.

"Mama!" Ellia cried.

If Ellia still thought and felt the way she had before her tenth ritual cycle, she would be very much like Marsai. But she had been set on a different path the day her mother died, thanks to Fan.

Sang had remembered how much their mother loved the Karta Coast. She and Fan were refugees of the wave that washed fishing boats all the way to the foot-hills of the western range. But the survivors had re-built, and by Ellia's Tenth, the land had bloomed again. The Karta Coast was their mother's homeland, and that was where their mother's ashes and funeral slats belonged. Together, Ellia and Sang had constructed the slats, then confronted their father and cousin Fan with their idea. But Fan overruled them, claiming that she knew what her Aunt Della wished—and fainted to end the argument.

So much had changed in one day, Ellia thought,

staring at the door. *And I promised to be true, Mama, didn't I?*

Ellia's knees cracked when she finally stood. She stretched and felt the circulation return painfully to her icy toes. Taking her jade oil lamp, she returned to her heap of pillows to try again to sleep.

Eight ritual cycles ago was the first time she had rebelled to do what she wished. Sang had dressed her in his own clothes, and together they had set off during the night to travel west with their mother's ritual slats. Their need to arrive in the Karta Coast before anyone could stop them from performing the needed rituals forced the twins to take a dangerous shortcut through the poorly policed Crow Well Forest.

Ellia shut her eyes to remember the first time she had run away.

Ellia had been scared in the midnight darkness of the forest. Though a thunderstorm raged above the leafy canopy, only rivulets of water seeped down the trunks of the trees. Blue lumin moss dappling the trunks lit the way.

Then suddenly they heard a small voice wail in pain. Sang and Ellia dodged immediately into some fallen branches beside the road. They saw a wagon—and something small just outside the circle of lantern lights.

Without warning, someone invisible in the dark shouted, "Move and you'll die!"

Ellia felt her heart in her throat; she froze where she crouched. The wagonmaster dove under the horses. Shots rang out.

The wagonmaster scrambled suddenly to the running board, caught up a rifle, and fired. The highwayman returned fire, and the twins saw the wagonmaster fall backward into the dirt. Moments later the highwayman appeared.

A fire feeding on spilled kerosene climbed the weathered wood of the wagon.

"Let's get out of here," Sang whispered into Ellia's ear.

Ellia swallowed hard. "The man's still alive." The boy tried to pull her away, but she held her ground.

"Blind priests!" came a cry from the flaming wagon.

"Where is your food?" the highwayman demanded.

Ellia, carrying the slats over her shoulder, suddenly skittered to the other side of the road. Sang scrambled after her. "Where are you going? *Ellia!*"

Ellia had obtained a better vantage point, and they could see the wraithlike, emaciated highwayman. He rubbed a horribly deformed and blackened hand against his shirt of rags, trying to rub off some slimy corruption. His hair was stark white in the firelight. He was no more than twenty ritual cycles old—Tagii's age!

"What is wrong with him?" Sang breathed into Ellia's ear as a sickly sweet smell swept their way. Ellia wanted to gag.

"Where is your food?"

"I have none," the wagonmaster said. He bled from the shoulder.

"That can't be. No!"

"It looks like you failed the Test. Why didn't you die?"

"Nobody asked me if I wanted to take any test Driver." The fire licked at the remaining horse's flanks, and it whinnied and kicked in fear. The highwayman crouched near the wagonmaster, pointing his pistol into the man's face. "There must be food," the highwayman said hysterically.

Ellia acted wholly on intuition. Seeing her opportunity to give the wagonmaster a chance, she launched one of the yellow funeral slats like a huge knife. It hit the damp ground point first and stuck. When the highwayman glanced away, the wagonmaster grappled with his assailant. They rolled in the dirt, tearing and punching at each other.

The gun went off.

The wagonmaster rolled a limp body off himself. Stunned, Ellia stood, unmoving, as the wagonmaster looked at her, then collapsed.

Ellia found the highwayman's bait covered toe to nose in gray muck: a little girl about Ellia's age, dressed in rags, shaking with fright.

Outlines blurred and darkened. Emerald-green fog condensed like the sulfurous exhalation of the other-world. In heartbeats an image coalesced: a spectre with a crippled arm. Its rags fluttered and waved madly as if blown by a gale. Green, very green, familiar eyes opened and burned like coals.

Ellia recognized her mother's face and screamed.

"Ellia!" a voice summoned, distant and warm. "Ellia! Wake up girl!"

Ellia fought the smell of rot and her own burning flesh. The next instant, she sat bolt upright in a ring of pillows. Blue glimmers of dawn shined through the window. The nightmare faded quickly, and she shivered as sweat evaporated from her back and neck. Fan was sitting beside her.

"Ellia, are you all right?"

"Yeah," Ellia said, regaining her composure. Her heartbeat calmed. "I'm sorry if I woke you."

"That's quite all right, Ellia. Were you having that nightmare again about the day you saved Terra from the highwayman?"

"Yes," Ellia said, looking at her hands. She wanted no one's sympathy, especially cousin Fan's. "Not enough sleep the last couple days, I guess."

"Do you want to talk about it, Ellia?"

"Not really."

"I'd be glad to listen. I realize I am no substitute for your mother, but I can listen. Being caught masquerading as a boy must have been frightening."

"It wasn't so terrible, and I really don't want to talk about it. Really, cousin Fan." Ellia hunched over, facing away from the woman.

Fan made a faint crooning noise, then lightly touched Ellia's back. The girl jumped and shivered as her back throbbed with the memory of the electric whip.

"Ellia? Is something wrong with your back?"

"No! Can't you just leave me alone!" Ellia screamed. She threw herself face down into the pillows and covered her head, but did not cry. She realized that she was being overly dramatic, but didn't care. She sighed and hoped Fan would just go away.

Ellia heard the sound of Fan crying. *No*, Ellia thought. *No!* She closed her eyes. *Now you've done it*. After a minute, she lifted the pillow off her head and straightened up to look at her cousin. She couldn't see the woman's face in the dark, but she could make out a faint cream-colored nightshirt.

"We had a word for a child like you when I was a little. A brat!" Fan said, breathing deeply to keep from sobbing aloud.

"What?"

"A brat! A girl who doesn't care anything at all for those who love her—a brat. I've tried with you. I've tried being good to you, tried treating you like my own daughter, but what do I get? Do I even get treated like a person when I am just being nice? Do I, brat?"

Ellia swallowed hard. "I'm sorry—"

"Oh, so you're sorry?" Fan sniffed loudly. "You think a word or two can repair this, too, do you? This time you hurt me, sliced me in half. I've not given you the punishment you deserve for your escapades. I've even allowed you to read the books you kept hidden in your room. I cannot remember all the times I gave in to you over the years, but every time I do all I get is a kick in the teeth in return. I can do for you, but you have to meet me at least halfway."

"You just don't understand."

"Oh, I understand all right. You're basically lazy and no good. Any decent girl would be willing to help with the housework, taking her rightful share. But you? You go off and do for you. Bury all of us, it would make no difference, huh? Or would it make things easier, perhaps? Ellia, you're selfish."

"I do care!"

"Yes, only about yourself!" Fan said, her voice rising in volume. "You couldn't prove to me you care for anybody!"

"I—I helped out yesterday with all the preparations, moving all the tables and—"

"I am talking about years of help. You are the eldest girl in this family, but what help have you given, all totalled? You've been gone a year and a half, and I have had to run the co-op practically all by myself. No, you be quiet. Your father can't be here all the time. He has to earn the money to get us fuel, to pay the taxes. That leaves me alone to do all the work. Tagii's wife is useless, but she'll learn to keep Tagii happy. You, *you* are supposed to take on part of the household workload. Cooking, cleaning, learning to be a woman as I learned. But I forget—you're not a girl, are you?"

Ellia closed her mouth and swallowed. "And last night? What do you call that? Do I care only for myself? What was my first thought? To run?"

"What are you talking about?"

"Who saved Shana's life last night?" *Let Fan belittle that!*

"Tagii did," Fan said slowly, in a calculated manner. "I am glad his father taught him how to shoot well."

"Tagii!" Ellia yelled. "Tagii?" Ellia gazed at her splinted and bandaged right hand, broken in the fight with the dogs. When she looked up at Fan, who was finally visible in the waxing dawnlight, she could see by Fan's expression that the woman believed every word she had said.

But I did *save Shana!* She had placed Shana on the barrel and attacked the dog with the torch! Tagii had killed the creature only after Ellia had warded it off. "Tagii?" Ellia asked again. Tears rolled down her cheeks.

"What is this?" a brusque voice asked suddenly. Ellia jumped. A black-haired young man taller than her father and at least as massive entered the room.

"I was talking with your sister, son," Fan told Tagii.

"Yes, loud enough to wake the whole house."

Fan ignored him, but Ellia spoke. "Did I do anything to save my baby sister's life last night, Tagii?"

Tagii yawned loudly. "I killed the mongrel that would have torn you to pieces."

"That's not what I asked!"

"Ellia," Fan growled, "watch how you talk to your brother."

"All I asked was whether or not my being there kept Shana from being torn to bloody pieces!"

"Ellia!" Fan cried.

Tagii moved closer and glanced at Fan. Ellia felt her face begin to burn as her brother said, "Melinu thinks the fact that you were in the barn with a torch attracted the dogs from the mess they made in the dried fish stores on the opposite side of the barn."

"And," Fan finished, "had you stayed out of the barn as you should have, Shana would have been in no danger."

"You cannot believe that!" Ellia returned.

Tagii's anger flared. "Don't address your mother in that tone of voice!"

"Fan is not my mother!" Ellia screamed.

Tagii backhanded his sister, knocking her into the pillows. When he raised his hand again, Ellia shrieked and scrambled away.

"I could care less if she is your blood mother or not!" Tagii yelled. "Cousin Fan has done more for you and the rest of us then Mother ever could. She felt responsibility for us even when *she* was not required to. Even if you don't recognize the debt you owe Fan for raising you, you owe Fan a debt you can never repay, my little sister, for taking care of Mother for all those years she was ill after giving birth to you. And if I ever catch you speaking to your *mother* that way again, you are going to regret it. Be glad I have enough principle not to tell Father of the way you have treated the woman he chose to run our family!" He turned and stormed out of the room.

Ellia rubbed her burning jaw. He had hit her!

"You'll never learn, will you, Ellia?" Fan asked after a moment. Ellia snapped her head around and glared at Fan. "With every privilege we give you, you take unfounded liberty. To think you'd take credit from Tagii for—"

"I did too save Shana!"

"You disgust me," Fan said. She walked over to the front door, opened it, and stood looking at the dawn. Then she faced Ellia. "And still you don't realize how much of a brat you are, do you?" Fan waited. "Do you?"

Crying, Ellia shook her head.

"What about what you did to your father, your blood, Ellia? What about that? Well, I'll tell you something, Ellia, that none of your brothers will ever have the nerve to tell you. Do you know what that is? Can you guess?"

Ellia shook her head again.

"You're the favorite, Ellia. You're your father's favorite child and were your mother's too. And they've spoiled you rotten. You wonder why your older brother dislikes you? Now you know."

"That's ridiculous."

"It's not so ridiculous. My family was a big one, I know about such things. Though you don't trust me, you can take my word for this. I have the task of balancing this family, making everyone feel equally attended to. The least you could do for the extra attention you receive is to try to fit into the family instead of fighting it every chance you get. This last time you hurt your father badly. When you failed to return at the end of the last ritual cycle, he didn't know what to think."

"I—"

"You what? You're a girl. What do you think he thought when you didn't return? Have you any idea how worried he was? Have you any idea how much he needed you to be around to make the loss of a child less? You're a girl. Perhaps you cannot imagine all the terrible, horrible things that could happen to a girl your age, but he could. You could be maimed, killed, even made pregnant!"

Ellia erupted into tears. The pillow in which she hid her face became wet. How could she have done that to Da? How? Her salty tears could never wash the guilt away.

"Are you quite done?" Fan asked suddenly.

"Yes, I'm done," Ellia responded, raising her head to look at Fan who still stood framed in the doorway. Orange rays of morning sun lit the fields beyond the house. Ellia wiped her nose.

"Well, perhaps now you understand what a brat is. She fouls all she touches, hurts all she loves. You are a brat and you know it now. I just hope you never forget. To be a brat is the worst thing a girl can ever be. It means unhappiness for her and all around her, but primarily for her. The brat that grows up still a brat is the one who has no choice of husbands and marries the worst. It means unhappiness, beatings, and sometimes worse. Men hate such women and have every right to hurt them to make them obey. I don't want that for any child I've raised. Can you understand that?"

Fan did not wait for Ellia to answer. "I am only trying to help you, Ellia. Do you forget that I conceded to allow you to read? I do want you to be happy, but I also want you to be part of this family. That I want very much. And please realize you can never be a boy, no matter how hard you wish."

Ellia sniffed again and closed her eyes. "I know. Don't you think I know?"

"You have always denied it, dear. But now I think you understand you can no longer deny it. You've had many years of many happy experiences, experiences that no woman has ever been able to have. Now it is time for you to grow up. You have a lot to learn. Do you think you are ready to become a girl again?"

"Have I any choice?" Ellia moaned.

"None at all. And now that you are part of the family again, I think I'll start by putting you in charge of Shana. The girl likes you, at least so far, and in ten dogdays it will be quite impossible for me to take care of her."

"Impossible?"

"I'm pregnant again. You'll have a new brother or sister soon after the new ritual cycle begins."

Ellia tried to smile, but could not.

Four

"*Ellia?*"

Ellia was lost in her thoughts. Redness rimmed her eyes again.

"Ellia!" Fan said louder, putting her hands on her hips. "Will you snap out of it! I need help carrying the groceries into the house." They had just returned from a trip to the general store near the highway junction.

Ellia said nothing as she dropped from the rear of the cart to the ground. Taking two sacks of fruit, she entered the house. Shana, carrying a small bag of rye flour, ran up behind her.

"Is something wrong, sister Ellia?" the little girl asked. Ellia shook her head, sniffing away the last of her tears as she placed her burden on the kitchen table.

"Yes, is something wrong?" Fan asked.

"These are the heaviest carrots I've ever—" Hagarra, Tagii's wife, began, then realized something was

47

wrong. "Whoops," she said, ducking her head and covering her mouth. She placed her bag with the others on the round table, then retreated for more from the cart.

"I'm fine," Ellia said.

"Don't play me for a fool," Fan said. "I could hear you crying back there all the way home. Are you upset about something, or are you not feeling well? Is it your time for the rag?"

Ellia gave her an evil look. "I'm not feeling well, that's all."

Fan nodded. "Well, you've done most of your chores for the day, and nothing is urgent. I think perhaps you'd better rest, and if you have a cold, take a potion for it."

Ellia lay back on the soft pillows in the common-room.

From the moment she had dried her reddened eyes and attended the breakfast table that awful morning, she had settled into the family's routine. While Sang and Tagii planted the fields of wheat, Ellia watched Shana and took on more and more of the housework. She hated the washboards, the crank wringer, and the clothespins; she liked even less peeling potatoes and scraping vegetables for the pot. Shana, who helped when her little hands were able, was one of Ellia's pure pleasures. But Ellia was more worried than ever—her father was expected home soon for the land blessing ritual. How badly had she hurt him? To make up for the pain she had caused him, she was trying to be a normal girl—but could that soothe a deep hurt?

A light rain started to fall, pattering rhythmically on the porch and the plastic film roof of the courtyard. The faint tattoo helped Ellia relax. Through the open front doorway drifted the scent of moist, cool spring air.

Ellia slept. She drifted on her own ship through a endless blue ocean to a world in which she had heard all good existed. She had no cares. Suddenly, through the pleasant mist of her dream, a dissonance intruded, the sound of a large fish landing on the deck. The fish flopped repeatedly against the wood planking.

Ellia opened her eyes and heard the same wet slapping noise she had heard in her dream, followed by footsteps. Then a familiar tall, broad-shouldered form filled the doorway. Ellia's father shook his plastic rain poncho once before tossing it over the clothesline hung for that purpose. Ellia's muscles locked, and her chance to run from the room before her father saw her passed as quickly as the impulse occurred to her. Ellia could define her relationships with Fan and Sang and other people in terms of compromises, loyality, friendship, or duty; when it came to her father, she had no such ability. He was simply "Da," and that made a difference. Heartbeats after she had seen him in the doorway, he turned and spotted her sitting amongst the pillows.

Shana walked in from the kitchen. "Dada!" she cried gleefully.

"Ellia!" the man exclaimed, his voice shockingly loud against the patter of rain. "Ellia, little girl!" he said with a smile. Ellia, weeping streams of tears, ran into his outstretched arms. He hefted her easily above his shoulders and swung her around just as he had when she had been Shana's age. Still weeping, Ellia laughed as her father embraced her tightly and set her on her feet. Ellia looked up and saw no hurt in the man's dark eyes or anger in his sun-tanned face. Her legs went weak with relief.

Then she looked behind and saw Fan. The hard line of Fan's lips scared Ellia almost as much as had the appearance of the dogpack leader. But when Shana ran up and Da swung her around, Fan's expression softened. He put Shana on her feet and knelt, reaching into a hip pocket. "And look what I have for my littlest girl." He pulled out a handful of plastic-wrapped crystals—green, crimson, and orange star candies.

When he ran out of crystals and received Shana's

kiss, he stood up and turned to Fan. "And I have something for you too, my big girl." He disappeared out the door. Fan's expression changed unpleasantly as she glanced at Ellia, then she smiled wholeheartedly again as her husband returned with a large, wet, gray ice sack. She looked inside.

"Fish?" she said. Her smile wavered.

"Fresh sea bass, caught yesterday. But that's for all of us—this is for you." He held out a long, fine strand of red and blue coral beads with a gold clasp at each end.

"Oh!" she cried. The sack struck the floor as she took her turn at hugging the bear of a man.

Ellia turned away and gazed out into the pouring rain.

"Ellia, little girl," her father called.

"Yes, Da?" Ellia said, smiling again.

"Did you think I forgot about you?" Ellia's heart skipped a beat. "Don't look so perplexed. I have a present for you, too, that's all."

Ellia's mouth dropped open. "Really?"

Fan immediately intervened. "No! Look, Ellia's been—"

"Fan, be reasonable," he said.

"Reasonable?"

"Fan—"

"Reasonable? Your daughter ran away for two ritual cycles. She deserves to be punished, if anything—not given presents!"

"Fan, please don't talk to me as if I were an idiot."

"But—I'm sorry, dear, but she did run away against your orders. One day she is going to get hurt! I'm only thinking of her," Fan finished sweetly. Shana, who had been sitting quietly counting her candies and trying to decide which one to eat first, looked up at Ellia, understanding that something was wrong. Ellia's father looked at his first daughter also.

"I have never ordered Ellia to do anything, Fan. My daughter has more intelligence than you give her credit for, and I don't think I could order her *not* to do anything," he said. Then he turned to Fan. "But you are right, I will talk to her about it." Ellia's heart beat faster; she was not to get off so easily.

"Achh!" Fan said, hitting her hips in disgust. She picked up the sack of fish she had dropped. "Supper will be in an hour." She left the room, taking Shana with her.

"Come with me, little girl," Ellia's father said, motioning with one hand.

Well, Fan did it after all, Ellia thought, following her father through the kitchen to his and Fan's bedroom. She sat on the canopied four-poster and rubbed her hand over the quilted spread as her father went through some drawers in his wardrobe.

"Here." He returned with a box wrapped in metallic gold paper. She guessed the gift was one he had intended to give her at the end of the last ritual cycle. Running away had been bad, but her decision not to send word home at the end of the ritual cycle was another thing altogether, she realized. *Fan is right*, the girl thought, *I have become a brat*.

Her father gently placed the box on her knees; the paper crinkled. Ellia looked at the heavy, golden box but left her hands folded in her lap. Without looking up, she shook her head. "No, I can't. Fan's right. I don't deserve it."

He chuckled, and his hand touched her chin, forcing her to look at him. "Whether or not Fan is right, this gift is for you now, not later, not in a dogday, but now."

"But—"

"You can well learn how to be a woman from Fan, but that doesn't mean you have to pick up her argumentativeness, too. Regardless of what Fan says, I'm charged to give you this. A long time ago both your mother and I decided on a present for you, and I purchased it for you last ritual season—"

"I'm sorry," she cried, and burst into tears.

"Oh, El!" The man sat next to Ellia and laid her head against his shoulder. "It's not as bad as all that! You're home now. Did something go wrong at your last shrineschool?" He gently touched her back, and she flinched.

"No," she sobbed. "It's—it's—I'm so sorry! I should never have stayed on over the dragondays last cycle. It was wrong. I should have at least sent word—" Ellia buried her face in her hands to hide her tears.

"Little girl, you know you did wrong. I could expect no better apology."

"You don't understand! Both ritual cycles I attended the Stone Coast shrine!"

"The what?" He withdrew his hand.

"Stone Coast," she whispered.

"I've allowed none of my sons to attend there; in fact, I ordered them not to go. And you went? A girl?"

"Y-yes."

"Of all the stupid things you could have done, Ellia, that is the stupidest. Learning to fight and kill has no place in my family."

"I'm sorry..." Ellia moaned.

"And they caught you, didn't they? You are home too early even if you arrived today to have stayed to the end of the cheedays."

"Uh-huh."

"They whipped you, didn't they?"

Ellia swallowed and nodded.

"Blind priests! They have no propriety at all. Fan is right. I've always feared that one day you'd get hurt. I don't ever want you hurt again—" He took a deep breath. "Ex-army officers always administer that shrine, and they have no business being near children, let alone deciding on the course of their education. It hasn't changed a bit, I am sure!"

Ellia followed the man with her eyes. "You went there?"

"It's not obvious? You knew your grandsire was army himself."

"I rather en-enjoyed it there, until they caught me." Ellia dropped her eyes to the unopened golden present on her knees.

"I enjoyed it once, too. You've always liked horses, just the way Shana does now. I liked them too. I suppose the old creosoted pole is still there behind the master administrator's offices?"

Ellia nodded her head.

Her father hissed. "I know that pole well. I was rather an embarrassment to my father, I was. I never could take orders well, and I embarrassed him one too many times. When I was only fourteen ritual cycles old, I took the Test. I never returned home after that." He paused. "Did you tell Fan what happened to you? The whipping?"

"No," Ellia whispered.

"Well, don't. I will the next time she brings you up, which she will, and I will paint a grim enough picture that she'll have to leave you be." He looked directly at Ellia. "You realize you have very much displeased me?"

"I do, Da."

"I just wanted you to realize that. I've put few real restrictions on any of you, but that was one of them. Under any other circumstances, or if you were Sang and had a chance of attending the Stone Coast again, I would punish you, and don't think I wouldn't. But I will allow it to pass this time. Being whipped to unconsciousness is more than enough punishment."

Ellia nodded.

"Well? Are you going to open the box, or just stare at it until supper?"

"I—I'd rather wait, really I—"

"Come on, little girl. I told you it is from both your mother and me."

"From Mama?" Ellia asked. "But how?"

"We talked about it long ago and decided. It's almost a ritual cycle overdue now. Open it."

Ellia sniffed, then nodded meekly. She turned the

box around until she found a yellowed strip of cellophane tape. She peeled it with a fingernail and unfolded the paper to reveal a white plastic box. Inside lay another box; she ran her fingers over golden-red wood that shimmered like satin. She removed the wooden box and placed it on her lap, and saw a little gold knob bulging out on one side. "Push the knob to the left," her father instructed.

Ellia did and the box clicked. Instantly the room filled with extraordinary music. Lovely bells chimed; a fiddle played in time with a seven-tone xylophone; a wood block clapped a staccato rhythm to punctuate phrases of a descending flute melody. The box weighed less than two kilos! Amazed, Ellia smiled as the tune went on into variations. Chimes tinkled like a mountain stream translated into music. Five minutes later, when the spring coil of the music box ran down, Ellia touched the knob and brought back silence.

"Say nothing," her father said quickly. "Your expression is enough."

"Da! It's so lovely!"

"Anything for my little girl," he said and accepted her hug.

"You said Mama helped you pick this gift. That was a long time ago. I don't understand."

Her father's expression became serious. "When you were approaching your Tenth, we began to realize you were growing up, that you wouldn't remain a little girl for many more cycles. You'd be a woman one day, and though I know you don't want to hear it, you are really no longer able to masquerade as a boy. You'll have no choice but to do what all women must. You're growing up, Ellia."

"No!" Ellia cried, tensing.

"Don't make this more difficult than it must be."

"Difficult? What do you call having to do 'what all women must'?"

"Ellia—" he warned.

"It's just not fair, that's all," Ellia said.

"Life is not fair," her father said. Ellia shivered. "But you'll do it, and you'll be happy too. Marriage brings its own special joys. We'll get you a good husband, see if we don't." Ellia felt on the edge of tears again. "But the worst part of being a woman, as far as we could decide, is moving away from your family when you get married. Your mother experienced that pain even before her marriage and knew how bad it could be. We hoped to ease that loneliness, that in the dark of winter when you cannot come to visit but have to tend to your children, you could have something wonderful to listen to and remember us by.

"We're going to start searching for a husband for you now. You could very well be married this time next ritual cycle and even be expecting an infant. We'll not settle for just any husband—your mother and I decided that long ago. But whatever happens, this music box is your special thing. You wind it like this with the key. The Collective merchant from whom I bought it likened it to a snowflake, never playing any two compositions identically. But it's special even without that." Her father finished cranking the box and touched the knob, and the mechanical symphony resumed where it had adjourned.

Ellia listened to the varying, watery tones and thought that there was little chance that her life could ever be as lovely as this music.

The seventy days of the dragon, the last of the 270-day-long ritual cycle, passed without event. Ellia joylessly did her chores as ordered by Fan, finding real happiness only in her time with Shana. Fan, in the twenty-fourth dogday of her pregnancy, felt marvelous and continued to run her family as strictly as always. When the shrine precinct called a fair to end the ritual cycle, Fan decided, with her husband's permission, that they should all attend. Even Marsai was there, dressed in bright orange wrapping, tagging along with Sang and what she hoped was her future family.

Ellia jumped into the back of the cart behind sacks of rye destined to be sold at the fair. Eyes narrowed, Sang gazed at her yellow sarong, green blouse, and the shell barrette that held her still short hair in a bun. Throughout the bumpy trip, Ellia caught his furtive, almost disapproving glances and wondered what was wrong.

At the fair, the twins left Marsai talking with Hagarra and Fan, and together they walked with Shana past stall after stall, eyeing the delicacies that a few bits of a barter could buy: sweet pies, fresh fish—baked, broiled, or raw—and grilled meats of all kinds skewered on sticks with fried vegetables. The air was filled with the sounds of xylophone music and hawkers' calls, and gray billows of smoke from sizzling barbecue pits.

"Ellia, you're beautiful today," Sang said suddenly.

Ellia's eyes widened. "Huh?" She stopped walking.

Shana bumped into Ellia's leg. "Can I have a pie, sister Ellia? Can I, please?"

The sun was hot, but Ellia felt cold. She quickly dropped a coin in Shana's hand and sent the little girl running off to the pie stand.

"I said that you look beautiful," Sang repeated.

"I don't think I like the way you said that."

"Well, it's true."

Ellia waited without expression for Sang to continue.

"Are you a girl or a boy?" he asked.

"A girl."

He sighed. "It took less than seventy days to make you look like a girl. You wear clothing wrapped to emphasize your form and colors to show off the highlights in your hair. You look eminently marriageable, thanks to Fan."

"Don't remind me, all right? It's really not so bad being a girl—"

"My ears are ringing. What?"

"It's not—"

"What's your name, girl?"

"Ellia." She wiped perspiration from her brow.

"You're not the El I know."

"I don't like the way you're talking to me at all."

"You don't? Some men talk to women only in that tone. Witness our elder brother and his wife."

"It's not so bad being a girl," she repeated, knowing the emptiness of her insistence. "I like taking care of Shana."

Sang just shook his head; his mahogany locks, cut shorter than Ellia's, flashed in the sun. In a low voice, he said, "This isn't the same girl who successfully masqueraded as a boy for more than a ritual cycle, managed to steal the finest horse in the precinct to get away, endured a public scourging without a sound, and finally escaped, while managing to keep her identity secret? Ellia Kellzi?" He shook his head again and sighed.

Ellia stood with her mouth open, then put her hands on her hips. "Who's side are you on, anyway? I thought you, like the rest of the family, were cherry-blossom happy that I had mended my ways."

Sang looked away. "Oh, I was," he admitted. "But that was before I had Marsai to compare you with. For a while I thought you were happy just being a girl."

"Sang, you must believe me. For the first time in my life, or at least in easy memory, I don't have to worry about being discovered. I can just go along with the world—"

"Like they teach all good girls in the shrines before they reach their Tenth ritual cycle?"

Ellia looked down, then drew a letter "E" in the dust with her big toe. "Look at Da. For the first time since—since forever, he doesn't have to be worried about what I'm going to do next. I can barely forgive myself for staying away over the dragonday holidays instead of going home. Gone for over a ritual cycle! What could he have thought?"

"That perhaps you were fending for yourself, perhaps enjoying yourself as any of his sons might?"

"What?" She looked into her brother's green eyes.

"Since the first time you ran away alone to school, he's tried to think of you as a boy. I'm sure he was worried then. I was worried! But he tries to understand. I think only Fan keeps him from saying so directly."

"If I could only believe that! How could you know? Fan said—"

"Yeah?"

"Fan said—!" It had been *Fan*, not her father, who told her how badly her disappearance had hurt him. So she had not misread her father's expression after all when he had first seen her again: he had only been happy to see that she chose to return to him, not angry that she had left.

Ellia had read into the situation exactly what *Fan* had wanted—Fan who stood to gain in her standing in the co-op if Ellia conformed; Fan who had purposely fainted at an opportune moment to make sure her Aunt Della, Ellia's mother, was buried locally instead of in her beloved homeland; Fan who was now her stepmother! Ellia gasped.

"In the last days you've acted more like a sister than I've ever known you to act," Sang said. "I've always thought of you practically as a twin brother. But since Fan—"

"Shut up, will you!" Ellia was shaking with rage.

Shana returned, peach-smeared and happy, and Sang bent down to catch her.

"Oh, thank you, Ellia!" Shana piped as Sang wiped her face. Ellia gazed in a different direction. In a daze, she saw women wrapped in sarongs in shades of brown, gray, and white. Ellia shivered.

"I'm going to the Southpoint shrine," Sang said. "The one near the hydroponics plant where father works. I'm going to see if I can get my requisite labors under his supervision."

Ellia nodded after a moment and unclenched her fists, then absent-mindedly removed the barrette to free her hair. She was suddenly aware of Sang's change purse being emptied into her own. She nodded at that also.

"Where are we going?" Shana asked plaintively as Sang took her by the arm. "Mama's that way, brother Sang." Ellia watched them disappear into the throng. Of everything, Ellia would most miss Shana.

Ellia jingled the money in her change purse, then sighed. She had about half an hour before she would be missed. She moved into the crowd in a direction she hoped would be away from her family and quickly counted the barters in her possession. She had enough for food for a few days, lodging, and some new clothes. There would be no time to change her hair color so she would say she came from the Karta Coast where red hair was common. She could easily describe the Karta Coast shrine if anyone asked about her earlier training; she had run away to that shrineschool the first time she had left home.

"May I help you, young lady?" a balding merchant with yellow teeth asked.

Ellia smiled, then nodded quickly.

"I have to get my brother a couple of blue shirts, like those in that pile."

"Indeed. And what size is your brother?"

"My size," Ellia answered. She was measured. The tailor packed up the shirts and counted the copper and silver barters he needed from her hand. Ellia went to another stall where she repeated the process for a pair of heavy, dark blue work pants. Then she purchased a carpet bag to hold her belongings and the cotton she knew she would need in a very few days. Finally, she bought a conical straw sunhat and a pair of boots.

Ellia was almost running by the time she neared the edge of the fair, but she stopped at the booth selling knives. Most adult women possessed knives, but never wore them; for a man a knife was an all-purpose tool:

for eating, prying open containers, not a few games of skill—and for cutting hair. Ellia had lost her own knife throwing it at the train in her escape from the Stone Coast shrine. She would need a new one, if for no other reason than not to stand out from other boys.

Ellia spotted a knife about the length of her forearm, its hilt set with stones the color of her eyes. She offered the merchant two-thirds of the tag price, and after appraising her for a few moments, he agreed. Glancing over her shoulder, she saw a large man in the distance paced by a tall woman wearing a sarong of the same yellow as Ellia's. She began to sweat suddenly. The merchant handed over her purchase. "And a sheath," she added hurriedly. Da and Fan were much closer, too close.

The merchant smiled. Ellia pulled a couple of coins from her purse, and he handed her a leather belt sheath. She ran her thumb lightly across the sharp edge of her blade, then sheathed the long knife with practiced grace. Ducking out of sight between the booths, she broke into a run.

Ellia's fears were quickly transformed into exhilaration as she ran through the tying grounds, past bullock carts and horse wagons and a couple of councillorcarries. Though those large lizards watched her with toothy grins, their grooms paid the girl no heed and she reached the cool shade of the nearby woods without being stopped. There the scents of pine and fresh loam made her feel better. She searched out a dense thicket where, hoping no one would intrude, she hacked away her girl-length hair with her new knife.

After changing into her new clothes, she headed back toward the fair, leaving her sarong behind. When she reached the tying grounds, though, she saw a wagon full of minors rolling away. Hastily she walked after them.

"Ho there!" one of the minors called as she approached.

"Ho back!" Ellia returned, waving. "Where are you headed?"

"North to the Fellbridge shrine," the spokesman replied as the wagon bumped over the rocks in the road.

"Might I hitch a ride?" Ellia asked, almost able to touch the rear gate of the wagon.

"Sure, if you can pay. We've put together funds for lodging and food and entertainment. Have you barters?"

Ellia glanced over her shoulder and saw Tagii. "Sure do," she said. She tossed up her bag, then accepted a hand up.

"Your barters first," the spokesman said. His almond-shaped eyes were black, his face freckled and spotted mildly with acne, his smile friendly. Ellia emptied her purse into her hand. Da, who made good money at his hydroponics job, paid all the taxes on the co-op and also provided well for Sang. Before a bump could upset her change, the spokesman nodded, one eyebrow raised.

"I should have known by all your new clothes. Welcome to our gang. What's your name?"

"Xander," Ellia answered quickly, then repeated the name in her head so she would not forget it.

"Well, Xander, I'm Tlezachi," he said. He introduced the rest with waves of his hand. "Looks as though you could treat us all with all you're carrying."

"A fine plum wine—" Ellia started, then checked herself. In most families only the girls drank wine; the boys were not allowed to drink until they passed the Test. Of course they did anyway. "Yes, for sure," she finished, gazing back at Tagii. When she saw that he had no interest in the blue-clothed minor with a sunhat, she sighed in relief and settled back onto a wagon seat. Tlezachi squeezed in next to her.

"Say, you have a twin sister, don't you?" the boy asked suddenly.

Ellia used every ounce of control to keep from reacting. Did he know Sang? She nodded.

"I thought so. I remember seeing you two walking together—your hair cued me. She's pretty, you know. I hope I can get a looker like her when I pass the Test."

"She's a brat," Ellia said, hoping to get him off the subject.

"Figures," Tlezachi said, settling back and tilting his sunhat over his eyes. "Girls with red hair are so pretty and yet so fiery."

"Yeah," Ellia agreed and laughed. She felt she could finally answer the question Sang had posed to her earlier: was she a girl or boy? *A girl, and I'll be damned if that prevents me from doing what I want!* She watched the woods pass by as the wagon bumped along, and she smiled once more.

Five

After a rowdy night at an inn, the group broke up at the train depot to buy tickets and find seats on the train. Ellia dropped into the soft cushions of a window seat and watched the trees and cottages whiz by.

"You do drink like a girl," a voice said suddenly. Ellia jerked around and was surprised to see that the speaker was not Comos, the boy who had become belligerently drunk last night and said the same thing. Instead she saw friendly Tlezachi.

Ellia's breath caught in her throat. "I don't know where my mind was," she said finally. "Hi, Tlee."

"I know where your mind was," Tlezachi returned, throwing his duffle bag on the shelf above the window. He plopped into the seat next to Ellia. "You were worrying about the placement tests and the type of labors required at the Fellbridge shrine. We all worry, don't we?"

"I've had more trouble with poor instructors and bad administrators, actually."

The freckle-faced boy folded his hands in his lap and nodded. "If you wish to pick something to worry about, that indeed could rate high on a list."

"Foolish, huh?"

"To worry about things you can't change? Perhaps in my case it's unprofitable, but for you? I noticed you managed not to get plastered last night. Something tells me you have nothing to worry about from bothersome administrators. You handle situations well."

"Thanks, but I did nothing special. Da—" Ellia swallowed "—Father lets us drink what we wish at home."

"Not terribly traditional. Frankly, I'm bringing it up because I'm embarrassed. You did my job last night, watching our collective purse. I guess I miscalculated."

Ellia laughed and so did Tlezachi. As the train wound out of the central mountains, passing the Blasted Hills where the Test was carried out and finally rolling north along the coast, Ellia and Tlezachi exchanged stories of their adventures in their shrineschools. Ellia avoided the subject of girls by shrugging it off, but Tlezachi was planning to take the Test at the end of this ritual cycle and was thinking of the advantages of early marriage.

When they arrived at Fellbridge, what they saw there discouraged them. Between the train depot and the distant ruins on which the Fellbridge shrine had been built lay a field packed with a good two-thousand minors. "Have you a second choice for a shrineschool?" Tlezachi asked, pursing his lips and shaking his head.

"Until I saw your wagon, I had made no choice," Ellia answered, surveying the field.

"Relying on chance all the way, eh?"

"You could say that, but I was in a hurry to leave the fair anyway."

Tlezachi raised an eyebrow at this, but was distracted by the movement of the train pulling out to roll down the track toward the north where a three-kilo-meter-long suspension bridge connected the Emerald Island with Emperor's Keep, the next big island. The ocean appeared as a solid blue pane of glass. "Why do you want this shrineschool so much?" Ellia asked.

"Simple. Fellbridge provides prerequisites for further education if you intend to attend the Council City university or the one at Southpoint after passing the Test. It assumes you are interested in building buildings, designing bridges, things like that—not just becoming a farmer. You have to have ambition to change yourself. You have that ambition?"

"Always have," Ellia replied. They sat on the edge of the platform, waiting for something to happen. Eventually they each purchased a roasted meat stick and walked together into the field to join the growing crowd of minors. With nothing to do but wait, Ellia snoozed away the afternoon.

"Hey, Xander, wake up!"

"Huh?" Ellia rubbed her eyes.

"Look," Tlezachi said, pointing in the direction of the late afternoon sun. Ellia had to squint to see the two emerald-robed figures and half a dozen red-clothed administrators walking toward the field. "This is where they tell us they have picked all the minors they need for this ritual cycle," Tlezachi drawled.

"Pessimist!"

"Blind optimist!"

The field became deathly quiet. Ellia was awed by the silence—how strange to be among so many people and still hear the priest's robes flutter in the sea breeze!

"Welcome, all of you, to the Fellbridge Shrine," the Master Administrator priest announced in a deep voice. A murmur passed through the crowd like a wave breaking on a beach. "Doubtless you have all realized we have a huge turnout this year, much more than we can possibly handle here."

A mass groan, accompanied by a noticeable movement toward the center, followed that announcement. The priest raised his hands, and everyone quieted.

"But this usually happens, so don't fear. We've made provisions to take care of the overburden and have always been able to accommodate all who pass our tests."

"That's what they always say," Tlezachi whispered in Ellia's ear. "Then they flunk fifty percent."

"Shush!"

The priest continued. "Many of you, I presume, have traveled from as far as the Hamure to sample scholarly philosophy and logic, which could lead to the priesthood, an administration seat, or a posting in the tech guild. Should this not be the case, do your comrades a favor: please leave now."

No one moved.

"Fine," the priest said. "We can handle all of you here or at our brother facility in the Open City. Some say that is the finest shrineschool in the Emerald Island, but I'm partial to Fellbridge myself.

"You'll obtain a basically identical education at both facilities. Labors in the Open City are more difficult and more demanding than they are here, but newer buildings, exposure to alien technology—many minors consider the extra work worth it. And it is work. If you cannot handle it, I don't recommend the Open City. I'll say nothing more. You decide. Everyone to the Open City, follow Priest Fumiko here to the tracks. The rest, stay seated."

Ellia stood. Tlezachi caught her by the sleeve. "Where are you going?"

"The Open City, of course. Sounds intriguing."

Tlezachi combed his right hand through his hair, then looked up at her. "It does, doesn't it? But I don't know. I need the 'in' to the post-Test schools. All my family has succeeded. I have no intention to be the first to fail."

"If you had decided to take the Test at the end of this ritual cycle, why'd you wait so long to come here?"

"I don't know. Procrastination, I guess."

"I don't think a M'admin priest would exaggerate the credentials of any shrine."

"I suppose not," Tlezachi said, looking at the crowd moving in the direction of the train tracks.

"You don't have to go with me, you know."

"I know, Xander," he said, looking back up at her. "Knowing somebody, though, makes it easier."

"Well, you'd better make up your mind because I'm going." The priest's words—"alien technology"—had evoked for Ellia images of autotrucks, wirelesses, and other bits of plastic technology that generally, except for high-tech novelties like her music box, did not seep down to the common man. She waited patiently while her new friend finally made up his mind to go.

Fumiko, the tinny-voiced master administrator of the Open City shrine addressed five hundred or so minors gathered around the rail platform. He wore the starburst medallion of a warrior priest; only that order could consecrate a battlefield or call down the wrath of the gods upon the enemy. He reminded Ellia of Mikitsu, the M'admin of the Stone Coast shrine.

"I don't like this Fumiko," Tlezachi said as he looked at the man's pale, bony face.

"I've seen as bad, worse even."

"Now I will distribute these forms," Fumiko began. "I want you to sign yours, tear it on the dotted line, and give one half to the supervisor who will be in your passenger car on the train. There is one thing I will stress: you have made a choice that involves a good deal of responsibility in exchange for all rewards. Follow the instructions of your master supervisor, as all errors will be dealt with severely. You have made the best choice of a preparatory school," he finished, crossing his arms over his chest. "Your master supervisor will instruct you in everything you require to know."

When the next train arrived, the master administrator boarded the first passenger car alone, and the minors piled into the next six cars, packing the train to capacity. Ellia and Tlezachi ended up standing, clinging to an aluminum rod suspended from the ceiling.

Their master supervisor had to shout to be heard over the sound of the wind coming through open windows and the clatter of the train wheels. "How many of you have attended the Open City shrine before? Raise your hands—if you can."

No one did.

"That's rare," the man chuckled, cleansing the air of the feeling of unease left by the master administrator. Ellia thought him to be about thirty ritual cycles old and probably from the Karta Coast, judging by the red highlights in his black hair. "My name's Ogawa," he continued, "and to make you all feel better, the M'admin neither teaches nor runs the religious services. You needn't worry about interacting with him in any fashion so long as you stay on your best behavior."

"That's good." Tlezachi whispered to Ellia.

"The other half of this"—the master waved the torn-off sheets he had collected from them—"is very important and should be guarded with your very lives. It cannot be replaced easily. This document allows you free access in and out of the Open City.

"Don't let the *Open* in Open City fool you. The designation has nothing at all to do with our view of the city as Emeralines, but rather it indicates a condition pertinent to non-Emeralines to whom most of the Emerald Island territories are forbidden. It shouldn't come as a shock to the majority of you that people with rather peculiar customs, appearances, and ways of speech live in the lands on the opposite side of the Dawn Sea. You will have a special opportunity to experience a way of life significantly different from your own. The best thing for you to do is not to judge what you see. Some sights will seem strange, indecent, or even disgusting. Don't judge. You will seem just as strange to others. All of you have different beliefs in different gods—you've all learned to keep your religious thoughts to yourselves or in the temple; you avoid arguments or worse that way. This is an identical situation. Just keep your thoughts to yourself all the time you are in the Open City and you'll do all right.

"And in particular, this applies to one, well, uh, oddity you'll surely encounter within the first few days here. Many of you who have heard of the Open City have probably heard of strange 'monsters' and such nonsense. Well, there are no monsters here, but there is another type of human being somewhat different from us that does visit often. Scientists comparing genetic structures claim that both species evolved recently from common ancestors. They call themselves the People and tend to be rather prideful and conceited, tied irrevocably to their concepts of honor. And for this last reason it is important that you not show any reaction when you first see them.

"They sometimes misconstrue human actions. If that happens, you are on your own. Don't fight them. The few who choose to fight generally die."

"Then why are they let on our island?" one minor yelled out over the train racket.

"Why? For a very good reason. About two hundred years ago, when their explorers found us, they discovered that we produce things they need—plastics and oil mostly. We exchange these for rare materials such as iron and magnesium, as well as bauxite and a few high-tech items they make better than we do. Chances are you all have in your possession something of foreign origin. The metal in your knife perhaps? The dye in your clothing? The expensive antelope leather in your boots? Or perhaps only the language you speak?

Yes, it is their language, and that of the humans who live in their lands, modified to be a little less harsh and more fluid. That alone hints at their power and the degree to which they could change our culture if they could trade unrestricted with the general public. Because we all profit by their visits here, we keep the Open City open to their vessels.

"But as I was saying, whatever happens when you first see one of the People, be careful—very careful. They are rather short by our standards, 140 centimeters tall on the average, but even so they are easily two to three times as strong as you or I. They are basically shaped like us, but their features are doglike: fur, claws, paws instead of feet, snout, and all."

Ellia, still haunted every time she ventured into the dark by the attack of the wild dog pack, spoke before she could stop herself. "Dogs?" She shivered.

"You," the supervisor said, pointing in her direction. "What's your name?"

Ellia swallowed once. "Xander, sir."

"You, in particular, be careful. Was there any reason for your reaction just now?"

"Y-yes. A good one, Master, sir." Ellia's hands had begun to sweat and stuck to the rod she gripped.

"You needn't call me by a title, Xander," he said reassuringly. "We aren't the Stone Coast shrine, and you don't have to be so jumpy. We aren't about to kick you out of the Open City unless we discover you are in danger."

"I realize that, sss—"

"Well, all right. And that goes for the rest of you. When you are given rules, you are being given guidelines to keep you alive and healthy. Understood? Yes, Xander, you were going to tell us why dogs bother you more than the rest of us?"

Ellia nodded. Taking a deep breath, she related what had happened, editing out any reference to her true gender.

"Good reason," Ogawa admitted. "But you must realize, the People are not dogs. We who live in the city consider them nothing more special than humans with a rather strange appearance. Be careful, understand? We like our minors to benefit from our shrine, and we get angry"—he raised his eyebrows—"when they don't."

Ellia laughed nervously and nodded. The lecture went on into the night as they traveled inland toward the northernmost tip of the Emerald Island. But throughout the trip, a fear that she had made a mistake grew inside her. Even as the minors were treated to their first glimpse of the lights of a modern city, Ellia was unable to escape that feeling of foreboding.

Electricity was no novelty to Ellia, but seeing an entire city lit up by roving, flickering, and racing multicolor lights astounded her. The Open City lay on the shore of a shallow, circular bay fifty kilometers in diameter, an incomparable harbor that supported a huge volume of trade. As the train snaked down the mountainside, nearing the city, Tlezachi pointed to a gigantic ship skimming out toward the sea at no less than 150 kph. Through the trees, they could see words written in neon light—names and catch phrases to attract attention to mercantile houses—glowing in red, blue, orange, yellow, every lurid hue imaginable. Would it seem to be night in the city at all?

Then the forest completely obscured their view with its hulking growths, and the train stopped to unload passengers. The minors stood in the cold night air on a long platform not far from the tallest fence Ellia had ever seen.

"Will you look at that," Tlezachi said. Ellia gauged the height of the monstrosity to be a minimum of fifteen meters. The uppermost links gave way to a bristly porcupine's coat of spikes on which two unlucky bats had been skewered, one still alive and fluttering in the blue-white glare that lit the main rail entrance to the closed

Open City. Men armed with rifles patroled the gate accompanied by a black, long-nosed variety of chee. "They are certainly serious when they say the rest of the Emerald Island is prohibited to outsiders."

"That is an understatement if I ever heard one," Ellia agreed.

While the train rolled out, Ogawa organized his group and marched them off the wooden platform. "The fence is electrified," he explained. "For those who don't yet understand the principle, that means it is deadly to the touch. It's like having lightning bolts on guard."

Ellia swallowed hard and looked up at the bats, hoping she had made the correct choice in coming to the Open City. She shivered and buttoned her collar to her neck, folding it up to protect herself from the hungry night.

The guards checked their papers, stamping them and jotting down identifying information in silvery ink. "Thin; mahogany-red hair, green eyes," Ellia's document said. She folded it and placed it in her pocket.

The minors were loaded aboard flatbed trucks, then driven through the forest and into the sparkling city itself, where people bustled along streets filled with horse and autotruck traffic. Again in the hills, the trucks finally turned into a drive lit by globes of mercury light and stopped, one after another, before a four-story, tan brick building. Ellia's teeth chattered from the cold as she and Tlezachi joined the growing group of minors on the sidewalk.

In a large refectory the newcomers were served a meal of rice mixed with curried beef and crisp vegetables, after which they queued up to receive bedding, supplies, and light red uniforms. Cubicles were assigned alphabetically. Tlezachi's was in a different part of the main secular building than Ellia's, but the two were not far apart. The day ended with medical checkups for all the minors.

Following an uneasy hour-long wait in a hallway lit

by fluorescent lights, Ellia was summoned. "Change into the smock now and we'll get this over with quickly," the doctor ordered as Ellia listened to the door close behind her. She saw the smock hanging on a peg, the shelves and shelves of herbals, the short man with blue almond-shaped eyes magnified by glasses. She swallowed hard.

"Don't just stand there."

"I don't want to go through this again."

"Huh?" He looked over his glasses at her. "We haven't time to dawdle here. What are you talking about?"

"I'm talking about having had an examination just yesterday at the Karta Coast shrine before they told me they had no place for me to sleep. I have no intention of being jabbed or poked at again. I tried to tell—"

"Physicians do not jab and—"

"I was told I was healthy," Ellia interrupted quickly to keep the man off balance.

"Healthy? You appear healthy, but—"

"But what?" Ellia said in a very irritated voice.

The man checked his clock and sighed. "If you're healthy, let's not waste each other's time." He waved toward the door. "Tell the next minor to come in, Xander."

Ellia turned and rushed from the room.

A poorly rested Ellia spent the next morning meeting instructors and priests, receiving new books, and learning her way around unfamiliar buildings. In the afternoon, Ogawa took his group by autotruck down the hill into the city proper to introduce the minors in his charge to a big city.

And big it was. They passed buildings five to eight stories high—huge for a land of frequent earth tremors—of ruddy brick and pale granite. On each block electric lamps were mounted on tall posts. Black wires spun out everywhere, a virtual spider's web to capture the sky. And the signs! The moment the truck left the residential quarter of town with its houses and apartment complexes, Ellia's eyes were assaulted by words and pictures. *Buy liquid sealer, buy seat covers, buy zero-attenuation light guides, buy powdered lubricants* —buy, buy, buy.

One billboard caught the eyes of all the minors: a pale-skinned woman wearing a yellow helmet and standing next to barrels of "catalysts." Her legs were bare to the knees, and her arms were completely naked. The woman's eyes were strange too, narrower, heavy-lidded, and her brow was more pronounced than in any Emeraline. The woman was no Emeraline, but neither was she one of the People. As the truck continued through the city, Ellia kept alert for her first glimpse of the strange creatures.

The truck stopped at an outdoor bazaar where the minors purchased their afternoon meal. It was there that Tlezachi's hawk eyes noticed the oddest sight yet. He pointed to a woman.

"Blind priests!" Ellia whispered under her breath. "And she's an Emeraline too!"

The woman saw Tlezachi pointing and reined her chestnut mare in their direction. Ellia's mouth dropped open. The loose, lacy material of the woman's sarong blew behind to expose her thighs and flapped in unison with the lace scarf tied around her straw sunhat. The woman was stunningly beautiful, with a silky complexion, finely rounded nose, obsidian eyes and hair. Ellia's breath caught, when the woman's steed, hooves clattering on cobblestone, pranced to a halt before them.

"Minor," she said in a loud, fluid voice, "hasn't your supervisor told you how impolite it is to point?" She spoke with a singsong, spicy accent.

"He has," Ogawa called from the truck halfway down the block.

"But we're new to the Open City," Ellia interjected.

"Please, if you can, Missy, forgive us." Tlezachi, still stunned, nodded vigorously.

The woman reined her impatient horse and looked down at Ellia. "Missy?" she said. "No one's called me that for ages. And I suppose 'sir' wouldn't do, would it?"

"Then what may we call you?" Ellia asked.

"Oh, Missy will do. Quite appropriate for you—at least for a few ritual cycles yet." She smiled momentarily, then patted her nervous mount. "I rather like being called Missy." The horse backed a few steps again, clearing the street of pedestrians.

"Your husband lets you ride a horse?" Tlezachi asked suddenly, recovering his voice.

"It's not a matter of somebody letting me," the woman returned. The horse swerved, and without thinking, Ellia reached out and caught the bridle.

"Bah, Kellen!" the woman scolded the horse. "Thank you much, Minor. I haven't the slightest notion what's got into the beast, really I haven't. Say, would you do me a favor? That booth that says 'Chicken on rice sticks'—could you get me one?" She flipped Ellia a coin.

"You—you can read?" Tlezachi sputtered.

The woman gazed skyward, then down. "Your supervisor is not going to be happy about how you learn your lessons, minor sir." Tlezachi reddened.

Ellia released her hold on the bridle strap, and the horse pranced a few meters away as Ellia headed for the booth. The vendor, all smiles, handed her a crackly, sticky stick with a filleted chicken breast skewered on it. "Pleased to be of service," he said, refusing the coin. Full of questions, Ellia shrugged and returned with the food.

"Keep the coin," the woman said, taking a big bite of chicken and nudging her horse away before Ellia could say another word.

Ellia felt surprised and offended at the same time.

Everything she had learned of womanly conduct had just been violated; the woman's indecent clothing and animated way of speech were especially shocking. Yet as unwomanly as "Missy" had been, she had been unquestionably feminine. Ellia suddenly wondered if she herself were unfeminine. The idea of a woman having the prerogatives of a male sparked a new desire in Ellia. How in the broad, green Emerald Island did the woman get away behaving as she did?

By the time Ellia had passed the placement tests and had been at the Open City shrine for four days, she had already asked three of her superiors about the woman in white lace. No one would give her a satisfying answer. "You'll find out when you get older," one man said. "Wait until you pass the Test, then ask if you still want to," another told her. And she couldn't ask directly what she really wanted to know: "Where did the woman get her privileges, and how could I match them?" She felt terribly frustrated.

Ellia and Tlezachi were quickly assigned requisite labors at the docks where they worked cleaning and unloading for non-Emeralines who paid the shrine-school for the service. Throughout the Emerald Island territories, labors performed by the minors kept the schools independent of all but minimal Council financial support.

Four days out of ten the minors rode down with Ogawa who escorted them to their assignments. Unless requested by a specific employer, a minor received a new job each day; Ellia had worked two different ships so far. As they walked down the row of warehouses and docks, the scents of kelp, fish, and oil reminded Ellia of the days she had spent at the Karta Coast shrine.

"Master, sir," a guttural, non-Emeraline voice called. "Please wait! We require your assistance!"

Daydreaming, Ellia did not notice the others stop, and she walked into the minor before her.

"Will you watch where you're going!" the boy said with an angry shove.

"Hey, watch it," Ellia returned, surprised, putting a hand to her knife hilt.

"Look," someone to her left whispered. "It's a shag!"

Shag? Ellia shot around to face the docks. There, animatedly talking to Ogawa, stood the first of the People Ellia had seen. The creature appeared much like a sheepdog molded into the form of a human. Ellia wondered how the shaggy beast could see: only the very tip of its leathery nose was visible in the haystack of white hair. Its red clothing stretched from groin to shoulders, leaving all its limbs free. It had been gesturing with a clipboard like the one Ogawa carried, but suddenly it stiffened and perked its floppy ears. The brown nose pointed toward Ellia, and her heart skipped a beat.

"Did you say that?" Ogawa angrily asked her.

"Said—said what? Sir?"

Ogawa looked at the shag, then back to Ellia. Narrowing his eyes, he said slowly, "You have your hand on your knife hilt."

Ellia looked down, realized that he was right, and instantly pulled her hand away. "I'm sorry, sir. It's my Stone Coast training, I guess. I apologize if I said something wrong, but I didn't say anything except to the minor who shoved me, sir."

"He speaks truthfully," the shag said. A feminine lilt in the growling voice betrayed the shag's gender. "The voice, it is wrong," she explained in a loud voice, then added, "Do not call any of the People 'shags' unless you are willing to fight for the right to do so. Do I make myself clear, Emeraline minorcubs?" Ellia gulped.

"I am truly sorry, Worthiness," Ogawa said. "I assure you it won't happen again. It is my fault that—"

"Oh, Master-sir, that is quite all right," the shag assured him. "Just feel fortunate the lesson was provided by one of the People who displays little temper."

Little temper! Ellia thought. She cracked a smile but caught herself quickly when the shag looked in her direction.

"And you state I may acquire two workers? We shall pay our fees by nightfall. We are desperate."

"Yes, two can be spared, at least for today."

"*Djo.* Thank you incredibly much. I select that individual"—the shag pointed her clipboard in Ellia's direction—"and any other you consider a hard worker."

Ellia's eyes widened momentarily. "Me?" she mouthed silently.

The shag nodded.

Ellia and a boy named Yuki trotted uneasily after the white-furred shag toward a ship called the *Star Sailor*. From bow to stern the *Star Sailor* ran nearly fifty meters, with passenger cabins forward of center, ahead of a stack and a tall mast which doubled as a crane to service the afterdeck. Five hatches punctuated the main deck area. A few large, wooden shipping crates lay scattered on deck.

"Sit here," the shag ordered, then entered the first cabin door. Ellia and her coworker waited in the sun for the shag to return. Many ships in port displayed the ravages of the ocean salt, but on the *Star Sailor* Ellia saw well-bleached teak planking, railing, trim. Everywhere else a spotless coat of bright yellow paint testified to the crew's love for their vessel.

The white-furred shag returned with a tall, blond, swarthy man with a middle-aged face and a young man's manner. A long, plaid scarf was wrapped around his neck. Ellia was surprised—the man had a cold! The last time Ellia had seen someone with a cold had been when her mother died as a result of one. The man didn't look very ill, though. He sneezed, then addressed the two minors.

"I am one of the owners and captain of this ship. Xander, Yuki, you two do not realize, perhaps, how much we appreciate procuring your services. This ship must be unloaded today, even if it takes into the night. Chriz here and I shall demonstrate operational procedures for the crane and other rigs. We can afford no mistakes. Upon completing our task, we will see if we cannot produce some barters to make profitable your time spent here. I think Xander shall operate the lift, and Yuki the crane." After showing Ellia how to drive the three-wheeled stacking vehicle, the captain retired to the cabin, leaving the shag to supervise and load the crane inside the hold. The boxes jangled metallically, and Ellia wondered what type of cargo they were unloading.

Her speculation was interrupted when a silver-haired shag came running up the gangplank. He glanced at the minors, but went directly to the hold. "I found the bastard merchant," he called down in a gravelly voice.

"Success?" Chriz cried back. "What were his words? Will he accept this shipment?"

"He claims it is late, but yes, yes, Chriz, he accepts it!"

"*Djo*, Hunter!" the white shag exclaimed joyously. Her furry hands appeared on the edge of the hatch, and she pulled herself up to the main deck. She skipped over and embraced the silver-furred shag with such gusto that she spun him around. He laughed, then returned her passionate kiss. They had no human lips, but what they did with their muzzled mouths open made Ellia wonder if they would suffocate.

"Thank the Huntress!" the silver shag cried when they separated. Hugging him, Chriz introduced Yuki and Ellia and complimented them on their hard work.

"Best tell the captain the news—it should cheer him," she said before jumping below. The older shag shook his head and made for the cabin. From the control cage of the crane, Yuki looked at Ellia and mouthed, "What was that all about?" Ellia shrugged. Then the silver-furred shag returned to a lift identical to Ellia's, and for the first time since they had begun, Ellia thought they might actually finish unloading the huge ship.

Midway into the hot, humid afternoon, they broke for lunch. Feeling a bit ill, Ellia only picked at the half of a roast fowl—turkey, they called it—provided her. Afterward, the shags began unloading nearly double the number of crates per craneload.

As the cargo was pulled slowly out of the hold, Chriz and her fellow took turns coming out of the hold to guide Yuki in placing the load. Chriz was standing on deck when suddenly a high-pitched buzz like a thousand maddened bees screeched out of the air near her head. She instinctively raised her right arm to cover her face just as the singing cable snapped. The sheared wire whipped around with a sound like gunshots.

An instant later, Chriz slid across the deck to lie covered with very human, red blood.

Six

Crates crashed to the deck. Chriz whimpered and tried to crawl away from the whirling wire and commotion before she slumped, unconscious.

Yuki paled and froze. Ellia gasped, then sprang from the protective cage of her lift and sprinted to the shag's side. She hoped what she had learned about first aid in the girlschool before her Tenth would also apply to this "other form of human being." The shag's forearm was slit open from elbow to wrist like a fish ready for filleting. The fur was slippery with blood, and Ellia had trouble finding the correct pressure points to control the bleeding. "Help!" she screamed. "Please!" But Yuki remained frozen like a statue.

The older shag scrambled out from the hold and slid to a halt beside the girl. "Huntress!" he cried.

Ellia was afraid she wouldn't be able to grip Chriz's arm much longer. Then she felt a tug on her left shoul-

der. She heard a loud tearing sound and glanced around
in time to see the silver-furred shag using her own knife
to cut off her sleeve. With Ellia's assistance, the shag
fashioned the material into a tourniquet, using the loose
end to close the wound farther down. The captain,
having rushed out the cabin door after Ellia's scream,
swore inarticulately, then rushed back inside—to the
wireless, Ellia hoped, to signal for assistance. When
Ellia and the silver-furred shag carried Chriz into the
cabin, the captain held the door for them. "I have summoned a physician," he said.

The sofa on which they placed Chriz became darkly
stained. When two Emeraline doctors arrived, they
immediately appraised the situation, shifted Chriz to a
table, then ejected the other three from the room.

When she returned to the deck, Ellia discovered
that her coworker had vanished. Lance, the silver-
haired shag, sat crosslegged in a corner with his head
in his hands. Ellia sighed and found a hose; with cold
salt water she rinsed the sticky blood off her hands
and off the teak planks of the deck. She retrieved her
knife, still wondering how the shag had taken it from
her without her awareness.

Already the sun had drifted noticeably toward the
horizon. Ellia grimaced as she spotted another autotruck pulling up. She strode over to her lift, pulled on
her gloves, and began hauling and loading the crates
already on deck. Finally Lance stood and walked up
to the silver cable with a tool kit. Brown dried blood
crusted a few of the strands that he cut using a huge
pair of snippers. He replaced the grippers and control
wires. Though his nose twitched often and he looked
ready to cry, he did not. He flung the pieces of cable
far into the harbor, then manned the crane. The captain, despite his cold, went into the hold to load the
crane.

Twilight approached quickly, throwing garish rays
of orange and red across the sky and bringing a welcome cool breeze whistling into the harbor. When the

doctors departed, assuring Lance that Chriz would recover, the work proceeded faster. Then Ellia heard someone calling her.

"Xander, Yuki!" Ogawa shouted. Ellia brought the lift to a halt. She stepped out of the cage and went to the railing.

"Yuki left, sir—" she began.

"What happened to you, Xander?" Ogawa said, his fingers drumming loudly on his clipboard. Ellia felt suddenly conscious of the thirty minors staring up at her torn and bloodied uniform.

"We had a small accident," she replied quickly.

"Is that blood?" he asked, squinting and moving closer to the ship.

"Yes."

The man turned pale. "What did you do?" he demanded, one foot on the boarding plank. Ellia heard the crane motor whine to a stop behind her.

"I told you, we had an accident." Exhausted, she felt peevish and added no details.

"Xander—"

Lance approached the railing then. Ogawa jumped backward. In a gruff voice, Lance said, "There indeed occurred an accident on board, master supervisor. Though I did not witness it personally, I will verify the fact."

"What? What happened, Xander? Tell me, instantly!"

Lance answered for her. "A cable to our crane snapped, and an end slashed open my mate's arm to the bone. Had it not been for your charge's quick action, she would have bled to death. The uniform, which we will pay to replace, provided a tourniquet. Is that sufficient explanation?" Ellia smiled at Lance's compliment.

Ogawa looked shocked. "Uh—yes, sufficient."

"Excellent, for now I wish to lodge a complaint against one of your group."

"Huh?"

"This Yuki who arrived with Xander—the People dislike any soul who runs from a serious situation, regardless of how insignificant the help he feels he can give. Extra hands may have proved necessary to save my mate's life, but as you see"—Lance gestured behind him—"Yuki is no longer present. He has violated a basic code of honor. Warn him to avoid meeting any of the People lest he be seriously injured," the shag finished with a dangerous growl. Ellia felt her skin crawl.

"I—I'll tell the minor what you said. I'm very sorry—"

"Why do humans never understand that each person is responsible for his own actions?"

"I—" Ogawa cleared his throat. "We are taking the minors back to the shrine now. Xander—"

The captain appeared to the other side of Ellia. "We are not finished yet, sir. We have lost one of the minors we contracted for, and one of our crew is incapacitated. Might we not retain Xander for a while longer?"

Ogawa shrugged. "We have to feed and—"

"We will take care of that."

"Well, you must realize Xander's responsibilities to labor are minor, four days out of ten, ten hours for each day. This assignment is proving excessive. Xander?"

"Our hold is four-fifths empty, sir, but they need it all unloaded very soon. I should like to stay and help," Ellia said as Lance patted her on the shoulder.

Ogawa thought for a moment, then jotted something down on his clipboard. Sighing, he said, "I guess there's nothing wrong with that. It's not a permanent assignment, but then—well, yes, I guess it will be all right."

"Thank you, sir," Ellia called down. "Will you excuse us? We have work to do."

The master supervisor nodded, then motioned his flock down the dock toward the next pickup. Ellia returned to her lift and found herself smiling. For the first time in her life, someone had honestly thanked her for her help. But they didn't know she was a girl, she remembered sourly as she pulled the levers and threw the lift into motion.

When the last crate was finally unloaded and payment received from the merchant, Ellia joined Lance and the captain in a sullen banquet. Overpeppered roast turkey and bloody undercooked beef, well-suited to the carnivorous habits of the People, were too rich for Ellia. At home everyone ate with their hands; at the shrines, spoons and knives were used; but the people from the People's Collective utilized two sharpened sticks, the manipulation of which confounded the girl. She picked at her food, exhausted; also, her overall aching told her that her period was upon her. The sooner she returned to the shrine, the better.

When the captain finally gave her a gold hundred-bartercoin and said he would summon transportation for her, Ellia felt only relief. But then Chriz awakened from her sedation and asked for Xander. Reluctantly, Ellia agreed to speak to her.

Chriz lay on a huge, half-oval bed, her right arm bandaged from her hand to just above her elbow. "You look rotten," Chriz commented.

"I feel rotten," Ellia admitted. Her glance took in purple draperies, a purple satin bedspread, rich paneling, and shelves filled with stuffed animal pillows—chee, tawny cats Ellia could not identify, hounds, and human dolls. And sitting beside the bed was a huge, tan and white, stuffed dog with one black ear flopped over its head and a red felt tongue lolling from its mouth. Ellia had to smile despite her dislike of dogs.

"Not what you expected?" the shag asked, her voice syrupy from painkillers.

"No disrespect, but you're right." Ellia was reminded of the ragdolls Shana loved so much and the few Ellia herself had once possessed.

"As you humans are so fond of saying, I am only human, too." Chriz slid her feet off the bed and found gold slippers shaped for paws. She wore a yellow satin robe. "The People love children, but we conceive so very rarely. Until Lance and I produce one of our own, my friends here substitute, albeit poorly." Chriz ruffled the fur and ears on the big dog, then rose.

"Are you sure you should be out of bed?"

"Oh, I feel pretty good, considering. Rather euphoric, too." Chriz chuckled. "The People's Collective may sail the oceans of salt and space and colonize the Korane and the mountains of Slen, our moon, but your people still train the best physicians known."

"That seems hard to believe, as advanced as your people reportedly are."

"Oh, but it is true. People travel across the world to the Open City for medical attention. It is one of your people's well-known trade items. As for me, Lance informs me that the surgeon believes I will escape this without a scar. Indeed, I can already see skin growing into the wound sealant. But more than anything, I wish to thank you for your actions and courage. Lance tells me I owe you my life. I thank the Hunter that unlike most Emeralines you are not frightened of us." Chriz offered her left hand to Ellia. Ellia swallowed hard and let her hand be grasped by the other. She shivered.

"You really look pale," the shag commented again, backing away a step or two. She sniffed the air once, then retreated another step, tilting her head slightly.

"What's the matter, Chriz? You don't look so well yourself." Ellia broke into a sweat as the shag sniffed the air again.

The shag's ensuing laughter was low and throaty. "Sooo, you *are* different from all the Emeralines I have met thus far!"

Alarmed, Ellia dived for the cabin door, but Chriz breezed across the room and kicked the door closed. With her good hand, the shag disarmed the girl before she could even think to reach for her knife.

"Wha—what are you going to do to me?"

"You misunderstand me."

"I didn't do anything!" Ellia said, squirreling across the wall away from the shag.

"Will you stop this, Xander!" Chriz threw away Ellia's long knife. "You have done nothing wrong."

"Then—"

"You make unfounded assumptions. Just calm your fears, will you!" Chriz said, sitting again on her bed. "I apologize for this," Chriz added. "I have scant experience dealing with humans, raised as I was away from the human reservations. Even being close to Peaessa for a year and a half failed to remedy that."

"Peaessa?"

"Yes, the crewmember you are replacing. We lost her just a few days ago."

"Lost?" Ellia asked, still too frightened to manage more than a syllable at a time.

"I thought better of you than this, Xander," Chriz said bitingly. Her pride injured, Ellia straightened and edged away from the wall.

Chriz nodded. "Peaessa fell in love with a Haywayee islander and jumped ship. We searched for her, but this shipment required delivery. We departed, hit a squall in transit, which forced us even farther behind schedule, then arrived this morning, and the rest you know."

"Oh," Ellia said.

"You are different, Xander, are you not?"

"Really, I don't know what you mean." Moisture began beading on her forehead.

"I saw the sparkle in your eyes the moment you saw all my friends lying about—that was my first clue. The second one floats in the air. I may risk insulting you in a graver fashion than my accidental treatment of you just now, should I prove to be wrong, but I do not think I am wrong."

"I really don't understand what you're trying to say, Chriz."

"Ho, ho, I am sure you *do* understand. You, Xander, are female!"

This is it, you've been caught again! Ellia told herself. What would it take to escape from the Open City?

"You are female, are you not, Xander?"

"I am," Ellia admitted.

Chriz chuckled. "I thought so. I thought so. My nose never tells me wrong!"

"What are you going to do with me? I saved your life, *remember*?"

"I have honor, my little girl," Chriz warned, then added in a much freer voice, "I would do nothing to hurt you."

"You sound just like my stepmother. She's said that enough times and each time stung me badly."

"I am sorry if you refuse to believe me. You interest me. Outside the Open City, are their women anything like you?"

"Do you mean, can the girls do what the boys do? No."

"Yes, that is the information I have. You are a maverick then, eh, Xander?"

"Maverick?"

"Near my father's horse ranch where I was raised, we could always find a herd or two of wild horses. The Ancients called these mavericks."

"That describes me, I guess."

"It is unfortunate that a hard-working, intelligent girl like you is driven to such—"

"Driven? I suppose I should stay home, bored and brainless, and just breed children and serve a husband like every other woman in history?"

"Please, Xander," Chriz said, raising a hand. "What I was attempting to say is that I find some Emeraline customs rather disgusting, and one I particularly dislike is the way they treat their females. I am a female, if you will recall, and can sympathize with you at least on that level."

"But that doesn't change any of the facts of the world. Men get what they wish for, and women rarely do!"

Chriz snorted. "They brainwash you expertly, but that is only to be expected."

"Huh?"

"Repeat a concept enough times—even one that has no basic validity—and people begin to believe it is natural law. Place some 'divine' reasoning behind it, make your important gods male, and the law that forces all the girls to grow into the familiar human pattern becomes unquestionable. You are a definite violation, I perceive."

"Can women, human women, actually choose their destiny where you come from?" Ellia asked with growing incredulity.

"Any woman determined to find her own way can, yes. Although sometimes there is the obstacle of clan ties since the People's Collective has no power in that area."

"It is difficult to believe," Ellia said in a low voice.

Chriz shook her head, then pointed at the girl. "It is a fine disguise you have maintained! Yet it does have one rather feminine flaw in it, does it not? Perhaps I can partially repay the debt I have incurred this afternoon and evening." Chriz gestured for Ellia to follow her out of the cabin. Both the captain and a very worried Lance were at the door when the shag opened it.

"What happened?" Lance asked, embracing his mate.

She kissed him on the nose. "I discovered Xander is a girl."

Ellia shivered nervously, but other than the openmouthed expression on the captain's face and a stunned silence from the silver-furred shag, neither reacted with anger or loathing. Ellia's eyes filled with tears, and she stared at the floor. Chriz took her hand and led her down the corridor to another stateroom with unfinished teak walls bare but for a few pictures of flowers.

"Peaessa's quarters," Chriz said, pulling Ellia through to another door and into the shower room and head. Chris sat Ellia down on the closed toilet fixture, then opened a compartment over the washbasin.

"Yes," she said, taking out a smoky yellow vial and shaking it like a rattle. "It figures. She left her supply."

"Of what?"

"Her protection. I guess she wants to start a family. These pills will solve a major difficulty of disguising yourself as a boy: human women utilize these to prevent themselves from conceiving, but with added benefit of delaying menstruation for long periods of time."

Ellia stood up. "Oh, no, you're not going to drug me!" The masters at one shrineschool had tried to drug her when she refused to identify her family.

"Oh, sit down," Chriz said. "Will you once and for all accept my apology for frightening you? I really have no intention of harming you."

Ellia looked up into the shag's fur-covered face and could see nothing human, nothing she could read, but she realized that she indeed was acting childish. "I'm sorry," she finally said.

Chriz's nose twitched. "The medication's effect is not permanent. If the dosage is discontinued, the effect wears off in about six days. After that you could conceive again, though I doubt you worry much about having children yet."

Ellia felt a twinge of guilt as she reached for the bottle: half the male Emeraline children died during the Test, and because of the rigors of repeated childbirth, women generally lived only half as long as men. Until the day that Emeraline medical science, which Chriz claimed to be so fine, filtered down to the average person as high-tech items had started to, acting to prevent having children, however briefly, seemed very wrong. Then Ellia recalled who was to take the pills and for what purpose. What had Chriz said about brainwashing?

As Ellia took the vial, she noticed that Chriz's hand shook almost as much as her own.

"Chriz?" Ellia saw the shag gulping for air.

Her voice became a throaty whisper. "I think you were right, Xander. I should not have left my bed." Ellia jumped up from her seat.

"Lance!" Ellia cried.

"What did I warn you?" the silver-furred shag accused his mate as he bounded in and gathered her into his arms.

"The surgeon said take it easy, I know," she replied. "Xander," she called over Lance's shoulder on their way out of Peaessa's stateroom.

"Yes?"

"Your name is not Xander, is it?"

"No, it isn't."

"I guessed as much. What is it then?"

Ellia thought for a moment as Lance placed Chriz back on her bed and covered her with the purple spread. "I can't tell you. What you don't know someone can't accidently get from you and track me to my family."

"Xander!" Lance said.

"She is right, dear," Chriz said, nodding as she propped herself up on a pillow. "But Xander is definitely a boy's name. Let us see... I am good with names. How about Greeneyes? That is *Verdjhua* in what linguists good-naturedly call Shaggish behind our backs. An excellent, very feminine name, I think."

Ellia shrugged. "Fairjewel?"

"Close," Chriz sighed. "Greeneyes is better. Promise you will take the pills as it says on the label, now. They won't hurt you."

She could read the pharmacy label, warnings, and prescription with little trouble, though it contained none of the contractions that made the Emeraline dialect of the long-ago-adopted Pecol language fluid and easy to pronounce. "'Twice a week,'" Ellia read aloud. "That's three days less than a dogday, right? Two doesn't divide into—"

"Every four days, then."

"Hmm," Ellia said, nodding.

The captain escorted her from the room. "A girl?" he said.

Ellia stiffened.

"You worry too much," he said, laughing. Together they went to wait on the dock for the hack. The evening had grown cold, and Ellia's teeth began to chatter.

"Chriz likes you," the captain said.

"What makes you think that?" Ellia asked.

"I have been around shags on and off all the years I have sailed the oceans. And Lance has been my partner most of the last twenty. I know Lance well and have come to know his recent bride almost as well."

"Recent?"

"Two years, I think, but they are not considered married by shag custom until they have had their first child. As far as the People are concerned, only the blood shared in a child binds them together. The People are rather infertile as a rule. I guess it is an incentive for them to keep trying, though I have never heard of a shag female who needs incentive. Chriz does like you. Her giving you a name is a good sign—generally, shags dislike humans."

"You said 'shag.'"

"The right has to be earned, and you have earned that and more today."

"Oh," Ellia said sleepily. "It's nice Chriz likes me, I guess."

"Lance and I discussed you, but Chriz's feelings about you settled it. Rather than replacing Peaessa, we would like to request your service on a regular basis."

She looked up at the man. In the light from the warehouses, she could see little save his blond hair. "But I'm a girl," she said.

"Peaessa was a woman, Greeneyes." He chuckled. "We require a capable worker, and you fit the job description."

Ellia sighed. "No one has ever paid me a finer compliment."

"You deserve every compliment. Besides saving Chriz's life, you quite possibly saved Lance's too. Losing another *Jarare*—almostwife—would have been too much pain for him to survive."

"Another life saved?" Ellia whispered.

Despite the lapping of the waves against the dock, the captain heard the pain in her voice. "What is wrong?"

Ellia took a deep breath and told the story of her saving Shana from the dog pack and then having her brother take the credit. She also related the story of Terra and how everyone forgot, even Terra, what had happened. Every time she saved someone, it seemed she ended being hurt instead. And the one time she needed to save herself by escaping, she was whipped. She could save others, but not herself—especially not from growing into a woman. She related the story of the horse chase and the whipping to her sympathetic listener.

"And ultimately it all occurred only because you are a girl?" He shook his head. "I admire your verve, Greeneyes. I possess no such courage myself."

The next day in town, after evading Comos—whom Ellia had disliked ever since he had been so nasty that night at the inn on the way to the Fellbridge Shrine—Ellia found a jewelry hawker selling silver lockets. She and Tlezachi each bought a locket to hold their passes, but Ellia's locket contained a second compartment in which she could hide her pills, along with a piece of cotton to keep them from rattling. Tlezachi raised an eyebrow but said nothing when Ellia ducked behind a cherry tree to fill her locket. She chucked the empty yellow vial into an open sewer drain, hoping that would be the end of her problems.

Later they saw another of the strange, privileged woman. She had hip-length, silky mahogany hair and wore the traditional gold robes and a sarong wrapped untraditionally around her hips so that in front it split to the knot at her navel while behind her it lay correctly in a train of fabric across the back of her palomino walking horse. Her feet and much of her legs were bare. She rode beside a purple-clothed councillor mounted on a gray-furred, bipedal councillorcarry that stepped high in imitation of the walking horse. When the councillorcarry eyed the pedestrians in their path and opened its mouth to hiss and reveal sharp yellowed teeth, everyone stepped aside quickly. And then the two were gone.

"You have a funny expression on your face, Xander," Tlezachi said.

"And with good reason." Ellia pointed down the street. "Explain that if you can."

"I can't."

"Well, I intend to find out."

"You like to bet? I'll wager that you'll fail today and you'll buy me dinner."

"Are you naturally pessimistic?"

"Me? No," Tlezachi said, putting his hands in his pockets and starting down the street. "No, just hungry and pretty near broke."

"And probably smarter than me, too," Ellia mumbled. She fingered the coins in her purse and searched the faces of likely street merchants to begin her quest for information.

Though they tried to avoid him, they eventually encountered Comos. He, too, was interested in the strange woman and was willing to assist with his purse. But even money failed to buy the answers they wanted.

Comos was neither rude, as he was so often, nor belligerent, but rather amiable. He showed them the vegetable market, a well-stocked herbalist, a beautiful hillside zoo, the theater district, the auction square where at least one shag could always be seen monitoring for the Collective NewsNet, and of course the restaurants. The bustling Open City was the financial nexus of the Emerald Island, matched in its metropolitan flavor only by the Council City across the bay—or so Comos told them.

"How do you know about all these places?" Tlezachi asked between messy spoonfuls of rice and fish. "You've been here only as long as we have, haven't you?"

Comos just leaned his chair back against the wall, watching the two finish the meal he had bought for them. "No. I've visited the Open City a number of times before. I've been here and to the Council City with my brother and my father. He was a petroleum chemist down—"

"You're the one to come to before chemistry exams, eh?" Tlezachi interrupted.

"Nah, not me. Chemistry's not one of my good subjects. My father's a merchant now for some of the people from his old company."

"Ah, then you're better in math?"

Comos chuckled. "A bit. Actually I am being primed to become a merchant also, once I pass the Test." He brought his chair forward with a crash and leaned on the table.

"I can sell anything," he said, looking at Ellia. His eyes were gray but looked red in the candlelight. Ellia shivered. Comos laughed disarmingly and reclined in his chair. He batted his rice bowl between his hands, then waved for the cook and ordered a short bottle of plum wine, a brand from the coastal plain of the Hamure. He tasted it, then poured the violet liquid into their glasses. Recalling the time Comos had said, "You drink like a girl," Ellia felt uneasy again.

During the next two dogdays, Tlezachi managed to land himself a permanent assignment to an Emeraline import agent on the docks, an actual paying job, though the pay was poor. Ellia spent her required days of labor with her Pecol friends when they returned from short trips to nearby islands. She enjoyed those days particularly because only then could she be herself. She didn't have to worry if an occasional giggle escaped her lips, nor did she have to watch her language to make sure she didn't swear. She even kept a little ragdoll in the stateroom where she slept when she stayed overnight; it had been Peaessa's, but its black eyes reminded Ellia of Shana. The Pecols didn't care if she read through their library after the work was finished. Chriz, whose arm had healed quickly, was constantly in Ellia's company, and they became good friends. Ellia could not recall happier times, though she and Tlezachi saw Comos more frequently than she would have liked.

One night, Ellia and Tlezachi were invited by Comos for an evening out. "The Steeped Tea Leaf?" Tlezachi asked as they looked up at the sign on the only eating establishment in sight. A wrinkled olive-green leaf was painted on the sign.

"That's what the instructions say, see?" Ellia showed Tlezachi the page. "Chee-horse-count Street and Fish Row."

"I guess this is it," he said.

"It isn't what I expected," Ellia said, folding the paper and shoving it into a pocket. A couple of the nearby buildings were boarded up, and the herbalist across the street stared at them when he thought they weren't looking. Factory soot swirled down the street every time the wind puffed, an indication of how long it had been since a street-sweep had been by. They buttoned their collars against the evening chill.

"Shall we go in, Xander?" Tlezachi asked finally.

"Comos said to wait for him," she answered. The streetlights flickered on one after another, but the one on their corner remained dark.

"Yes—'Wait for me'—that's what I said," a voice commented behind them.

Caught off guard, Ellia whirled around, hand on her knife hilt. "Comos! You sky-staring idiot!"

The boy laughed. Behind Comos, six other minors

in red appeared walking up the street. "I'm glad you waited," their host said, greeting them with a councillor heart salute. "I apologize for being late, but you'll find the evening well worth the wait." He proceeded to introduce his companions. The way Comos had frightened Ellia intensified the unease she usually felt around him.

Ignoring the queasy feeling in her stomach, she followed the rest into the Steeped Tea Leaf behind Comos. They left the swinging, louvered door behind them and walked down a stairway toward blue-green illuminations such as Ellia had seen in books containing illustrations of underwater life. The walls were of the gray, roughhewn rock of an ocean cave and even smelled faintly of kelp. Music with a definite thrumming beat floated in the air.

In the main room, simulated sunlight streamed from a crack directly above the stairs and reflected off a ceiling encrusted with huge shells and green gemlike stones. Tables were arranged in a circle about a clamshell stage. The floor, though dry, looked as if the tide had just retreated.

"You approve?" Comos asked Ellia.

"It—it's incredible!"

"Indeed." He smiled and turned to greet the proprietor.

"You'd never guess this place by its humble exterior," Tlezachi said into her ear. Ellia chuckled. Her earlier fears were vanquished by awe. The mellow music—zithers and buzzy, brassy, deep drums—seeped from the walls; Ellia could not locate the source. A man dressed in sea green led them to a crescent-shaped table where one continuous bench with individual cushions provided enough space for all of them and gave a fine view of the stage. Ellia sat beside Tlezachi. The waiter stood a chalkboard menu on the table. When the order pad came around, Ellia wrote out her selection of fried squid in fish sauce, then sat back to see what would happen next. As the tables in the main cave began to fill, a few bottles of wine were brought. Smiling, Comos poured for Ellia.

The meals came quickly, steaming and smelling delicious. Then the stagelights brightened, and the tempo of the music sped up. Every face turned toward the center of the restaurant.

Ellia dropped her spoon in her lap when she suddenly realized why none of the men in the audience had brought their wives.

The woman on stage wore a stunning, metallic green and gold sarong, which was really two lengths of fabric tied together over her hips so that a bare leg could be exposed to her waist. To the rhythm of the music she slinked around the clamshell stage as a powerful cat does in the forests of the upperlands. She seductively undulated her hips, then walked on the tips of her toes as if treading on a cloud. Her talent defied gravity. Whirling to face her audience again, she rotated her torso and gyrated, causing the ruby beads tied in her black hair to sparkle and click together.

"Do you think she's one of the women we saw on the horses?" Tlezachi whispered in her ear. The dancer was unwrapping her sarong. Ellia couldn't help but stare.

"No," she said. "Definitely not." The women they had seen displayed intelligence and an independent self-confidence while this slip of a woman had vacant green eyes.

"She is beautiful, though," Tlezachi commented, enraptured.

"Lovely," Ellia agreed. She drank down the remainder of her glass. *Has the woman no pride?* Ellia wondered.

She calmed herself. She must remember her disguise—she did not want to be caught again. Since the other minors obviously enjoyed the show, she must too. After this, she thought wryly, she would more easily accept the lot Fan offered. Ellia tried to smile but grimaced instead.

The sarong and blouse finally fell to the stage in three long strips revealing a loose, gauzy black top that displayed well-endowed curves when the light struck just right. The show ended with much applause, to which Ellia added her own halfhearted gesture.

"Wasn't that fantastic?" Tlezachi said.

"Sure."

"Doesn't it make you want to hurry up and take the Test?"

Ellia laughed at Tlezachi's predictability. She felt better knowing she had a friend next to her—but what would he think if he found out the truth about her?

"Am I glad you got Comos to invite me! There is nothing more lovely in the world than a woman, don't you agree?" Tlezachi continued.

"I agree."

"Is something wrong, Xan?"

"Huh? No." Ellia picked at her food.

"Well, Xander"—Ellia gave a strangled gasp when Comos startled her—"do you approve of my choice? You know, you really ought to loosen up a bit. That's the second time I've startled you tonight."

"Well, I apologize. Sure, I approve. Marvelous dancer that, and the food's delicious."

"Good, good," he said, and smiled at Ellia and Tlezachi. "I've arranged other entertainment for the evening also, entertainment which it looks like you can well use, Xander ol' boy."

"What?" Tlezachi asked.

"I told you my father was formerly a chemist—"

"Yes, that's about all we know about your family," Ellia interrupted, her tongue loosened by the half bottle of wine she had consumed.

"You should talk," Comos said.

"Huh?"

"Look at our friend Tlezachi here. I can name his

brother and sister, Hoshi and Tane. His father has worked plastics, his brother is a geophysicist. I can practically describe his home and doubtlessly could find it if I had a mind to. But you? What do we know of you? You have two sisters for sure, one of which looks like you—"

"A twin," Ellia offered.

"Is that Shana or Elta?"

"All right," Ellia said, putting down her empty glass. "I stand corrected. One good mystery deserves another, I guess. I'm sorry."

"That's all right. We're all friends here."

In your own mind, Ellia added silently.

"As I was saying a while back, my father was a chemist once, and now he is a merchant. He sells all sorts of items, but he specializes in products that make people happy," he continued, winking at Ellia. "You know, incense, herbals, and—"

"—and contraband," Ellia finished for him. The atmosphere froze as Tlezachi and the rest stared at her.

"That is unfair, Xander. If you were an adult, you'd be able to get most of it without restriction."

"But I am not and it's not allowed."

"As if it mattered!"

"It must, otherwise—"

Comos sighed loud enough to cut Ellia off. "You need this, perhaps for medicinal purposes." He gestured, and an incense burner of what looked and felt like cinnabar was passed to him. It fit easily in Ellia's palm and in it burned a little black cone giving off a line of indigo smoke. Ellia quickly pushed the gift away and glared at Comos.

"No," Ellia said flatly.

"Remember your manners, Xander," Comos returned. "I'm just trying to be hospitable."

Ellia's nose tingled from the pungent smoke, and her stomach tightened. She had to maintain control. "No," she repeated, beginning to sweat about the collar.

"It won't hurt you," Comos said. He skidded the tray across the table under his nose and inhaled. "Though, I admit, cloud smoke could have a better scent," he said, coughing. He smiled crookedly.

"I've never—" Ellia began, hoping for Tlezachi's support.

"There's nothing wrong with it, really," Tlezachi said, giving her a strange look.

"Tlee?"

"I guess we've all tried some contraband at some time, Xander, *haven't we*?"

"Never—"

"It's for you, too, Tlezachi," Comos said, scooting the tray in the minor's direction. Tlezachi took a whiff, then sneezed violently. Ellia licked her lips.

"Really, Comos. I don't want to," she said and swallowed. "At least, not now."

The minor's smile was contemplative as he stood and shrugged. "Suit yourself. At least let me pour you more wine?"

"Please," Ellia said, giving a sigh of relief. She saw the minor lift her glass and the bottle, then she gazed at Tlezachi. A disturbing, dissociated smile drifted over his freckled face. He sighed dramatically and took a bite of his fish steak. Ellia looked back and saw Comos swirling the purple contents of her glass.

This will be my last glass, Ellia decided and took a swallow. The wine tasted slightly bitter, and she wrinkled her nose. She gazed through the smoky liquid at the stage. The wine was clear. The dregs of the bottle, she concluded, and finished the glass. Doubtless she would be the one to help everyone back to the shrine just as she had been the one to get everyone to bed at the inn. She knifed another piece of squid and chewed as she listened to the music.

Then she began to notice that her squid lay on an exceptionally beautiful sauce. Ellia cracked a smile, then laughed and took another bite which she chewed with thorough consideration, thinking about the angle of her teeth and the correct pressure on the biting surfaces. Before her eyes, lights began dancing a watery dance in time with the music. When she looked down again at her plate, it had transformed. "Tlee, look!"

"Huh?"

"At my plate. Isn't it so pretty? I couldn't have done it myself if I tried! It—it just happened!"

Tlezachi moved his head slowly and looked. "Is it aliiivvve?" he asked, his mouth open, his eyes goggling.

"Noooo," Ellia said, then giggled. Horrified at herself, she put a hand over her mouth, then giggled again. The giggles were bubbles escaping from her mouth, and she could not contain the effervescence. "Time to gooo," she said, then attempted to stand. The world began to whirl about her. Her head felt as light as goose feathers, floating and twirling in the breeze. A moan escaped her like honey from a tipped bottle, every so slowly. All through her body the vibrations moved like pleasant hands, soothing and petting. Her muscles felt rubbery and weak. She settled back into her seat where she swayed with the music glowing warmly inside her like a child growing in her womb. At one point, something excited her, and she reached over and kissed Tlezachi the way the shag Chriz had kissed her mate: open-mouthed.

Presently she blacked out.

The next thing Ellia knew, she was lying outside under the stars, and her skin itched. Dew glistened on the grass by slenlight and moistened her clothes. She saw mountains, a dark line of forest far away, fields of stubble closer, and in one direction, nothing at all. Did she hear surf? As she walked toward the sound, she could smell salt and kelp on the cool breeze.

Heart pounding, she continued up to the cliff and looked down at the familiar rocky, boulder-strewn shoreline that gave the Stone Coast its name.

She shivered and sat on the thin grass. As she tried to reason the whole thing out, she dug with one hand, feeling the damp dirt collect reassuringly under her fingernails.

Then she froze. Danger condensed out of the cold night air like sea fog. Something panted heavily not five meters from where she sat. Turning her head ever so slowly, she saw two dark silhouettes.

Chee!

Without thinking, she sprang backward toward the drop. She heard the chee spring after her as she skidded off the edge. An instant later she knew she had made a mistake. After a short downslope, there was nothing.

She screamed as she tumbled into the void . . .

Seven

Ellia hit the floor of her cubicle head first. Scrambling to her feet, she struck her head again on an overhanging shelf. Furious, she kicked her bed.

Suddenly she realized how much her arms and legs itched. She scratched through her clothes, remembering that once when she had been very little, a medicinal potion for a sprained wrist had given her a bad case of hives. Ellia dived for her carpet bag and found a tiny mirror. She sighed in relief: she found only a few red marks, all on her neck. She threw the mirror back into the bag with all the venom she felt for Comos.

She been drunker than drunk last night—and she had acted like a girl. She hoped Tlezachi didn't remember her kissing him. She hoped no one remembered. How much had Comos seen? Who had returned her to her cubicle? And what had happened during the time she could not remember? Her head began to throb.

She opened the curtain closing off her cubicle. Yellow light streamed in from high arched windows along the maze corridor, dazzling her eyes and causing them to water. Midmorning! Ellia moaned.

Exhausted, she made her way to the *Star Sailor*. Chriz waved to her. "Hail, Emeraline!"

"Morning, Chriz. How's the schedule?" Ellia smiled and stopped at the ramp to the ship. The captain had taught her some shipboard etiquette.

"Fine, just fine, Greeneyes. Lance departed to locate the merchant. Well, do not loiter. Work must be done!"

They worked through lunchtime, waiting to eat with Lance. By the time midafternoon ushered in a southerly breeze and clouds, over half the hold had been emptied, but Lance had still not returned. Worried, the captain left to search for the missing shag. Chriz took over his job. While Ellia struggled with boxes from the hold to the spidery grip of the crane, the shag ran the lift and the crane alternately.

At nightfall, the captain returned. "Oh, your husband had been sighted," he said, "but our paths failed to intersect. Something else is wrong, though. Our merchant friend is nowhere to be found, and I doubt Lance located him either."

Chriz's mouth tightened to a long line. When black sky had finally replaced the orange sunset, Lance finally returned.

"Where have you been?" Chriz cried.

"And why have you not sent us word?" the captain added sternly. But they halted at the sight of the shag's posture of complete failure.

"No luck finding the merchant Nosaki?" Chriz asked.

Lance nodded.

Chriz hissed loudly and began to pace. "Hunter," she said in a low voice. "Not this time, not this time!"

"What else did you discover?" the captain asked.

"I searched everywhere. I went to the import agency first—"

"We know that. I went searching for you."

"Yes, I guess Chriz would have sent you. You know about the merchantmart and the auction square, yes? I checked the warehouse and found it leased now by someone else, then I went to the autotruck rental agency, then to the hotel. Nothing. I searched the restaurants where we held our meetings as well as the agency he claimed digitized his designs for him. Just an hour ago I stopped by the Collective Embassy to see what legal action we could take, and found this." He handed a note to Chriz.

"Damn Emeralines for contracting and linking words until they make no sense!" Chriz muttered.

"It says our contract is void," Lance stated.

"What! I cannot read this *merdthe*!"

"Calm yourself, Chriz," the captain said.

"What! Hunter, hear that? He wants me to calm myself!" she yelled, brandishing the note. "King of the Dron, what does the thing say?"

"He told you, Chriz," the captain put in. She whirled around as if she were ready to bite his head off.

"I could read it," Ellia volunteered weakly.

"No, it's business," Lance said.

"Don't be a fool," Chriz returned and gave the paper to Ellia.

"You're sure?" Ellia asked the others. The captain shrugged, and Lance said nothing. Ellia glanced at the illegible scribble. "The man obviously didn't pass his first writing course."

"What does it say?" Chriz asked impatiently. "Exactly."

"It's dated chee-goat, that's the twenty-ninth of this ritual cycle, or two days ago. It says:

> *To Lanzaqurrt, Pursur d' Star Sailor:*
>
> *D'ntract fectif as of d'chee-dog-drag'n*
> *count prev'cycle tobe 'sider'd void per—*

Ellia cleared her throat and shook her head weakly. "In speaking, contractions work well, but nobody writes them! I'll expand them. Let's see . . . The contract effective as of the 203rd day of the previous ritual cycle is to be considered void per section dragon, part chee, of the contract which states: 'In the event the initial or cheecount shipment should be late or delayed by any circumstances, it is to the purchaser's discretion whether to accept said merchandise, being as the product is tightly scheduled, the supplier taking all responsibility,' et cetera." Ellia scanned the remainder of the page. She checked the blank flip side. "It goes on to apologize and expresses the hope that the loss of the contract should not cause too great financial burden. Can he do this?"

"He just did," the captain said.

Chriz growled. "If I could get my hands on that human." She swallowed her rage for a moment, then kicked a metal pail and sent it clanking down the deck. "He can't do that!"

"We signed—"

"Hunter! Have humans no honor?" Chriz blurted.

"Some humans do," Ellia put in, then eyed the mountain of wooden crates stacked on the deck and on the dock. "What can you do about it?" she asked.

"If that human lived in the Open City—"

"But he does not!" Lance yelled back, suddenly angry. "I have tramped all over this inhospitable town all day, and I suffer a headache. Yell once more in my ear, my almostwife, and I will dump you in the ocean and let that cool you off!"

Chriz opened her mouth, but shut it when Lance took a step in her direction. She retreated to stand next to the captain. "It is just not fair."

"Of course not," Lance returned. "For us."

"But it was my first sale!" Chriz said. The fur over her eyes began to glisten with moisture. "Damn, damn and fry the man," she said and began speaking in a guttural language Ellia could not understand at all.

"Is there nothing we can do?" Ellia asked the captain.

"I doubt it. It is difficult enough to obtain restitution against an Emeraline when you are obviously in the right, but with a contract that states outright—"

"But he accepted the oxcount shipment!"

"Yes, but all the contract mentions is 'if it is late.' It was late. I approved this deal for Chriz because this Nosaki appeared a decent businessman. Because of the margin we purchased at and the fact that the manufacturer will only buy back at half what he sold it at, we face a fantastic loss."

"Can't you sell—"

"Titanium structural elements in specific sizes? I have no clue to what he even needed them for."

Ellia just shook her head, then sat down on the deck with her back to the cabin door, feeling useless. She hated to see this happen to her friends, the only people in the world besides her twin to have accepted her for herself.

"Greeneyes?" Chriz asked, sitting on her haunches and touching the girl's shoulder.

"No," Lance warned immediately, then spit a string of Shaggish syllables her way.

Chriz responded in kind. "It's worth a try," she finished.

"You haven't any right to involve the child."

"Let her decide, eh?"

"What is it?" Ellia asked, looking into the white shag's face. "If I can help, I will."

"The possibility exists. Could you smuggle one of us out of the Open City?"

"What? You aren't serious? Have you seen the fence?"

"Yes, twice. Could you do it?"

Looking at the only other human on deck, Ellia nodded. "It might just be possible, if I dyed his hair red—"

"No, not the captain," Chriz said. "Me."

* * *

"I don't want to fill out those papers and neither do you," an irritated clerk told Ellia. "It takes fifteen days to complete a pass."

"But it seemed so simple when they gave us ours—"

"On the train, I know. And didn't they warn you how hard it would be to replace? They did, I'm sure. The shrine does the paperwork en masse; that and the fact that you minors have legal anonymity until you survive the Test makes it all easy at that point." The man sighed. "Haven't you noticed that nobody cares who you are each time you arrive at a shrine? They only care if you pass the exams. Everything is left to your responsibility—learning, labors, and this slip of paper you've lost. Why not try searching for the pass again? Now I would have to treat you as an adult application, and that would mean researching your family background and everything else. Would your parents appreciate that?"

Ellia shook her head.

"I thought as much. I am sure you'll find it, just give yourself a chance."

So much for getting Chriz her very own passport, Ellia thought as she left the office building. To implement her plan, she needed papers. She could have borrowed Tlezachi's, but she had been avoiding her friend ever since Comos's party. Finally she had no choice.

After searching all his usual haunts inside the shrine complex, Ellia finally found Tlezachi reclining on an orange sofa in a sunny reading room, his feet propped up on the armrest. "So there you are," she said.

He placed his book on his stomach and smiled pleasantly. "Oh, hi, Xander."

"Hi? I've been looking all over for you."

"Why? I've been here since class let out." He chuckled.

Ellia was in no mood for flippant answers. "I need a favor."

"I thought there must be a reason you were back so early on a laborday."

"Come on, Tlee, I'm serious. I need to borrow your pass; I misplaced mine."

"Your pass out of the city?" he asked. Having known Tlezachi for some three dogdays, she expected him to jump up and offer to help her find her lost possession. He seemed lethargic, confining his movement to looking around her neck for her locket. She had removed it. "How did you lose it?" he asked finally.

"I don't know," Ellia answered, sounding appropriately disgusted with herself. "But I need to run an errand for the *Star Sailor*, and I need a pass."

Tlezachi's eyes narrowed momentarily. "But you don't look like me."

"I know. But they don't really read it."

"Oh," he said.

"Can I borrow it, then?"

"You won't lose it?"

"I'll guard it with my very soul."

"All right then." He pulled his locket over his head and handed it to her by the silver chain. He seemed to have barely the energy to do that. His pleasant smile struck Ellia as uncharacteristic, but she shrugged it off.

"Thanks," she said.

"You'll be careful?" he asked again, looking up at her.

"I said I would be."

"Good," he returned and reached for his book, dismissing her.

Despite her own deceit in obtaining Tlezachi's pass, Ellia felt hurt. Tears in her eyes, she swallowed her pride and turned to leave. But then Tlezachi spoke.

"Comos's party was interesting, wasn't it?"

Ellia stiffened. "In many ways," she finally answered.

"Yeah." He chuckled. "I found out the reason you kept from getting drunk at the inn." He chuckled again.

Her breath hissed between her teeth. "What'd I do?" she asked, blushing.

Tlezachi craned his neck to look back at her. "When you get drunk, no halfway for you. You laugh, you cry, you sing, and you pass out. I remember little really except that I helped you back to your cubicle with Comos. Tried to change you into your bedclothes, but you balled up tighter than a fist." Tlezachi laughed again and relief flooded through Ellia: he didn't recall the kiss. "You really seemed to enjoy yourself," he added.

"I hated it!" Ellia returned violently. "I hated it. The insolent bastard drugged my drink when I wasn't looking!"

"You seemed to need it at the time."

"What?" she yelled. "What!"

"But you're right, Comos is a bastard, albeit a smart bastard," he said, nodding to himself. "I saw him pour a vial of purple crystals into your drink, but by that time I was too far gone to warn you. I would have," he added sincerely.

Ellia didn't know what to say to Tlezachi. "Thanks for the pass."

"Sure," Tlezachi returned and opened his book. "Just don't lose it." He smiled. As she left, Ellia merely shook her head.

The hot day ushered in a cool night, and shivering, Ellia hugged herself for warmth. Ellia patted the soft, pink nose of the horse whose halter she held, then reached over and patted the other.

"Docile animals, are they not?" Chriz asked.

Ellia hadn't heard the shag's cheelike approach and was startled. "Pretty much so," she said, quickly regaining her composure. But the thought of what they were going to do tonight set her on edge. Smuggling a shag out of the Open City! The sheer immensity of the fence emphasized the desire of Ellia's fellow Emeralines to keep the People off their soil. Though she had gone against the rules all her life, sneaking a Pecol past the gate felt criminal to her. But what Nosaki the merchant had done reeked of an unfairness similar to that Ellia herself had always faced. She shivered.

"You look cold," the shag said, and handed her a short cape. Ellia wrapped it about her shoulders, then turned to appraise the white shag.

The effect was shocking. Chriz had reproduced one of Ellia's uniforms for herself. White fur protruded around the red cuffs and the curved neckline. Ellia was reminded of a nightmare she had had in which one of the dogs in the barn had worn Fan's clothing. Ellia suddenly hated what she was doing.

"What is your opinion?" Chriz asked, pirouetting.

"Too good," Ellia replied. Someone who had seen few shags might at a glance mistake Chriz for a short minor.

Chriz chuckled, then asked, "Have you ever ridden a horse bareback?"

"No. We herded the cattle from the saddle. Better on the horse's back, they told us."

"True, but also better on your rump." She bent down and picked up a blanket. "This will help. You will need to be able to walk when we arrive." She threw the blanket in the back of the wagon.

Ellia held the horse while the captain loaded three crates into the wagon; the cargo was their excuse for leaving the Open City. Lance came down the gangplank.

"You are all prepared to leave," Lance stated.

Chriz took a deep breath. "Greeneyes?"

"I'm ready," she lied.

"Ready then," Chriz answered.

"I still dislike your plan," the silver-furred shag said. He approached his almostwife, closer than Ellia would ever think of approaching another person, and looked down at her. "I refuse to give you permission to go."

"And you will stop me?" Chriz asked.

"Has a male ever been able to restrain a female whose mind is made up?" he asked and smiled hesitantly.

"Never," Chriz returned. "I got you, my love, did I not?"

"You did by trickery and shenanigans, you lusty, white-furred enchantress—" He broke into Shaggish but was interrupted by Chriz's kiss. Ellia turned away. "Is there nothing I can do to persuade you out of this foolery?" Lance asked a moment later.

"Nothing," Chriz insisted.

After a long pause, he said, "I hope you really know what you are doing. Neither of us have children to perpetuate us, and there exists no greater sin. Be wary of danger if you can."

"Then you are giving me your permission?"

"Yes." The shag sighed.

Chriz jumped up to kiss him again. "I will return before dawn, and then we will make something of the morning. Who knows? Perhaps children?"

"I hope so," Lance replied as Chriz mounted the buckboard beside Ellia. The captain wished them luck and waved them off.

Ellia clicked her tongue and flicked the reins to urge the rented team forward. Chriz reclined on the long wooden seat, arms, shoulders, and head covered with a blanket. Ellia drove the horses through town toward the gate she had chosen the night before.

"Why you?" Ellia asked suddenly as the horse clopped down the deserted avenues, the crates rattling behind.

"What do you mean, Greeneyes?"

"I was wondering why it was you who decided to go and not Lance. I mean, it seems to me that Lance should be the one taking action—"

"Are you insinuating that Lance is acting cowardly?"

Ellia's breath caught in her throat. "No, not at all. I—"

"Another human stereotype, that males act and females remain home protected. The People differentiate no real sex roles. After our children are weaned, Lance would be just as likely to raise them as I would. Is that wrong?"

"No," Ellia answered. "But I think if I ever have children, I'd rather raise them myself."

"I, too," Chriz returned. "I have always longed for children. Always."

"Not me."

"Yes, but that is your own choice, so far," Chriz said, reflective. "The stereotypical male always lusting for war, conflict, and power, generally fearing and misunderstanding his woman who provides him with fodder for battle—that has always been an affliction of your species. Archaeology tells us that your ancestors solved the problem for themselves by letting some old religions mutate in the century before the dron attacked this world. The old religions didn't survive the dron, but we encourage a similar spiritual state today on the human reservations."

"I don't like the sound of that," Ellia said honestly. "'Reservations'." She pulled the eight reins and sent the horses trotting out of the city, past the residential quarter lit by big yellow incandescent lamps.

"Reservations?" Chriz echoed. "It was the Onnakine Treaty that gave humanity the entire central part of Southern, leaving us the Bahas to the equator and Subarctica with all its forests."

"I suppose you got the best lands, though."

"Yes," she answered, "for us, just as your species obtained the best climates for themselves. Onnak the Discoverer was a human, and he prevented the extinction of both our species when the dron began re-learning technology. He saw to it that a mixed republic came into being that would allow humans to co-exist with the People. Thus as it worked out, you received the climate we dislike—temperate regions—but the one best suited for your species. I like the snow especially."

"With thick fur, I guess so. But the way you said 'reservations,' it seemed like you had control—"

"But we do."

Suddenly the great electrified fence made sense to Ellia.

"You see," Chriz continued, "we prohibit internecine warfare and regulate land usage by the same laws that apply to ourselves, thus we prevent the human population from exploding beyond bounds. It is not as callous as it seems, though," she added quickly. "The human population has always and will always outnumber the People. We grant both people, human and shag, every freedom and have no jurisdiction over family or clan decisions. Since the treaty, my species has lived in peace with your often xenophobic species."

"But before?"

"You do not wish to know."

"What happened before?"

Chriz took a deep breath. "Archaeologists have reconstructed an earlier technological period. They say that long ago the people of Earth discovered a method to propel ships quickly through the void between the stars. There they met the Dron who, born of a world like our own, considered us unbearable competition in their hunt for habitable planets. In any case, it seems we blasted each other beyond easy recovery of technology somewhere around a thousand years ago. My species regressed to savagery just as yours did."

"Yes. And?" Ellia prompted grimly.

"Humans hunted us once, and we often returned the favor with relish."

Ellia fell into a brooding silence as she reined the horses through the dark over the blacktop road leading to the fence. They crossed the railroad tracks, emerging into the blue-white corona of light that illuminated the gate.

"We're almost there," Ellia warned. She took a moment to arrange the blanket over Chriz to appear casually wrinkled. Satisfied, she took up the reins again and tightened her cape collar against the night air. Finally she spotted the guard who patroled with a leashed pair of black-furred chee, and waited until he returned to the forest's edge from whence he had come. Having timed the guards' rounds the night before, Ellia began ticking off the seconds in her head.

Then with a flick of the reins, she urged the team forward. The gate-guard sighted them almost immediately; they rolled to a stop before a peppermint-striped wooden barrier as he stepped from his protective cage.

"Good evening, minors," he said. He wore a black Stone Coast military uniform, but the youthful lilt to his voice confirmed that he had not yet spent the years of service battling the dron on the continent which hardened some until they saw no joy left in the world. Like all the other guards, he shouldered a rifle. Ellia noted that he narrowed his eyes as he scanned her apparently sleeping passenger.

"A freezing evening, actually," Ellia returned quietly.

The guard laughed, putting his hands in his pockets and returning his attention to Ellia. "Yes, very. I've had much better assignments. Say, what are you doing traveling so late?"

"Delivering a couple of crates of pipes that must be delivered before morning. The Pecol I've labors with left these out of the last shipment. He's paying us extra for this run so I don't care."

"Yeah, who needs sleep anyway," the guard chuckled and extended his hand wordlessly.

Ellia paused a calculated length of time, then said, "Oh, yes." She reached into her pocket and retrieved her own and Tlezachi's pass. They crinkled as she placed them in the man's hand.

"Xander, no family name."

"Yo," Ellia answered.

"And Tlezachi Cohssan?"

"That's him, sleeping," Ellia said, trying to smile.

The guard studied the blanketed form of the shag. "Uncomfortable place to sleep," the man observed and quickly handed back the passes.

"Definitely. You have to admire some people's ability to sleep anywhere."

"Why's he along, then? Not to keep you company?"

"Obviously. He'll drive back—and he had better help me unload, or he'll not get paid."

"He ought to be awake to give me his pass, you know."

"I told him that," Ellia answered, her heart pounding.

"It is regulations—"

Thinking quickly, she threw up her hands. "I'll wake him then." Dropping the rawhide reins against the wood footrest, she added, "But I hate when he gets cranky."

"Aaaah, forget it," the man said while Ellia gave Chriz an initial shake. Chriz groaned and shifted position; her movement exposed one hand, but the guard did not notice as he gazed past the two. Ellia turned around and saw the guard with the chee emerging from the forest. *Blind priests!*

But the first guard was already past the draw gate. He touched a black square on the gate with a key and rolled open the metal fences. Then he returned and raised the gate by resting his hand on a counterbalance.

A click of her tongue and a flick of the reins, and the wagon jerked ungracefully over the gate rails. Ellia glanced over her shoulder.

"What a night," she heard the guard say to the man with the chee. "Can't even get a minor to strike up a conversation."

Ellia slapped the reins against the horse's rumps and drove quickly into the night.

"You did it! You actually did it!" Chriz cried, peeking from under the blanket, then throwing it off altogether. "Praise the Hunter and you, Greeneyes!"

But Ellia felt no jubilation. What had she done? A shag outside the Open City!

"It was too close."

The shag sniffed the air once. "Yes, I guess it was. I can smell the fear in your perspiration." Ellia gulped as the shag put a hand on the girl's knee. "Those trees over there. I think there is enough of a clearing there to hide the wagon."

The wagon rolled to a rest out of sight from the road. In just a couple of minutes Ellia had unhitched the horses and replaced their harnesses with the bridles and blankets Chriz handed her.

Ellia watched then as the shag stripped off her disguise and threw it in the back of the wagon with the crates. She noticed that the shag's fur thinned only slightly about her chest. Ellia guessed that the People wore clothing only to satisfy human proprieties and was only marginally shocked when the shag merely buckled on a belt from which a couple of silvery objects hung. When the shag returned for her horse, Ellia tightened her cloak against the cold. "Won't you be cold?" Her breath condensed in the air in front of her mouth.

"You forget, Greeneyes, I like the cold. I was born in Subarctica." Ellia examined the shag from paws to muzzle, pausing only at the black leather belt, and she decided once and for all the shag wasn't really undressed.

"What are those things?" Ellia asked, pointing at the devices that resembled skeletal hands.

"My claw knives?" Chriz asked. Her mysterious laugh sent shivers down Ellia's spine. Chriz mounted her horse and waited for Ellia to follow. "They are souvenirs from my virgin days. They represent another reason why I would be more likely to take action than my mate would be."

"Than Lance?" Ellia asked. "Why?" Their horses stepped up onto the road where hooves clattered against the packed gravel.

"How old do you think I am?" Chriz asked.

"I—I don't know."

"Well, I am not as old as Lance, for sure, but on the other hand I could easily have had children by now, even though my species takes so long to conceive. I spent my youth protecting my people, fighting the dron!"

"A soldier? You have dron over there?"

"Yes, and we do. I used to be less fashionable and shaved around my eyes so I could see better. Skin-faced warriors they call us." Ellia saw a fang-baring smile by slenlight as Chriz reined in her horse. "We also prevent our human friends from nullifying the treaty and attacking us. No human attacks a skin-faced warrior and expects to live. Ha!" Chriz flicked the ends of her reins across her mount's rump, and the animal bolted off at a gallop.

Ellia's eyes widened. She would have to trust Chriz; she could do nothing else but abandon the shag. At her signal, her horse took off after its companion as if racing the wind.

The seaside village where Nosaki lived was nestled in the cliffs on the opposite side of the bay from the Open City and about ten kilometers from the Council City. When they eventually came to a sign that said, "Nosaki, Shipwright," they turned to follow a private road until blocked by a high wooden fence with a gate secured by a bulky, metal lock. Chriz dismounted to examine the lock in the dim light.

"I would say he values his privacy," the shag whispered.

Ellia glanced at the hefty fence. "I'd say rather that he fears his neighbors."

Chriz snorted. "Possible, yes, possible." Chriz guided their horses off the road, then wrapped their reins around a fence rail. Grass and leaves damp from dew crumpled under Ellia's feet as she dismounted and scrambled up and over the fence after Chriz.

"What are we going to do?" Ellia whispered.

"I shall have a frank discussion with Nosaki, that is all."

"You're not going to harm him?"

"That would be disadvantageous. He must purchase our second shipment. I must simply convince him it is in his best interests to fulfill his contract, that is all. However, he may be obstinate. We shall see." They trudged parallel to the dirt road, toward the cliffs and the bay.

Suddenly Chriz halted and threw an arm across Ellia's stomach. Chriz's houndlike ears perked as she scanned the bushes, the knee-high grass, the clumps of trees all painted silvery by the gibbous slen. Ellia herself detected nothing, but her heart raced.

"What?" Ellia whispered.

"Remain still!" Chriz said quickly. Ellia froze. Chriz squeezed Ellia's arm reassuringly, then padded about five meters to her right while pulling her claw knives over her hands like gloves. When the shag sniffed at the night breezes, even Ellia sensed something was amiss.

That instant, a pair of chee broke from concealment, bounding toward Chriz. Ellia had her knife in hand before her next heartbeat.

The first chee sprang, and Chriz went down. The two furred creatures rolled, and Ellia heard a crack, then saw Chriz jump through a backward roll to stand ready again. The second chee circled and loped in. Chriz jumped aside, whirling and lashing out with her knives which sparkled with silver glimmers. The great cat jerked the shag through the air as Chriz's knives sunk in just past the animal's ears. The beast snarled in pain and tumbled head first, then rolled, injured and shaking, to its feet.

Chriz hit the snarling animal just below the right temple so hard that even at a distance Ellia could hear the animal's skull crack. The chee collapsed like a ragdoll.

The fight had lasted just half a minute. Ellia sheathed her knife—how useless it seemed!

Sure that the second chee was dead, Chriz returned to the first one and delivered a death stroke. Then she shivered and collapsed to a sitting position.

Ellia ran to kneel beside the white shag. "Are—are you all right?" She refused to look directly at the chee, but her peripheral vision took in the gory scene of torn fur and muscle. She looked instead at the blood that drenched the shag's arms.

Chriz sat, gasping. "I believe I fractured my wrist."

Ellia did her best to check the wrist. Chriz whimpered once. Suddenly what had happened dawned on Ellia. "You saved my life!"

"Aaah," Chriz said. "The animals would not have injured us. They would have held us clamped in their jaws until we passed out, then gone and fetched their master."

Ellia shivered. "I hate chee," she said, then continued her examination of the shaggy wrist. "It looks like it's just sprained."

Favoring her injured left hand, Chriz stood with Ellia's assistance, then as if in afterthought bent down and touched the chee. Ellia was horrified to see the shag put her blood-covered fingers into her mouth.

Ellia released the shag's shoulder and retreated. "Hunting mountain cats is illegal," Chriz said, mostly to herself, then turned to Ellia. "But I have. Good eating, if you have strong enough teeth." Chriz must have seen the disgust on Ellia's face for she jerked her hand from her mouth, said, "No use procrastinating," and began walking.

Soon they heard the muted sound of the surf. The road jogged left, and the dense woods gave way suddenly to a view of a whitewashed, plank-sided mansion. Slenlight illuminated the upper story, but the lower level was shrouded in darkness. Open black shutters about each window gave the house an air of stately sturdiness. Outside a shoulder-high stone wall that enclosed a finely manicured courtyard, Ellia smelled orange blossoms. "What now?" she whispered.

"I enter and discuss business with Nosaki."

"Just you?"

"Yes."

"I won't let you. You're hurt and—"

"I am better trained at this," Chriz hissed.

"And what happens if you meet others besides Nosaki? That's a big house." Chriz began walking around the fence looking for a gate and said nothing about Ellia following her. When they found the knee-high gate, they stepped over it. When a sliding door proved to be bolted inside, Ellia followed the shag around the house to a window. Chriz pulled up on it, and the sash scraped against the wooden casing. Chriz turned and smiled, then disappeared through the draperies.

Ellia accepted a hand up and scrambled easily over the sill, but clumsily fell to her knees on carpeting. Her eyes adapted quickly to the darkness inside. She swallowed, stood, and followed Chriz, keeping a hand on the shag's furry shoulder to guide her past the ghostly shadows of furniture, then through a door into a slenlit hallway. Ellia felt exposed in the dim light.

"Here," Chriz whispered into Ellia's ear. The shag pointed to the sliding glass door they had seen earlier, then removed the restraining rod and opened the door, letting in cool, fruit-scented air. "Since you insist on assisting me, you shall watch the door to the hall. If you spot someone approaching, I want you to give a yelp and run outside. We shall rendezvous later. Understand?"

Ellia nodded. From where she stood, she could see most of the unexplored hallway and the staircase, which Chriz stealthily climbed. Presently Ellia heard the sudden tattoo of feet, someone jumping, then running—then nothing. She closed her eyes and tried to calm her breathing as the muffled sounds of an argument drifted on the night air.

The girl smiled for a moment when she thought what kind of impression the shag would make, spattered to the elbows with blood. She only wished Chriz would be quieter. What if someone else was in the house? Ellia strained to see down the dark hall.

Half a minute ticked by, then a tall man wearing a gray cloak materialized out of the murk. When Ellia saw that he carried a rifle at the ready, she quickly scrambled back into the room. She should have realized the merchant would have hired a guard and trainer to go along with his chee—if he treated Emeralines as he had treated the Pecols, doubtless he had suffered a house invasion before.

Ellia squeezed through the open sliding door, then slid it shut. A light burned in a window above. Breathing hard, she skulked around the courtyard looking for something to throw and nearly bumped into a tree trunk. Fruit trees! She snapped off two pears. With quick aim, she pitched one pear, then the other—the second hit the window pane. Chriz appeared at the cracked window, saw Ellia, and threw open the sash.

"A rifleman's on the stairs!" Ellia called in a low voice.

"Hurry! Hurry!" Nosaki cried to his guard.

Chriz turned from the window, her ears erect. She hurled a final warning at Nosaki, then Ellia quite clearly heard a Shaggish curse followed by, "Hunter!"

A shot shattered the night. Ellia screamed as Chriz came flying out the window amidst a rain of glass and wood splinters.

The shag hit the ground in a roll and bounded to her

feet. Ellia was halfway to the stone fence when a second shot rang out. The third whizzed by her ear. Terror nearly doubled Ellia's speed, but even with her head start, Chriz passed her. The shag executed a somersault vault over the wall at a dead run, but Ellia had to halt to get a foothold. Though trees obscured the guard's view from the window, he continued to shoot. Another shot sounded the instant Ellia crested the wall. She heard a double explosion and the next thing she knew she was in the grass, the breath knocked out of her. "I've been shot!" she gasped out.

Chriz, already some distance away, spun and came rushing back to Ellia's side. "Where?" she cried.

"My right arm."

Chriz cursed and pulled Ellia to her feet. As the shag half-carried, half-dragged her down the road, Ellia thought only of the growing fire in her arm and her foolishness in going along with Chriz's scheme. When Chriz threw her over the outer fence, Ellia managed to land without further injury. While she waited for the shag to climb the fence, she fought to catch her breath. She touched her ripped sleeve and elicited fiery, disabling pain.

Chriz hit the ground next to her and caught her up in furry arms. Seconds later they mounted the same horse, Ellia ahead of Chriz. The shag grabbed the other animal's reins and yelled in Shaggish—the horses bolted into a gallop.

Once on the bay road again, Ellia held both sets of reins in her good hand while Chriz examined her wound. The girl endured waves of dizzying pain. "You caught a ricochet," Chriz said. "It is barely bleeding, but your arm is going to be bruised for weeks."

They stopped at a beach so that Chriz could wash the blood off her fur and clean Ellia's wound. But it was only a short respite, for they continued onward immediately. Ellia was thankful to finally see the wagon.

The shag readied the team, donned her minor's uniform, and resumed her position under the blanket, her head against Ellia's thigh. Ellia noted that Chriz had not removed her tool belt; she assumed the omission was due to exhaustion, and since the claw knives were hidden by the blanket, she kept silent. She snapped the reins, and they were moving again.

"We're almost there," Ellia whispered as they crossed the tri-rail tracks set into the road. Behind the glaring mercury lights of the gate, the predawn sky seemed black again. But when the guard greeted them, Ellia saw that the one thing she had not counted on had occurred—the same man who had let them out of the city still manned the post!

She considered turning back to try again later, but she knew that suspicious persons were always searched coming through the gate. She knew, too, that the guard-chee outside the gate could easily outrace the wagon, and they would be better trained than Nosaki's pets. Ellia hissed a warning to Chriz and prayed for good luck.

The black-clad guard recognized Ellia and her companion instantly. "Still sleeping?" he asked with a tired chuckle.

"Yeah," Ellia returned, handing the guard the passes. "He exhausted himself."

"Sure he did, eh?" After a simple scan of the passes, he walked to the fence, unlocking the exterior and interior gates and throwing them open. But when he returned, he did not give back the passes. He glanced past Ellia at the cargo in the wagon.

They had neither opened nor dumped the crates as they had planned!

"What happened to your shipment?" he asked, pointing with the passes.

"Uh—they're defects, defect returns," Ellia said much too quickly.

"Identical markings, and they look untouched."

"Resealed them. Don't want them to rust on the ship back to the Collective."

"Oh." He nodded and Ellia unconsciously sighed.

Giving the passes another look, the guard stifled a yawn, then handed back the pieces of paper. "You know," he said, "I really ought to check you both against your descriptions."

"I'm me."

"Obviously, but what about Tlezachi?" He circled around the front of the wagon toward Chriz's side.

"Don't wake him," Ellia said desperately.

"It is regulations."

"Don't, please."

"Why?" he asked, shifting his rifle.

Ellia gulped, then detected Chriz's arm creeping toward her waist, toward her belt and claw knives. *Blind priests, say something!* "Don't touch him, he's ill!"

"Ill?" the guard stopped short; he clicked off the safety on his rifle.

"Yes, that's the real reason we left the Open City tonight. It was to take him to a skin specialist in Tarmentter. He told me it wasn't contagious, but—ugh!"

"Really?" the guard asked. He made a face as if he smelled something rank and halted just a meter from Chriz. Ellia saw the warning sign of doubt dawn on his face.

"In the middle of the night?" The guard's free hand flashed forward. The blanket snapped as it came off.

Eight

Lightning-swift, Chriz drove her good hand into the skeleton of her claw knife. The guard sprang back and raised his rifle. Ellia threw herself sideways over the shag. Stabbing fire leapt up her arm, yet she snagged the blanket in midair before it could expose Chriz's weapon.

Together, they tumbled off the plank seat, the blanket on top of them. Agonizing pain in Ellia's arm caused her whole body to convulse. She whimpered. The guard retreated another step, agape.

"A shag!" the man hissed. "A dogtail, rotted shag!" The man glanced around, then without lowering the rifle, he crept closer, keeping his eye on the shag.

"It was only a dare!" Ellia cried, then gasped as the guard threw the blanket back over Chriz.

"Blind priests! Get back on that seat!" he said in a loud whisper. Ellia complied, and the guard retreated, rifle still trained on the blanket, to lift the crossing gate.

"Damn, dogtail minor, how stupid can you get! I'm
not about to be flogged and shamed because you accepted a juvenile dare! And don't expect to get away
with it again—if there weren't witnesses to me not
following regs and letting you two through earlier, your
Pecol friend would be dead now." He glanced around.
"Get out of here!"

He whacked one of the horses on the rump, shocking it into a gallop. The wagon bumped over the first,
then the second guide rail for the sliding sections of
the fence. As the vehicle raced down the interior road,
Ellia fumbled for the reins.

Chriz's shock wore off first. She threw off the blanket and climbed back onto the seat. As Ellia began to
regain control of herself, Chriz stripped off the offending uniform and threw it in the back, then waited
with hands in her lap for Ellia to say something.

"I don't think I like you," Ellia said suddenly, turning to glare directly at the bangs of white hair hiding
the shag's eyes.

Chriz remained still, then sniffed loudly and looked
away. "But I like you," she said in a low voice.

"This whole fool maneuver was your idea. We nearly
got killed. Twice!"

"Nothing is easy."

"Looking for danger is stupid!"

"Ah, but we succeeded!"

"Yeah, but was it worth it? So much risk for so little
return! You can pound on a rock all day, but if it's
water you want, you'll do better to collect your sweat."

"Well, I am satisfied with the result."

"Yes, and you'll have a few gray hairs tomorrow,
I'm sure. It's all because of your selfish pride!"

"Honor."

"Honor that is self-centered is too expensive. Did
you think of me? Did you think of me when you wanted
to avenge your honor?"

"You volunteered!"

"To help a friend—and that was *my* foolishness."

"Greeneyes!" Chriz cried, her mouth hanging open. As Ellia gazed into the dark wall of forest, Chriz broke into loud, sobbing tears and buried her face in the bundled blanket. Ellia felt a twinge of regret, yet she refused to listen or to look at the shag—the pain in her right arm mirrored her pain at being sorely used. The horses pranced down the lane through the residential sector of the Open City.

Suddenly the shag turned around. "What did you think I was? Human?" Her voice cracked.

"No," Ellia said simply, watching the waving manes of the horses.

"You cannot judge me by human—" the shag yelled, then groaned when Ellia's reply penetrated. Out of the corner of her eye, Ellia saw the shag collapse like a heap of rags, panting. Chriz remained silent until they entered the dock quarter.

"Greeneyes?"

"I'm here."

"I apologize," she said weakly. Her voice was barely audible as she added, "I still like you, Greeneyes."

Ellia sighed guardedly. She blinked a few times as her reserve of anger finally poured out of her to leave her empty. But without anger, the hurt remained as ugly as a puddle of blood on a white sheet.

Yeah, your honor's been bruised, just like Chriz's, eh? Ellia swallowed. She had volunteered. She had helped plan. She had violated laws she knew were important; and she had done it to help people whose friendship she valued.

"Greeneyes!" Chriz cried. "Don't shame me, please! The Hunter watches us all."

Ellia turned and saw that the shag suddenly had her claw knives on again, the points resting against her furry throat. Ellia coughed. She knew too little to treat the shag as she had. Chriz had been—was—a warrior. *Nothing is less forgiving than military honor!*

"Chriz," she said, pulling on the reins. "Don't do it."

"I—Greeneyes, it hurts," the shag sobbed. "You have saved my life, thrice, and what repayment have I offered? What?"

"Chriz!"

"How worthy are my actions? I do not deserve you as a friend—"

"Don't say that either," Ellia commanded. "Chriz—I'm sorry."

The shag froze as if slapped. The claw knives over her throat shook for a second, then she let them fall to her furry lap. "Sorry? Sorry for what?" the shag asked, facing Ellia.

"I'm acting just as haughty as you, worse perhaps."

"That is quite impossible," Chriz said with conviction, again avoiding Ellia's eyes.

Ellia took a deep breath. "I'll accept your apology if—if you'll accept mine."

"I have seen myself today," Chriz returned. "I have battled again the flaw that expelled me from the society of my warrior sisters." She took a deep breath. "How about us forgetting the whole matter?"

"That would be impossible."

"I suppose." The hair around Chriz's mouth formed a shaggish smile. "Friends?"

Ellia smiled and offered her hand.

"*Djo* Hunter!" Chriz quickly shucked the claw knives and brought her furry hand into a clasp.

The dawn light had metamorphosed from orange to yellow by the time Ellia entered the cubicle maze in the main secular building. She could hear rustling and the beginnings of conversations as the other minors began to rise. Her eyes felt dry with fatigue, and the thought of facing the day nauseated her. She needed a shower. She spent five minutes under steaming water, scouring her skin, then luxuriated in a warm, massag-

ing stream. Her puckered wound, now covered with
the same wound sealant used on Chriz's arm, throbbed
dully, but she did not care: the medicament looked like
skin, and already she could feel a warm glow as if
tissues were being stimulated into healing. In a few
days, the Pecols assured her, there would not even be
a scar.

Barely able to keep her eyes open, Ellia staggered
through the halls, heading for her cubicle. Passing
Comos, she tried to ignore him, but the minor was
determined to speak to her. "Morning, Xander," he
said with his most affable smile.

Ellia grunted. "Morning," she said. She rubbed her
bloodshot eyes with the thumb and index finger of her
unhurt arm.

"Hard time sleeping last night?" Comos asked,
standing between her and the staircase.

"Yes," she snapped. "You could say that. Right now
I want to return to my cubicle and get some sleep to
make up for it."

"But you'll miss classes!"

"I guess I will."

"That's too bad. And you, the best student in the
Open City. If you're having trouble sleeping, studying
too hard, perhaps I can get you something to remedy
that."

"Oh, I'm sure you can!"

"You know, Xander, I've been trying to connect up
with you since the evening we spent at the Steeped
Tea Leaf together—"

"And I've been doing everything in my power to
avoid you."

"Hmmm," he said, nodding. "That could explain it.
Yes, it could indeed."

"Look, do you mind? I want—"

"I've invested a lot of time—"

"Invested!" Ellia tried to get past the red-uniformed
minor, but he deftly blocked her way.

"Yes, invested. Time, money, effort, all in an attempt to show you some of the pleasures in life. I've displayed my wares"—Ellia made a disgusted noise—"and I should think you'd find something you'd like."

"And you think I'll forgive you for pouring that purple stuff in my wine?"

"If you saw me pour the violet cannonshot in your drink, why'd you drink it then?"

"I didn't see it! Tlezachi did. I'm not *that* stupid."

Comos smiled. "If you say so. Still, you sure enjoyed yourself. I've never seen a person more jubilant or playful or flying quite so high as you were. A truly wonderful reaction."

Comos's words suddenly evoked memories of that night along with pleasant sensations she had managed to block out.

"I can get you cannonshot just as easily as that other thing you prefer," Comos said.

"I don't want it."

"You like it, though."

"If you do not step out of my way this moment, I will walk right through you, Comos, and don't think I wouldn't."

Comos chuckled. Furious, Ellia walked forward and pushed the minor with both hands toward the stairs. Comos stumbled backward. Hands whirling, he lunged for the handrail.

"Stupid, dogtail—" Comos yelled as he clung to the rail, then righted himself to stand five stairs down from the landing. But by this time Ellia had stalked past him, down to the second floor. "Blind priests!" she heard as she turned into her cubicle maze. She walked on angrily.

Comos caught up to her as she reached her cubicle. He grabbed her wounded arm and spun her around.

Ellia let out a scream, felt her head whirl. Then anger won out over pain, and she ripped her arm out of the surprised minor's grasp. Sleepy faces peeked out of cubicles to see what had caused the commotion.

Ellia held Comos in her stare, then her rage hit its peak, and she threw open the curtains to her cubicle. She grabbed her sheathed knife and belt; holding the sheath in her trembling right hand, she slid out a decimeter or so of shining metal. Every witness disappeared into his cubicle.

"I'm unarmed," Comos said.

"So much the better." Ellia laughed weakly as wave after wave of pain washed through her body.

"You wouldn't—"

"You are right there, Comos," she said with deadly slowness. "Your blood would likely corrode the steel. But I could easily beat you to a pulp with the hilt to stiffen my fist—and don't think I wouldn't."

The minor gulped, but stood his ground. He licked his lips, then looked into Ellia's cubicle and spied the two lockets lying on the bed.

"What about that?" he asked, pointing.

"About what?"

"The pills in that locket of yours, that's what!"

Ellia quickly covered up her surprise. "Don't you believe in medicine?"

"Unregistered with the shrine physician? I've read the records."

"It was made specifically for me and I didn't wish—"

"Ha! A story if I ever heard one. I saw with my own eyes when you emptied a yellow vial into your locket and then threw the evidence into the sewer! Look, Xander, I can replace anything and at a better price."

"In this case, I do doubt it," Ellia said. She was no longer amused. She bared her blade completely, dropping the sheath to the floor, and took one step in Comos's direction. Like a scared rooster, he turned feather and ran.

"I don't forget," he warned from the end of the hall.

"I'm sure you don't," she muttered under her breath.

* * *

The next morning Ellia did not see Tlezachi in their mathematics class. Realizing suddenly that lately she had not seen her friend in any of the classes they shared, she marched to his maze and rapped on the wall. "Tlee? She waited. "Tlee, are you ill?"

Tlezachi made a few sleepy sounds, then went silent.

"Tlezachi? It's late. Don't you think you'd better wake up?"

"No."

"Tlezachi, it's Xander."

"I'm sleeping," he said.

"Come on, Minor, wake up. You are missing classes."

"And sleep too. Oh, all right. Wait a minute." She heard the sounds of fabric moving against fabric, a wooden box closing. Wrapped in a robe, a shockingly pale Tlezachi pulled open the privacy curtain and sat back on the narrow bed. "Morning."

"Are you feeling well?"

"Yeaaah." Ellia could tell that he was not well.

"Why don't you get dressed and we'll go see if we can't bribe a snack out of the cook so you don't have to wait until afternoon."

Tlezachi gave a pained sigh, then nodded. Ellia closed the curtain for him and waited. When he rejoined her, she returned his locket.

"You found yours?" he asked. Ellia nodded and pulled hers out from under her shirt. They ate together and studied together, but the boy remained pale, sailing the doldrums for the next few days.

Then without warning the lethargy Tlezachi had displayed the day Ellia had borrowed his locket returned. He showed no interest in studying for the exams. He became unpredictable, and Ellia actually began to dread his company. But he refused to go to the shrine physician.

Tlezachi shrugged off his behavior, swearing to study

twice as hard, but in the dogdays that followed, he became weirdly depressed.

Finally, to preserve her worn sanity, Ellia had to avoid her friend altogether. When her Pecol friends came to port, she retreated to their ship for several days. But she felt guilty—to abandon a friend in need was not in her nature. Chriz sensed Ellia's ill ease and asked her about it.

"Obviously something is amiss with your friend. I am sure that if you really attempt to discover the problem, you will. Have you so attempted?"

"I've tried," Ellia sighed as the shag toweled dry her rain-soaked hair. "He just shrugs it off as nothing."

"Well, you are going to try again, Greeneyes." Chriz handed her the damp towel, then walked across the salon toward the wheelhouse. When she heard the shag summon a hack by wireless, Ellia just stared at the wood floor and shook her head.

At the entrance to the main secular building, Ellia stamped the water off her boots, put her rain gear away, and set off in search of her friend, but Tlezachi was not to be found. She finally gave up and went to her cubicle, but when she pulled open the curtain, she nearly stopped breathing. Her mattress had been turned over and her bedding thrown on the floor. Her carpet bag had been emptied.

"Kantilphanes," she whispered, putting her right hand over her locket. She backed out of her cubicle, bumped into somebody, and spun to face a dark-haired minor she knew from some of her classes.

"Guess you haven't been here in the last couple days?" he asked.

"N-no, I haven't." Ellia turned and peered into her ruined quarters.

"Everybody's cubicle was searched for contraband two days ago, thanks to your friend, Comos. I wish somebody would have the courage to inform on Comos to the M'admin."

Ellia compressed her lips into a thin line and shook her head. With the minor's help, Ellia righted her mattress, fixed her desk, and sorted her papers.

An hour later, Tlezachi knocked at her cubicle wall.

"Xander, may I speak to you? It—it's Tlezachi."

Ellia had been reading by lamplight. She placed the text down on her desk, then stretched to open her curtain. "Sure."

The boy swallowed visibly. "Evening," he began.

"Sit down," she said, patting the gray flannel blanket on the bed beside her. He remained standing.

Tlezachi looked pained and was very pale. His gaze shifted everywhere; he looked at everything except Ellia. She narrowed her eyes as Tlezachi said, "I came to ask a favor."

"If I can help, you know I will."

"Could I b—borrow about twenty-five barters?"

She almost asked him why, but shrewdness made her reach for her purse instead. "I could loan you more if need it." She opened the pouch and poured into her palm one gold coin and the equivalent in glittering, jingling bronze and silver.

Her friend licked his lips and stared at her hand. "No," he said suddenly. At first he had trouble tearing his eyes from the coins, then solved the problem by closing his eyes and retreating. "No. No, I can't."

"Tlezachi!" she called as the minor pitched over then caught himself as he retreated out of her cubicle.

"I'm sorry, really I am." He disappeared out of view. Ellia stuffed her coins in her hip pocket and followed the boy.

Presently Ellia faced the green curtain that shut off Tlezachi's cubicle. "Tlee—"

"Go away!"

"Tlezachi—"

"Go away, Xander, please."

Ellia began tapping her boot on the floor. "You came to me, Tlee, asking a favor. This time I shan't depart until you explain yourself." Ellia heard a groan; he didn't open his privacy curtain, though, and his rudeness infuriated her. "Tlezachi," she said very slowly, "will you let me in?"

"No."

"But Tlee—"

"If you wish so badly to do me a favor, leave me be!"

"You know I can't do that," she replied, then she did something she would never have even considered doing otherwise: she threw open his privacy curtain.

"Blind priests!" he cried. Ellia smelled stale eucalyptuslike fumes; when she flipped the light switch, she saw the remnants of a red wax candle melted all over the desk. Tlezachi cursed and shielded his eyes.

"Are you going to explain all this foolishness?" Ellia asked, her fists on her hips.

"No."

"Look at me." Flushing with anger, she shouted, "Look at me!"

"No!"

Irritated, Ellia reached over and slapped his hand from his face.

"You want to fight or something!" Tlezachi yelled back. "Can't you just let me—"

"No, Tlee, I can't," she interrupted, reaching into her pocket and then holding out a handful of change. "You asked for a favor. Here's the money you wanted. Take it."

"No, I—" he breathed deeply "—no. I really don't need it, really. Thank you anyway."

"You're lying. Don't lie."

"Really, Xander—"

"You can do anything but lie to me, Tlee."

"But—"

"But nothing. Come take the barters, Tlee," she said, inching closer, placing her hand before his face. He tried to strike away her hand, but Ellia was faster. "Rude, very rude."

Tlezachi groaned. "Why are you tormenting me?"

"You are tormenting yourself."

"Stop!" he yelled suddenly. "I don't even deserve to be your friend."

Ellia sighed. "You're the second person to say that. Will you let me judge, huh? Are you going to take the money or not?"

"No! I said no."

"Are you going to take the money?" she repeated, her voice scaling louder. "Or am I going to have to ram it down your ugly throat?"

"Xander!"

"You can either take the barters or—or you can tell me why you refuse to take them. Either will do."

Tlezachi closed his eyes in pain. "I can't do that!"

Ellia moved closer. "One coin at a time, huh, Tlee? How does that sound? Remember, you are only borrowing them. I'll expect repayment."

"Please!" he cried. He hid his face in his hands.

"Well?" she asked. For a time, Ellia listened to him cry. Then, in a more friendly tone, she said, "Tell me, Tlee."

"I've insulted you either way it goes!" Tlezachi stared at the curtain. "I checked your cubicle after they did the contraband search," he said suddenly, "but found no money."

"You—you *what*?"

"I—I—I wanted to wait, but I looked anyway, fi—figuring I—I wouldn't find anything. I should have waited for you to return, but I couldn't. I was desperate! I knew you'd loan it to me, Xander, but I couldn't wait!" He dropped his gaze.

"Why?"

Tlezachi shook his head vigorously and refused to look at her.

"*Why?* More than anyone, I have private things I'd never let anyone see. I want to know what made you so desperate."

"Private things? Oh, I know," Tlezachi said sud-

denly in a condescending voice. Ellia was startled—
did he remember the kiss?

"Know what?"

"About the contents of your locket. A good way to
escape a contraband inspection."

"It's medicine!"

"Sure. Where have I heard that one before?"

"Tlee, I'm a bleeder," she said, giving him the half-
truth the situation demanded. "I need that medicine."

He groaned. "That explains the report that you
dodged the medical check-up. Afraid he'd send you
home saying dock work was too dangerous? *Blind*, I've
insulted you again."

"No, you haven't, really. I like you, Tlezachi, and
something is terribly wrong. I know it. The question
is, are you going to tell me what?"

"I—I can't." He moaned. "Do yourself a favor and
forget me."

"I can't forget you," she said simply.

Her tone proved more effective than all her earlier
bluster. Ready to burst into tears, he spoke one word:
"Comos—"

"Blind Priests!" she shrieked. She kicked the wall
so hard her boot left a depression in the lath.

Comos had managed to addict Tlezachi to a mood-
altering drug. A thimbleful of "Mountain Snow" burnt
with a heavily scented candle and inhaled in a single
deep breath relaxed one instantly and brought a weird
clarity that magnified every feeling. The hangover
brought chills, nausea, and a tendency toward magnified depressions.

Jitters came to Tlezachi as if caused by an icy wind
as Ellia escorted her friend out of the main secular
building. For three days they skipped all their classes
to spend every waking minute in the woods where no
one could overhear Tlezachi raging. The foul names
Tlezachi's dementia dredged up, the anger Ellia en-

dured, the unexpected attacks she fought off, and the bruises with which she was left—she would never have gone through it all if she had felt she had a choice. But curing her friend had become her responsibility, even when he spit on her.

Yet even worse, when on the depressed side of his pendulum mood swings, Tlezachi required comforting that Ellia was loathe to give. It exposed her too much, making her disguise seem—to her—more transparent than summer air. But when Tlezachi needed physical comforting like a child Shana's age or even an infant, Ellia gave without question. For hours she hugged him and rocked with him, watching as the sun filtered through the trees to give them warmth. Only the wind blowing though the leaves masked the sound of his crying.

The experience left Ellia aware that she too required comforting and contact. It was a lonely revelation, a need that could become a craving, an addiction in itself. Each night, watching Tlezachi fret under his blankets in the woods where she had made camp for them, she knew the seeds of womanhood had germinated. The warmth of a well-tended fire was no longer solace.

Eventually, though, the pendulum weakened, finally centering. From then on Ellia accompanied Tlezachi as often as possible, even to his requisite labors when she was free, adding the emotional support the lack of which she judged to be the cause of his addiction in the first place. She vowed to do anything she could, short of revealing her disguise.

But still there was Comos. Every time Comos saw Tlezachi, Ellia was there and if he had been angry at her before, losing Tlezachi to her made him livid. He refused to forget—and that spelled trouble.

The second dogday after Ellia had worked her cure, Tlezachi's employer asked him to stay late to complete packing rush orders. As was her habit, Ellia arrived with the homebound shuttle and remained to assist her friend. Together they finished the task quickly; the proprietor of the clearing house was grateful enough to flip them a ten-barter piece as he padlocked his doors.

"Theater or dinner?" Ellia asked, turning the silver-nickel coin over in her hand.

"I'm hungry."

"Dinner, then?" she said.

"No, both," Tlezachi decided, and they rushed off into town for rice and fishcakes from a street vendor, then to a tragedy of the classic type about the end of the warlord era. By the time they left the theater, the streets had emptied, and the air had become uncommonly brisk. Hands in pockets, collars up, they rushed toward the single path to the shrine.

"Ah, Xander, and if it isn't Tlezachi!" someone said without warning.

"Huh?" Ellia spun around, heart pounding. She watched, hand on her knife hilt, as Comos and two companions approached, their bootfalls echoing loudly on the shadowy street.

"Just who we wanted to meet," Tlezachi hissed. Ellia suddenly wondered if Tlezachi wore the short sword on his hip only as an ornament.

"So what are you two minors doing about town tonight?" Comos asked, halting two meters from them. Seething inside, Ellia managed to remain silent.

Tlezachi answered. "Theater and dinner."

"Fall of the Warlord? Yes? Decent story." Comos nodded. "Expensive tickets also. You have extra cash, Tlezachi? Huh?"

Ellia narrowed her eyes. "No, he hasn't," she spit. She held Comos's eyes when he looked at her; after a moment he shrugged and appraised Tlezachi again.

"We've all seen how Xander's been *mothering* you recently. We've wondered where you've been disappearing to, haven't we, boys?" he said to a chorus of chuckles. Both Ellia and Tlezachi flushed at this. "Why don't you ask your mother to leave? I think we have business to transact."

Ellia began to hiss; she was too angry to speak.

"She's losing air," Comos laughed. "We'd better find her a rubber patch before she deflates completely."

"Watch yourself," Tlezachi growled. His hand wavered near the hilt of his short sword.

Bravo! Ellia thought.

Comos lost his humor and narrowed his eyes at Tlezachi. "You watch yourself, eh?"

"Then give me a good reason to," Tlezachi answered. "I'm not throwing insults at your giggly friends now, am I?" Ellia saw that, like Tlezachi, Comos wore a fashionable short sword while the other two wore more useful long knives like her own.

"You want a good reason? How's deciding not to sell to you, or making sure no one else does? I can do that, you know, Tlee."

"In that case I might just insult you for my own good!"

"Tlezachi," Ellia cautioned as she noticed Comos's companions unsheathing their weapons.

"I'd be careful what I say if I were you, Tlezachi," Comos warned. "My friends have been known to hurt people."

"As oxen carts have been known to run over people?" Ellia asked. Comos's friends tensed.

"Come now, let us be civil about this matter, Tlezachi. Tell your girlfriend to leave. Perhaps then I might be persuaded to give you a price break, maybe even a free sample of a new, stronger blend of Snow."

"No," Tlezachi said, unstrapping his scabbard and pulling out his sword. "And if you don't stop insulting my friend, I'll make you sorry." Ellia did not know whether to applaud her friend or berate him for his stupidity.

"What?" Comos said. "You by yourself against us three? You'll get hurt."

Ellia snorted. "If you were the one who picked your bodyguards, I'd say you had better worry that they may run away."

"Ha!" Comos returned with forced levity. "Why don't you just turn around and toddle back to your mother, Xander—"

"I'm warning you," Tlezachi snapped. "I'm Stone Coast trained." Ellia looked at him with amazement; Tlezachi had never mentioned that part of his past.

"As am I," Ellia quickly added. "Last ritual cycle, in fact." She shifted her knife from her right hand to her left and then right again—a calculated show-off maneuver.

Tlezachi added, "Still wish to insult us, you mangy rooster?"

"So this girl has training. I don't think much of Stone Coasters. They caught a girl masquerading as a boy there last cycle, which demonstrates the difficulty of their vaunted training. They whipped her. Was that you, Xander?"

Ellia grinned.

"You haven't a gram of intelligence, have you, Comos?" Tlezachi returned. "Most women I've met at least have the sense to resign in a no-win situation. But then again, there are few women as dumb as you."

Comos's right hand fluttered. Recognizing his gesture as a signal, Ellia attacked. She took two quick lopes, then kicked, disarming her opponent immediately. Before his knife hit the pavement, a spinning backward kick in the stomach sent the minor to the ground while the cat yowl that had escaped Ellia's throat reverberated off the dark storefronts.

Instantly she spun around just in time to jump away from the sweep of Comos's blade. But she was not quick enough, and he hit her on the right ear with the flat of the blade. Head ringing, she kneeled five meters from the minor. She fought double vision. Two images of Comos coalesced into one, and she saw that he was waving for her to come back to him. "What's the matter, Xander? Is the flat of my blade too much for you?"

"No," she hissed, waiting to be sure her dizziness would not incapacitate her. Tlezachi and the remaining bodyguard were circling one another. "No," she repeated, measuring distances, gauging Comos's skill by his stance. She saw signs of hyperventilation and elation: evidence of poor training.

Ellia lunged, yelling as if to wake the entire city, but dodged Comos completely. "Sorry," she said, and kicked Tlezachi's opponent in the side. Her companion completed the maneuver, knocking the knife from a suddenly palsied hand.

Ellia spun around. "Well?" she asked, gesturing with her knife. Her vision swam, and she saw Comos shimmer like a distant object on a hot, hot day. The girl focused on her knife, then on Comos's sword, and her opponent solidified again.

"Rather a dirty trick," Comos said with less bluster.

"So?" Ellia said, shrugging. "Say you apologize and we will forget the whole thing."

"Me? Apologize? To a girl?" He laughed.

"Unimaginative, very unimaginative—besides being dumb," she said.

Comos lunged. Ellia yelled again as she kicked out. The edge of his sword cut into her boot, splitting the sole in half, and the shock sent her tumbling off balance. But she had succeeded in knocking the sword from his hand. She hit the pavement rolling, endeavoring not to slice herself with her own blade, but blood flowed from her shoulder as she came up in a squat. Comos, stunned, was still standing, holding his right wrist. His sword lay two meters away.

"I'm disarmed," Comos said, finding his voice.

"That you are," Ellia said, taking every second she could to rest, catch her breath, and prepare.

"What are you going to do now?" he asked. One glance showed him that Tlezachi had his hands full making sure his two disarmed bodyguards remained useless. Comos's eyes searched for his short sword.

"Wait for you to concede defeat, what else?"

"Then you're dumber than you look!" he cried quickly. He lunged sideways for his sword, but Ellia was faster. She struck his exposed left side with a fist reinforced by her knife hilt. Then she whirled and knocked him to the ground with a swift heel in the rear. Finally she crouched behind him and caught him up in a choke hold. Chuckling for effect, she pressed the edge of her knife up against Comos's larynx.

"Try something and I might slip," she hissed into his ear. "And don't think I wouldn't."

Comos swallowed.

"Still want to call me an ignorant girl?" Ellia asked. She chuckled, then stopped, disliking the sound of her laugh.

"Bastard," he said quickly, tensing.

"At least you give equal time to both sexes. How about making this easy and apologizing, then we could just forget it."

"I won't. You won't kill me."

"Slitting a scrawny throat like yours would be as easy as chopping off a chicken's head, which I've done more times than I can count," she lied.

"You wouldn't," he said.

"Apologize, that's all I ask. I received a slash tonight. I see nothing to keep me from reciprocating in kind."

Comos swallowed again, then after a moment said, "I apologize."

"For what?" Ellia prompted.

"For calling you a girl," he returned rapidly.

"And?"

"And for bothering both you and Tlezachi tonight. Isn't that enough?"

"Sure is," Ellia said, pulling her knife away and giving Comos a quick push. As he sprawled on the cobblestones, she grabbed his sword. Then she and

Tlezachi collected the remaining weapons. "You won't be needing these again," she said as Comos looked up at her. "And don't call someone a girl unless you know for sure you are addressing one. I'll lose these tonight, no doubt," she added, "so don't come looking for them."

Leaving Comos on the ground, Ellia and Tlezachi retreated. When they turned a corner, they sent the extra weapons spinning into a smelly sewer, then ran until they reached the dirt path up the hill.

"Do you think humiliating him was wise?" Tlezachi asked as they hurried up the hill.

"You mean, do I think he will attack us again? Ask yourself that."

Tlezachi thought for a second. "He's confronted you twice and lost. He may be dumb, but he's not stupid."

"Precisely . . . I hope." She sighed.

"Oh my, your arm!" Tlezachi exclaimed as they walked under the first lamp on the path. He made Ellia stop, and rolled up her sleeve to examine the cut. The wound was four centimeters long and shallow. Her red uniform was stained darkly, but the bleeding had almost stopped.

"And I did it with my own knife," she said, shaking her head.

"It's really not bleeding badly."

"A cut like that, why should it?" she asked as they resumed marching up the path.

"But you said you were a bleeder!"

"And I bled."

"But not much. Tell me the truth, is that stuff in your locket really for bleeding? Huh?"

Ellia took a deep breath. Should she tell him? "It's medicine, all right," she said, "and it stops bleeding too. It does something else on top of that, but it doesn't make you fly like the contraband Comos sells. How about this: when we leave on the train for our homes, I will tell you all about it." She laughed. "You'll find it very interesting, perhaps enlightening."

"Knowing you, Xander," he said, nodding, "I probably shall."

The dogdays that followed came and went without further confrontation with Comos. He avoided both Ellia and Tlezachi whether they were together or alone. Ellia found it difficult to believe, but she had to conclude eventually that the minor had actually admitted defeat.

By the time the ritual cycle was two-thirds complete, Ellia found herself thinking more and more about Tlezachi. Late at night in her cubicle, she would think of how she would break her secret to Tlezachi. She must preserve his friendship past the end of the cycle! But how to tell the truth? She didn't feel right just coming out with it. She could drop clues until he could make no incorrect guess. Then again, she could kiss Tlezachi as she remembered kissing him that unfortunate night. The thought caused her to giggle, especially at the impropriety of it. Ellia felt suddenly very much kin to Marsai.

Soon the dragondays would arrive, and Tlezachi would learn the truth. Ellia liked Tlezachi—enough to enjoy the idea of marrying him. He would understand her special needs: to read, to travel, to learn, to enjoy life. And then there would be children, children like Shana. Da would be so happy.

And so would she. Had she indeed "discovered boys," as Marsai would say? That thought caused her to smile.

Nine

"*Hold there,*" Chriz said, grunting as she tugged a rope taut and lashed it around a handy cleat. "There."

Ellia let the rope go, then helped Chriz heave a tarp over the excess cargo they had stowed on deck. Mopping her forehead on her sleeve, she looked over her shoulder.

"Are you expecting someone?" Chriz asked.

"Yeah. I'm waiting for Tlezachi." She scanned the docks and the warehouses lining them. The sun, near setting, sent dark shadows angling everywhere. "He said he'd meet me here and together we would catch the homebound shuttle."

"You have had your friend on your mind a lot recently," the shag observed as she tied down the eyelets of the tarp to the deck. Ellia belatedly did the same.

"Yes, I guess I have. We're good friends."

"Have you told him yet?" Chriz asked.

"No. But I've thought about it. I'll tell him, soon."

"But you are waiting until he is fully cured until you tell him?"

"No, that's not it," Ellia said. She shucked off her workgloves and sighed. "In fact, I think there is no danger of him becoming addicted again. He's stronger than he thinks. He has sight of his goals again—and me for a companion!" Ellia laughed.

"You seem significantly happier than the day I first encountered you, Greeneyes."

"I try not to think of my future problems anymore," Ellia said soberly.

"Look, Greeneyes, I believe I can complete the stowage myself. You have been more than a help."

"Thanks," Ellia said, trying to smile. As she searched for Tlezachi again, she spotted on the dock two burly masters who she did not recognize. Wishing Chriz good sailing on the return trip to the People's Collective, she walked down the gangplank toward the red-uniformed masters. Again she thought it strange that she didn't recognize them. Long hours in the sun had hardened their swarthy faces.

"Evening," Ellia said as she approached.

"Are you Xander?" the shorter of the two asked.

"That's me."

"We haven't caused you to leave your labors early or anything like that?" he asked.

"No. In a few minutes everyone for the shrinebound shuttle will be by."

"Good." The man smiled unpleasantly. "We're assigned to take you to see the master administrator. You distinguished yourself on the last exams, and he wishes to meet you, personally."

Ellia sighed and glanced over her shoulder.

"We've ordered a hack to take us to the master administrator's apartments. Will you follow us to where we instructed it to meet us?"

"But I was waiting for someone—"

"I'm sure he'll understand when you tell him to-night. We don't want to keep the master administrator waiting, do we?"

"Definitely not," the other master agreed.

"I guess Tlee will understand," Ellia conceded. She followed, flanked by the second master.

"Oh, yes," the spokesman said suddenly. "You'll give me your knife."

"Huh?"

"Fumiko is a priest," the spokesman pointed out.

Ellia shrugged. She unbuckled her belt and handed it into a beefy hand. But as they walked onward, she noticed that both men carried long knives on *their* waists. When they turned the corner into an alley, they found a short, thin man in the black clothing of a merchant awaiting them. The same man had worn a black uniform the last time Ellia had seen him. She gasped.

"Master Administrator!" She grabbed for the knife hilt she suddenly remembered was not there.

"Nice to meet you again, Xander," Mikitsu said in a controlled, deprecating voice.

"I've never met you, sir," she said, sweating and swallowing hard.

"You disappoint me, Minor. I can remember when your hair had a less flashy tinge."

"I was born with hair this color, sir. Are you sure you have the right person?"

"I have the right person," the master administrator said, nodding. "And you had hair a darker color once. That puzzled me when I first read my friend Fumiko's records on you. You stand out prominently. Good exam scores—amazing, but you received help because of your charms, yes? Then there were the complaints about fights breaking out over you. Interesting, or at least I thought so. But your scores caused Fumiko to discard the complaints about you. He thinks they were placed by a contraband trafficker."

"*Comos!*"

"I thought it significant," he continued. "And I remembered Hanssan's description of a mahogany-haired minor. Your brother? It was stupid of you to allow yourself to be so easily disarmed, Xander—or is it Elthen? Or perhaps it is something else? Would you like to tell us your true name?" He smiled with unsavory intent in his dark, feral eyes.

"You can rot—"

"Xander!" a growly, shaggish voice interrupted. Mikitsu's lackeys whirled around, but before Ellia could consider running, hands clamped her forearms like vises on wood. She struggled fruitlessly. "What is going on here?" Chriz asked.

Ellia saw in one glance that the shag was unarmed and felt her hopes dashed. The shag was strong, but could she prevail against two huge, armed humans?

"This minor is under arrest for contraband violations," Mikitsu answered. "I am truly sorry if the minor caused any problems on your ship." Ellia's mouth fell open at the man's lie.

"Well, that explains it," Chriz said. "I am new to the ship, and, you understand, I have never observed a human quite as clumsy as this creature. Broke open a couple of crates, it did."

"I wouldn't doubt it," Mikitsu returned quickly, nodding.

Ellia found her voice. "This is the master administrator of the Stone Coast shrine!" The pressure on her arms increased sharply.

Chriz growled low in her throat, a gravelly sound to set nerves on edge. "Master administrator? Is that special? You Emeralines fascinate me."

"The minor's misinformed," Mikitsu said sourly. "That M'admin has been retired from his post for almost a ritual cycle. Honestly, we must be going—"

"He thinks I'm the girl he whipped—ouch!"

"A girl?" Chriz asked. "Does that mean female?" Chriz was stalling, Ellia realized.

"The contraband's gone to her—his head, I'm afraid. Drugs do that, confusing the identity," he finished, wavering a hand near his right ear.

Mikitsu's lies proved to Ellia that he was not acting in an official capacity. He had whipped her when operating within a set of rules; what would happen when he operated outside them?

"This is true?" Chriz stalled again. "How can I recognize the symptoms better and prevent having this happening to my ship again?"

"Really, worthy sir—" Mikitsu began.

"I am female," Chriz said dangerously.

"E-Excuse me, worthy, uh, worthy female, but we really must be going."

"Going? But why? I have queried you with a reasonable question, and you have not provided an answer. We pay an outrageous fee for labor. If it is that your men have not the strength required to hold the cubling, I would gladly assist."

"That won't be necessary," Mikitsu answered. "Your best source of information is to be found at the Trade Interest Center near the harbor master's buildings, worthy."

"But I asked *you*," Chriz insisted. Ellia's lower arms throbbed with the loss of circulation.

"What can I say? I'm not well qualified in this area. I go where I'm assigned."

"Sure you do!" Ellia exclaimed. "Yow!" She squirmed to no avail, on the verge of tears.

"And paranoid too," Mikitsu added. Ellia stopped struggling when she gazed beyond the white-furred shag to see another person in a red uniform approaching. Chriz noted Ellia's reaction and glanced over her shoulder to see Tlezachi. Puzzled, the minor ran toward them.

"That means it is dangerous? That is why I require this information. Can you not understand?"

"Tlezachi!" Ellia cried. "Give your sword to

Chriz—" A hand gagged her. Ellia bit down with all the viciousness she could muster. Mikitsu yelled out in pain.

Tlezachi skidded to a stop as he recognized Mikitsu. "That's the master administrator of the Stone—"

The hand gone, Mikitsu cursing behind her, Ellia used the only weapon left to her. "I'm the girl he whipped last cycle, and he's going to hurt me!"

Tlezachi's eyes went wide. He instantly grabbed his sword below the hilt and tossed it pommel forward to the shag who jumped to a safe distance to catch it.

The man to Ellia's right drew his sword. "We're Stone Coast Military trained," he stated.

"But I am a veteran warrior, human mouse," Chriz said, wildly brandishing the sword. "Humans do not attack skin-faced warriors and expect to live!"

Ellia heard a shout, and around the corner of the building she spotted red uniforms heading her way across the docks.

"What is going on here!" Ogawa yelled, running with his hand on the fashionable short sword.

"They're frauds," Tlezachi yelled. "They're trying to rob Xander of his money!"

"What the—?" Mikitsu yelled. Without his military finery, the man must have realized he was not instantly recognizable. Mikitsu's other man released Ellia to draw his sword. Ellia quickly slammed her free hand into the base of her other captor's sternum. He coughed, and Ellia was free.

An arm tightened around her waist, crushing the air out of her. Chriz and her opponent disarmed each other; a bloody gash opened on Chriz's leg. The shag pounced.

Ogawa yelled, about to join the fray. Unable to breathe or struggle, Ellia blacked out and was pushed to the pavement where she cracked her head.

Tlezachi hauled her, half-conscious, to her feet. Mikitsu lay on the ground, balled into a fetal position. Tlezachi screamed words indiscernible to her fogged brain, then jerked her so hard he nearly wrenched her arm from its socket. Blood from a cut on her forehead streamed into her eyes as she stumbled down the alley.

"Come on, girl!" Tlezachi yelled, pulling even harder. Barely balanced, she ran with Tlezachi toward the street. Panting, she grabbed hold of the building to halt them both.

"I've got to go back!" Ellia cried between breaths.

"What for?" He tried to pull her on, but she stood rooted.

"I can't leave Chriz like that! If she gets hurt—"

"With no weapon and blood in your eyes?" he asked, drawing a finger across her forehead. His touch stung. He drew a red line across the wall. "With you gone it'll end, if you told me the truth."

"I did," Ellia said. Tlezachi pulled again, and she allowed herself to be led. After running most of the way down the street toward the next alley, they heard a shout behind them.

"Halt!"

She glanced over her shoulder to see the red uniform of the man she had decked earlier.

"Hurry, Xander!" Tlezachi cried. They turned into a dark and shadowy alley that offered neither doorways nor other hiding places. Their boots clattered as they ran onward. A third pair of bootfalls sounded behind them. At the alley's end, Tlezachi dodged left toward the setting sun, running at a pace Ellia could barely match. She extracted her hand from his grasp; he glanced back but said nothing.

They dodged down more streets and alleyways, hoping to lose the man.

"To the left!" Tlezachi yelled as they exited an alley. Ellia's boot heel found a curb. She careened forward, hands out to break her fall.

She screamed as she skinned both hands and nearly rammed face first into a fruit cart. In a daze of pain, she felt Tlezachi roughly haul her to her feet.

"Xander!" he cried, shaking her. She couldn't answer.

"He's covered with blood!" came another voice as Tlezachi caught hold of Ellia's hand and again dragged her behind him. Her blood mixed with tears as she stumbled after him. She saw only the crimson ghosts of the people they shoved out of their way. They dodged into a new, dark alleyway. But regardless of the loss of precious seconds, they had indeed escaped their pursuer.

Ellia waited alone in another alley and was finally able to catch her breath by the time Tlezachi returned.

"Are we safe?" she croaked. Though she tried, she could not look her friend in the eye. She kept blinking and looking at the grimy alley road.

"We're safe," he said, sighing. "I've never seen someone so persistent in my life."

"M'admin Mikitsu inspires persistence, as you should well know."

"I know." Tlezachi was quiet for a few seconds. "So you're that Elthen they caught last ritual cycle."

"Yes," she said. Ellia swallowed hard and still didn't look up.

"Look, I realize you're a girl. I don't think less of you for that. To do what you've done as long as you did—then to get caught isn't something to be ashamed of. Without Mikitsu, nobody would have known."

Ellia looked up. "You don't care that I'm a girl?"

"I didn't say that. I said that I just didn't think less of you. Perhaps now I think better. You are extraordinary by any standard."

Ellia managed a little smile. "Hadn't we better get out of here?" she asked.

They threaded stealthily through the backstreets and alleys of the Open City. Later as night fell, they bought supplies. Though Tlezachi looked as bad as Ellia did with his shirt torn at the collar and a bruise turning blue on his chin, she let him go while she sat on the stoop of a darkened store. "I need time to collect myself," she told him, handing him her purse.

Tlezachi returned carrying a bottle of antiseptic and cotton. Gently he cleaned the cut on Ellia's forehead, then the scrapes on her hands. Later Ellia, her hands hurting badly, took a needle and thread from Tlezachi's inexperienced hands and mended the rip in his shirt.

"Thank you, Xander," he said as Ellia leaned forward to cut the thread with her teeth. His voice made her aware of how close she was to him, and she moved away. "Or should I call you 'Elthen'?"

"My name's Ellia."

"You're your sister!"

"You could say that," Ellia returned, smiling.

"You know you're beautiful?"

Ellia laughed.

"I'm serious."

"You just like red hair."

"Maybe," Tlezachi said, then paused. "Your Xander persona was exceptional. I didn't even realize all those days in the forest while you were so close—" He swallowed and looked away.

"When what happened today can be the direct result of a flaw in your disguise, you strive for perfection whenever you can. I've had a lot of practice."

"I suppose you have. But it seems so difficult—"

"It's worth it," Ellia snapped.

"Even after what happened today?"

"Even after having my blouse ripped off my back and being whipped to unconsciousness!" she said, glaring suddenly at her friend.

"I'm sorry," he said in a faded voice. "I guess I take it for granted. Sometimes it even seems boring to me. The soporific school books, the labors, all of it. I guess that's why I attended the Stone Coast shrine and nearly got killed by a horse halfway through the ritual cycle."

"But think of life without any of that, not even the

choice of seeking something adventurous like the Stone Coast."

Finally he said, "I never could understand my sister, how she doesn't care about reading or traveling around to shrines. I think I'll go fetch us something to eat, then we'll decide what to do next. All right, Ellia?"

After fishcakes and apple juice, they decided to leave the Open City before someone thought to wait for them by the fence.

At the gate, blinding lights glared blue-white on the gate guard who watched them approach and also illuminated a guard walking a pair of black chee on leashes. Ellia shivered.

"Perhaps you had better let me go alone," she said. "If they are looking for someone, it'll be me."

"Any more avidly than me? I hurt our old M'admin pretty badly."

Ellia nodded, and they continued toward the gate. "Let me talk, though. This I've had practice at."

"Evening," the guard said. "You two look like you've been through a scrape recently. Escaping justice?" he asked good-naturedly.

"Not today—maybe tomorrow." Ellia smiled. "We're going to visit our families in Telmetter."

The guard chuckled. "Your passes, please."

Ellia took hold of her silver chain to pull her locket from her shirt. Then she heard Tlezachi become upset.

"My locket," he said, patting his chest, then his pockets. "I can't find my locket!"

"What?" Ellia said, turning to face him.

"I've lost it! The rip in my shirt—he must have snapped the chain."

"Blind!" She turned to the guard, who shook his head.

"Sorry. It is regulations. I need to see all passes."

"Maybe if I returned to the docks—" Tlezachi offered.

"You might meet someone you would rather not,"

Ellia interrupted. "Is there no way?" Ellia asked the guard.

He shook his head. "You would not believe how often this happens. If we started letting people in and out of the city without passes, then what good would the fence be? Besides, Minor, you would find it impossible to re-enter the city without your pass. Go back and get it. It'll save a lot of hassle."

"Blind," Ellia said again under her breath.

"You go without me," Tlezachi said.

"No!"

"Look, it's more important that you get to Telmetter!"

"And it's not important for you?"

To the guard, Ellia moaned, "We just *have* to leave."

"Why?"

"It's very personal," Tlezachi answered. "We heard about it only an hour ago, and we rushed out here."

"Yes, you looked rushed," the guard observed with a laugh.

"My aunt's dying!" Ellia suddenly cried. She looked at Tlezachi.

Her heart skipped a beat before he took her cue. "We're cousins. We must go or it'll be too late!"

The guard took a deep breath and shrugged.

"But—"

"Look, you two. If that is a pass, I can let one of you through. If you have a telegram or something to prove what you say, I'm sure you can obtain a special pass if you've really lost yours. An offer of money would probably expedite matters, if you'll take my advice."

"Money?"

"Never mind, blind it! I see others coming down the road. Give me your pass!"

Ellia took a deep breath and handed over the piece of paper.

She faced Tlezachi and had a sudden feeling this

would be the last time she would see him.

"You'd better be going," Tlezachi said, interrupting her thoughts.

"I'll wait outside for you," she whispered.

"And if I'm delayed—or even caught? They might go looking for you."

Ellia looked down.

"Tell me where you live, Ellia, then I could—"

"Could be forced to tell where I live if caught?"

"I wouldn't!"

"Do you really want to take the chance? I'll tell you, if so."

Behind her the guard crinkled the paper of her pass. "No," Tlezachi said.

Ellia had an inspiration. "Well, then tell me where you live. I'll send word to you sometime after I arrive! My twin brother, Sang, will do it for me."

Tlezachi quickly told her where he lived in the mountains south of Ellia's farming valley home. Ellia nodded. "Sang will take my message to you," she said again, more to reassure herself than Tlezachi.

"You'd better be going."

"Yeah, I guess so," she said, smiling back at the impatient guard.

"Farewell," Tlezachi said, offering his hand.

"Thank you, Tlee. I'll miss you," she said and clasped his hand for a long minute.

On the other side of the fence, she gazed sadly back through the metal links. Tlezachi waved. She waved quickly, then strode away from the lights as quickly as she could. Once in the dark, she broke into tears.

She trudged down the road in the darkness with only the melody of the crickets for company. After a while she even stopped wiping her tears. How had she allowed this to happen? Why was it so hard to forget Tlezachi and put today behind her?

Some time later she ran out of tears, but not out of hurt. And she had no hope of more happiness in the future. She would have to conform this time; Fan would give her no other choice. Even Ellia had to admit that she had matured: her new curves were probably discernible to anyone who had some reason to suspect she was a girl.

A black cloud surrounded her as she walked. Her achievements, her adventures, her experience—all in the garbage heap! Her eyes burned, and the muscles in her jaw twitched as she fought to master her emotions. She mustn't cry again, she mustn't!

She wondered how far away the railroad was; she had lost track of time and of her steps. The night was cold, and she was hungry. Hungry? Ellia gasped. Tlezachi had *purchased* her last meal using the contents of her purse!

She felt her pockets desperately, but found no reassuring lump. "Blind priests!" she cried to the night. She sat, shook her head, and turned out her pockets. That produced a one-barter copper. Ellia closed her eyes in pain.

She sat at the edge of the road, her legs crossed, feeling no urge to move. She began to rock, but the hurt refused to go away. She shut her senses to the outside world until she no longer heard the insects of the night. Why her? Why did she have to be born a girl? Why did she have to learn then what it meant to be a girl?

"Ellia?" a voice said. "Is that you?"

Ellia shrieked and jumped backward, her hands flailing, her heart beating wildly. A strong arm caught her.

"It's you," Tlezachi said drolly. When Ellia stood on her shaky legs, he released her.

"Blind priests!" Ellia cried between gasps. "Don't you know—not to sneak up—on someone like—like the ghost of a chee?"

"Well, if you hadn't been sleeping—"

Her rage snapped as quickly as it had formed. "Tlezachi!" she moaned and hugged her friend. "Tlezachi," she cried. "I'm so glad you came!"

"I'm glad I found you."

She sobbed quietly for a few minutes while he cradled her head on his shoulder.

"I'm so glad you came," she repeated in whisper after a long while. "I was so afraid I'd never see you again I could not even move."

"And I was afraid I wouldn't find you," Tlezachi said into her ear. She shivered as he ran an arm down her back. Chuckling, he added, "You left your barters with me and I had to return them."

Ellia snorted, then she laughed too. Then she reached out, grabbed her friend's head, and kissed him passionately as she had seen Chriz do to her mate. Tlezachi gasped, but presently realized what was happening and returned the kiss.

"What was that about?" he asked finally.

"That's for doing whatever you did to the master administrator of Stone Coast shrine," Ellia replied, smiling.

"Well, let me have another shot at him!" Tlezachi growled, boxing at the air.

Ellia obliged him with another kiss. The dark, the chill of the air, the impropriety—she was thrilled!

Tlezachi gasped for breath. "What was that for?"

"Oh, for getting me out of the city and away from the man who chased us and, uh, for returning when I needed you so badly. I'm so glad you returned!"

"And I'm glad I found you."

Ellia smiled as she grasped his hand. Together they began to walk, then Tlezachi spoke again. "What about the time I stood up for you with Comos, the night when he insulted you by calling you a girl?"

Ellia giggled. An open-mouthed kiss—a true shag kiss—left Tlezachi staggering. Ellia felt gloriously weak.

"Do that again," Tlezachi warned, "and I might forget I haven't taken the Test."

Ellia laughed. Once she would have been appalled to hear such a compliment, but she was no longer the same person. She took her friend's hand firmly, and they continued on. In the night darkness with Tlezachi, Ellia decided she might not mind having been born a girl.

Or even becoming a woman.

Ten

By the time the two trudged up the dirt road into Tle-zachi's hometown, the sky had already brightened with the pastel blue and orange of dawn. The snow-covered shattered peak of Ji, the tallest mountain on the Emerald Island, stood out majestically in the distance. The morning birds burred and trilled raucous greetings to the dawning sun.

The architecture of Tlezachi's town was very different from that of Ellia's rural co-op. She saw one- and two-story houses painted in pale yellows and browns, built richly of milled planks, brick, and heavy bark shingles. Lush gardens and gaslights lining the blocks spoke of wealth and community pride.

"This way," Tlezachi said, leaving the main road for an uphill path through the residential part of town. Ellia had trouble keeping her eyes open; the few hours of sleep on the train after so many hours in line at the depot had hardly refreshed her. "You didn't tell me how you got out of the Open City so quickly," she said.

Tlezachi's breath steamed in the morning air. "Count the barters in your purse."

Shrugging, Ellia poured the coins into her hand. "That's not right." She recounted.

"Something that the guard said to us struck me as strange. Halfway back to the city, I searched around for a small slip of litter. I presented that, along with a gold barter—it worked!"

Ellia shook her head. "A gold coin has never bought anything more precious."

"Oh, stop that, will you!" Tlezachi said, blushing. "Say, look there. See that yellow, two-story near the streetlamp that just went out? That's my house!" But a plaque lettered in flowing black brush strokes read Feechi—not Cohssan.

"You didn't use your real family name at the Open City, did you, Tlezachi?" Ellia asked as they walked from the gravel road directly to the front door. "Your name *is* Tlezachi, isn't it?"

"Yours is Ellia?"

She nodded. Tlezachi knocked on the door. A moment later, an old woman greeted them. She wore a white sarong and was even taller than Fan. Wrinkles covered the golden skin of her face; silver-gray hair was tied severely atop her head. "Grandmama," Tlezachi said, bowing his head to the aged giantess.

Holding his head by the temples, she kissed him. "Grandson." She looked at Ellia. "Oh, you brought a friend."

"I'm Xander, Ma'am."

"I met him this ritual cycle at school," Tlezachi added, looking at Ellia, then at his grandmother. "I hope there is no reason he cannot visit us."

"That's for your father to decide. You are going to have to explain to him why you are home so many days early—and that bruise on your jaw. Your mother is going to be very upset. Meanwhile, we'll put on some extra breakfast for the both of you." For the first time the woman smiled. The sandstone of her face seemed to protest as if the smile were a foreign movement. As Tlezachi and Ellia followed his grandmother through the house, Ellia saw rich, dark wood furniture, red carpeting, books, and electric lamps. Tlezachi's family was well off, Ellia thought as they entered a modern kitchen.

"Lee!" somebody cried. Ellia saw a skillet crash to the floor.

"Oh, Mama!"

"Don't 'Oh, Mama' me! What happened? Why are you home?"

Tlezachi's mother was a decimeter shorter than Tlezachi and had the same freckly face and large black eyes that Ellia found endearing in him. The woman stepped around the sausages she had spilled on the floor and lifted Tlezachi's chin to examine the black and blue mark. "Tell me now."

"Nothing's wrong," Tlezachi protested, not meeting his mother's eyes. Ellia suddenly noticed a tall girl who resembled Tlezachi sitting at a square table opposite the stove. The girl looked as if she were about to burst out laughing. She wore a yellow sarong.

"There must be," Tlezachi's mother insisted, on the edge of tears.

"What did I tell you?" Tlezachi's grandmother said quite pointedly to her grandson.

"Stay out of this, Jan!" Suddenly the woman looked past her son. "And who is this?"

"His name is Xander," Tlezachi quickly said.

"I don't mean to cause any trouble, ma'am," Ellia said.

"I'm sure you don't," she said. "Do you backtalk your mother like this child?" she asked.

"No. My mother died almost ten ritual cycles ago."

"Oh. I'm sorry." She blinked and looked at Tleza-chi. "Nothing is wrong, is it?"

"Nothing," Tlezachi stated irritably. "Really."

Tlezachi's mother nodded. "Your father is the one you must explain it to. He'll probably understand better than I do, anyway." She looked to Ellia. "Xander, is that your name?"

"Yes, ma'am."

"None of that, please. Feechiwife will do. Do you like sausages?"

"I do," Ellia said in a little voice, nodding. From a box filled with ice, Feechiwife fetched fresh links to replace those she threw in the ashcan.

"'Feechiwife will do,'" Jan muttered sarcastically. The younger woman returned to the white porcelain-coated range, and Tlezachi's grandmother left the kitchen.

"Xander," a smooth, pretty voice said.

"That's my sister Tane," Tlezachi said into Ellia's ear. "She's weird."

Tane giggled. She appraised Ellia from foot to head, then dropped her gaze and giggled coyly again. Tane's hair glinted a much darker red than Ellia's own; the two girls were the same age. "Like I said, weird," Tlezachi repeated.

The sound and smell of sizzling sausages filled the kitchen as Feechiwife set the table for two more. Ellia and Tlezachi sat across from Tane, who fiddled with a drawstring pouch lumpy with salt. Ellia gazed out the gauzy draperies at the house across the way and the mountain in the distance. Then she caught Tane's furtive glances.

Tane had obviously discovered boys.

"Shouldn't you be helping your mother?" Ellia asked finally.

Tane giggled. Without looking up, she answered, "I do the dishes and the grocery shopping, mostly."

"Are you overworked?" Tlezachi asked sarcastically.

"Yes," Tane huffed.

"You would think so."

"You think that because you learn how to read and write and ride smelly horses—"

"You know I don't like riding—"

"Smelly," Tane insisted. Her eyes twinkled in the morning sunlight.

"Oh, do be quiet," Tlezachi said.

"Mama!" Tane whined, then immediately said in a low voice, "I will not be quiet. You don't know what you're talking about. You don't know what real work is!"

"Ugh! You try taking classes in history and math, then keep everything straight in your head—"

"I can't help it if you have a soft head. You can't impress me that way."

"You don't understand."

"Oh, I do, Leezy," she said. "You have it easy. In a few ritual cycles I'll have my own family to care for, and that is the hardest work in the world!"

"Both are hard," Ellia said softly.

"How would you know?" Tane asked. Ellia shook her head.

Tane eyed Ellia strangely, shrugged, and dropped her gaze to the tabletop again. "You probably wonder how I get away with talking the way I do? It's a cultivated talent. It upsets my father, but I don't care. I expect to nab myself a strong man, and that is all I care about." Tane eyed Ellia coquettishly for an instant.

Tlezachi laughed, and Tane instantly turned red.

"Tlezachi, what are you doing home?" a deep-voiced man asked. Ellia looked up and saw a taller, swarthy, older version of Tlezachi standing in the doorway.

Tlezachi swallowed visibly and stood. Ellia stood also. "I ran into a bit of a problem in the Open City."

"Does it have anything to do with the bruise on your jaw?" the man asked.

Tlezachi nodded.

"And does it have anything to do with the Open City shrineschool?"

Tlezachi shook his head.

"You didn't give our family name on any of your records, did you?"

"No, I didn't, Father," Tlezachi said and swallowed hard again.

"In that case, we won't worry too much about it, Mei," he said to his wife, who turned from the sausages and another pot whose contents she had been studiously stirring. "We'll eat as soon as the food's ready."

"It'll be done very soon," Feechiwife answered sheepishly, scraping at her cast-iron pan.

"And what's your name, Minor?" Tlezachi's father asked.

"Xander," Tane answered for Ellia. Her father favored her with an unhappy look.

"That's right, sir," Ellia said and accepted the man's hand clasp.

"I am always glad to meet a friend of my son, though I wish it could be under better circumstances. He periodically gets himself into trouble, but at your age I guess that's inevitable. Will you have breakfast with us?" Tlezachi's father asked her formally.

"It wasn't your son's fault, what happened, sir," Ellia stated.

"El—Xander, you don't have to," Tlezachi said.

"And let you take the blame before your family? It wasn't really my fault either, but last ritual cycle I attended the Stone Coast shrine. Near the end of the cycle, there was a misunderstanding over a horse and I was punished for it, though the administrator had no right to do so—"

"They think they have all the right in the world," Tlezachi's father agreed, nodding.

"The man must have gotten into trouble over the situation. He tracked me to the Open City where he intended to apply just a bit more justice. Tlezachi helped me escape."

A smile broke on the man's face.

"But why didn't Tlezachi just say he saved Xander's life?" Tane asked.

The man raised an eyebrow. "Tlezachi?"

The boy gulped.

Ellia took a deep breath. "The man who attacked me was the Master Administrator of the Stone Coast shrine."

"The what?" Tlezachi's father said, stunned. He turned to his son. "Was that the bastard who ruled you had to ride horseback when obviously horses don't like you?"

"Yes," Tlezachi said guardedly.

"Ha! I hope you hurt him."

"I'm afraid I did," Tlezachi admitted, beginning to grin but unsure of his father's tone.

Tlezachi's mother gasped. "Lee!"

"You stay out of it, Mei," his father said, reaching out to clasp his son's hand. The woman turned immediately and faced her cooking fires. "I do not sanction attacking people," Tlezachi's father continued. "But on the other hand, helping Xander was a very proper action on your part."

Tlezachi smiled, but looked toward Ellia. "Remember the letter I wrote you, Father, a few dogdays ago? Xander is the friend I told you about who helped me through the crisis."

"Is that true?" Tlezachi's father asked, his dark eyes appraising Ellia. It took her a second to realize that they were referring to Tlezachi's addiction.

"It is, sir," she said.

"I am glad to meet you, and honored. No matter how hard I could try, I would not be able to thank you enough." The man paused, then asked, "What are your plans for taking the Test, Xander? Have you thought about it?"

"I have," Ellia admitted. She got a momentary reprieve as Tlezachi's father directed his wife to serve the gritty wheat porridge and sausages.

"Well?" he prompted after taking a bite from a sausage.

"I haven't made any real plans yet. I am younger than Tlezachi, really."

"How much?"

Ellia sipped some milk from her glass to settle her stomach. "About Tane's age."

"Ah, that's good. I would not mind having you as a member of my family, if you know what I mean."

Tane's eyes widened, and she dropped her spoon into her bowl. Her eyes swept Ellia again, then she crossed her arms over her chest and stared out the window. Tlezachi broke into uncontrollable laughter.

Tlezachi's father thought his son's amusement was directed at Tane, but Ellia knew better.

After breakfast Tlezachi led Ellia up the red-carpeted stairs to the room that had been his brother Hoshi's. It had a wide sash window, a bed supported by a brass frame, a dresser, and a wardrobe with floor-length mirrors on each door. Ellia walked to the reflecting glass. To her own eyes she looked less boyish by the day, but she still appeared to be a waggish, lanky adolescent boy as long as no one had reason to suspect her being a girl. She examined her green, almond-shaped eyes: They were bloodshot, as red as the soiled uniform Ellia wore.

The door closed behind Tlezachi.

"Don't you think we had better tell your father the truth?" Ellia asked, facing her friend.

"No, I don't," Tlezachi said. The bed creaked with age when he sat down.

"May I ask why?"

Tlezachi looked up at her. "My father has always had a certain method of dealing with a woman. Tane and he are always at odds for what little bit of independence she shows. Do you want to be treated the same way?"

"Definitely not!"

"Well, then you understand. Right now Father likes you very much—"

"Yes—he'd like to marry me to your sister!"

The two laughed. Tlezachi got up and rummaged through the wardrobe. "You see," he said, "if he comes to think of you as a boy, and at the very least an intelligent person, he'll have more trouble treating you as he would an ordinary girl."

Ellia shook her head.

Tlezachi tossed her a purple and red plaid flannel shirt. "If my attitude ever becomes condescending, make sure you tell me," he said.

"Don't worry about that." Ellia smiled.

"Hoshi is about your size. You'll find a robe in there and most else you'll need."

"Thanks." As soon as Tlezachi left the room, Ellia lay down and fell asleep.

"Ellia Kellzi of co-op 454 in the north of the Ji shrine precinct. I won't forget," Tlezachi said.

"I'll send my brother to greet you. You'll recognize him."

"Don't make me wait too long," Tlezachi said, taking her hand in a clasp of friendship. Ellia tingled with the memory of the kisses they had shared. With a wave to Tlezachi's father and mother, she walked down the gravel path toward the depot. After six uneasy days, she was ready to face Fan.

What would happen when Tlezachi's father discovered the truth about Xander? Ellia made Tane appear the model female. Ellia would never let a man control her. She was sure that Tlezachi would always take her feelings and needs into consideration, but living with his family could be worse than living at home—competing with three other females would be impossible!

She thought about Tlezachi's plan to apply to the universities after passing the Test. Once they married, she would be traveling along with him, and she knew he would do everything he could to get her access to facilities and texts. It could work. And with the pills supplied by Chriz, there would be no children immediately to spoil an ideal situation...

Of course, that was assuming the shag was not injured or dead or prohibited from Emeraline soil! Ellia could not fight a feeling that she had abandoned her friend in her time of need. How could she have run?

The train ride home was miserable, hot, and long. When Ellia finally walked down the dusty co-op road, the sun was so low behind her that her shadow reached the front porch long before she did. When her bootfalls sounded on the stairs, a little girl swathed in orange stood open-mouthed in the doorway. "Sister Ellia!" Shana giggled gleefully and ran to hug her half-sister at the waist.

"Shana, how's the cutest little sister in the Emerald Island?"

"I'm not cute!" the little girl responded. "I'm beautiful! Sister Ellia, I'm so glad to see you!" Shana's eyes sparkled in the sunset light. "I missed you."

Ellia smiled. "I missed you, too. Where's your mother?"

Shana's voice lowered to a furtive whisper. "Mommy doesn't like you too much."

"I'm in the house," Fan said, standing in the doorway. The tall woman, wearing a cherry-red sarong, squinted at the two girls.

"Hello," Ellia said, putting a protective hand over Shana.

"So you have returned. And I thought today was going to be a perfect day."

"Mommy, that wasn't nice!"

"You, Shana, into the house." The little girl ran into the house in tears. Ellia eyed her stepmother. The woman was unchanged: black hair, black eyes, slim figure.

"Shana was just greeting her sister," Ellia pointed out.

"You look just like Sang," Fan sneered, appraising Ellia's boots, repaired uniform, and close-clipped red hair.

"Thank you."

"I did not mean it as a compliment, girl."

"Regardless, I'll take it as such." Before the woman could say anything, Ellia asked, "Say, do I have a new brother or a new sister?"

"A sister." Fan smiled. "We named her already—after my aunt. Little Della looks just like me."

"Della?" Ellia said, stunned, then angry. "You named her after my mother!"

"No, your father and I named her after my aunt."

"How dare you!"

Fan shrugged. "When you bear your first child, you'll be able to name it whatever you wish, girl. Then again, you might have to settle for a husband that won't even give you that right." The woman chuckled.

"You haven't any idea of how many men might be attracted to me as I am, have you?"

"Dream on, girl," Fan said, facing the door. "I will feed only girls who look like girls at my supper table. You had better be wearing a proper sarong, and I had better be able to see the matching polish on your toenails. Understand?"

Ellia fumed. But when later she entered the dining room a few minutes later, she wore a close-fitting orange sarong, and there was orange polish on her fingernails—and toenails.

Shana applauded in glee as Ellia pulled out a chair and sat.

Just wait until Sang brings Tlezachi here, Ellia told herself. *Oh, Fan, your expression will be well worth the trouble.*

In the days that followed Ellia made certain everyone noticed her, including most of the married men as well as the two sharecropper sons who hadn't gone to shrineschool this ritual cycle. Fan pretended not to see Ellia's femininity, but Ellia sensed her chagrin and was delighted.

In her free hours, Ellia told of her many adventures or read aloud from books the other girls fetched from their fathers' bookshelves. She even listened to gossip like any other girl. The rest of her time Ellia spent caring for Shana.

Sitting in Tagii's room after sunset on the second day into the Dragondays, Ellia heard Shana cry out in glee. Ellia tossed under the bed the novel she had been reading and cut through the courtyard to the common-room. Hearing her father's voice, she took a couple of seconds to arrange her hair and emerald sarong.

Everyone in the room—Shana, Sang, Da, Tagii and his wife, and even Fan—went silent as Ellia made her entrance. Sang wore a green minor's uniform wrinkled from many hours of travel. Her father, displaying two days' worth of scruffy beard and wearing soiled brown overalls, appeared even more stunned than his son. "Is that you, Ellia?" he asked, incredulous.

Ellia just smiled.

"Ellia?"

"Da!" Ellia cried. She ran into her father's beefy arms to be swung dizzily around. In tears, she hugged the big man when he set her down.

"You're beautiful, little girl," he said, awed.

Fan, looking formidable in her chocolate-brown sarong, remained quiet longer than Ellia had expected. "I must speak with you," the woman interrupted in a deadly serious tone.

Ellia felt her father's irritation. "Couldn't it wait, dear? Sang and I have only just returned."

"And I have been waiting a dogday. This is too important. It should only take a few minutes."

"Fan—"

"Look, Toyru," she returned. "If you do not agree with how important this is, I shall gladly apologize to everyone in this room."

Ellia's father took a sharp breath. He nodded, leaving his daughter with a terrible feeling in her stomach as Fan led him into the kitchen.

Someone tapped her on the shoulder; she whirled around. Sang stood next to her, his green eyes scanning her from head to green-painted toes. "You got caught again?"

Ellia took a deep breath. "Yes. What else is new?"

Sang chuckled and shook his head. He gestured, and Ellia followed him out the front door.

Not far from the house, he halted and held her before him. She was very conscious of his eyes sweeping her feminine costume in the twilit dark.

"You're beautiful today."

Ellia remembered Sang's conversation with her the day at the fair. "I know," Ellia smiled back. "I intended it so."

Sang's eyes narrowed. "Are you the same Ellia I remember who attended two ritual cycles at the Stone Coast shrine?"

"No. We all change."

"To spite Fan can be dangerous."

"That's not the only reason I am dressing like a girl, Sang, really it isn't."

"I should hope so!" Marsai said so abruptly Ellia jumped into Sang's arms.

Heart beating double time, Ellia turned and spat, "Don't do that!"

"I'm sorry." Marsai had evidently raced to look good the moment she had seen Sang returning home; Ellia could smell her heavy lemon perfume.

"Hi, Marsai," Sang said, happy to see her. "You look beautiful, too."

Marsai giggled and looked away. "You say that just because it's true."

Sang coughed. "Girls!"

"You said you had a reason for dressing like a girl?" Marsai prompted.

"Oh, I have a reason—a very good reason!" Ellia giggled. "All girls have a reason for looking pretty, don't they, Marsai? You should know."

Marsai eyes went wide. "I get it! To get boys interested in you?"

"Obviously!"

"El?" Sang asked, bewildered. "What's happened to you?"

"She's discovered boys," Marsai said instantly. Ellia and Marsai giggled in unison.

Embarrassed, Sang said, "I imagine, looking as nice as you do, you'll have no trouble getting some boy interested in you, though I can't imagine any I'd like as a brother-in-law, nor any that would tolerate you as a wife."

"Sang!" Marsai cried.

"It's true," Ellia admitted soberly. "I know it. For that reason, I took it upon myself to find myself a prospective husband. He is named Tlezachi Feechi, and he was a classmate of mine at the Open City shrine-school."

"Oh, El, I'm so happy for you!" Marsai said, taking Ellia's hands. "He knows about you, of course. I mean, that you're a girl?"

"He knows!" Ellia said in a syrupy voice that caused Marsai to laugh in delight.

By the time Ellia finished describing Tlezachi and relating their adventures together, even Sang nodded his approval. "As soon as you ask it, it would be a pleasure for me to go fetch your friend for you. And you're right, Fan's expression will be worth every gram of effort spent. But one thing—Fan is dangerous. I suggest you immediately go and tell Father what you have told Marsai and me. That's the only antidote to Fan's poison. How many days has she had to plan?"

Ellia swallowed and shivered. "She—she wouldn't."

"You're prettier than her, Ellia," Marsai observed.

Ellia gasped, understanding and immediately denying Fan's possible motivation. The girl felt chilled when Tagii called, "Ellia! Come into the house."

As Ellia entered the warmth and light of the house, she noticed that only Tagii's wife sat among the pillows on the floor. She cradled Tagii's sleeping son in her arms. Where was Da? Ellia took the time to adjust her sarong, tying it tighter at the waist, before pushing open the door to the kitchen.

Ellia found Fan pacing alone. The smell of fish stew hung oppressively in the air. Fan acknowledged the girl's presence with a predatory smile. She walked over to the big black pot on a low fire and stirred it thoughtfully.

"Do you need help cooking?" Ellia asked civilly. Fan sipped a spoonful of the stew.

"Sit down," the woman ordered.

Ellia noticed a chair pulled out for her at the table. She shrugged. "I think I'd rather stand."

"I said, *sit!*" Fan yelled. When Ellia failed to obey immediately, Fan flashed out and struck the girl in the chest.

Ellia fell into the seat. She coughed and gasped for breath. "Blind priests, Fan! Are you trying to kill me?" Ellia shrieked, rubbing her sternum.

"Shut your foul mouth, you ungrateful brat!"

"Ho, don't start that again! Thought you could control me by preying on my fears, did you? Well, my conniving cousin Fan, it won't work any longer. I can see right through you."

"Shut your mouth!" Fan screamed.

Where is Da? Ellia wondered as Fan approached her. She gulped and tried to revive her dampened bluster. "I can see right through you," she insisted again.

"So what?"

"I am a number one embarrassment to you, aren't

I? And that's all that matters, isn't it? If I were a stepson—oh, you'd be proud. But I am a girl. I save people's lives, I read, I write, I travel, and you don't. You're also jealous because I'm so much prettier than you."

"Jealous? Of you?" Fan chuckled. "How ridiculous."

"Oh, it's true. But you would settle for a girl like Terra, half-mindless because of her past, wouldn't you? You would like someone who talks endlessly of potential husbands, helps simple-mindedly around the house, and looks pretty—and that's the way you're raising Shana! Isn't it?" Ellia finally understood Fan's expression that day when Da had returned to find Ellia home from the Stone Coast. What had been Fan's reaction to the embrace? How would Fan profit from marrying off her aunt's daughter? Less competition, perhaps?

"Oh," Ellia breathed, "you are far worse than I ever thought. I am ashamed to be related to you."

Fan's anger flared as a fire will when a new log is thrown into it. She approached like a spider.

When Fan stepped within a half-meter of Ellia's seat, Ellia flinched, expecting to be slapped. But instead, Fan reached into a small cardboard box and Ellia heard something rattle. When Fan grabbed Ellia's left hand, the girl saw a black chain. Then something cold and hard clicked on her wrist. Ellia shrieked.

A locking pony hobble! Fan reached for Ellia's right hand. "No!" Ellia cried and tried to push away. But it was too late.

The other iron shackle clicked around the wrist. Fan let go. Off balance from trying to escape, Ellia tumbled over and knocked the back of her head on the floor.

Fan chuckled. "Try running away now, brat!"

"Ellia!" someone shrieked. Crying, Shana looked at Fan, then at Ellia. She wanted to say something, but youth and agitation twisted her tongue. Beating her hips with her fists, she finally let out another screech before running from the kitchen.

Swearing uncharacteristically, Fan ran after her daughter into the courtyard.

Ellia sat up and crossed her legs. Her head spun.

"Blind priests!" Ellia yelled, pounding her fists on the floor, clattering the chains. She felt nausea building. Moaning, she closed her eyes to fight it.

"Ellia?"

A large, warm hand reached out and took hers. Ellia's chains rattled. She forced her eyes open and saw her father; Sang kneeled behind him, all the blood drained from his face.

"Look!" Ellia cried, displaying the pony hobbles. "Look!" she cried again, her voice cracking. "Why?"

Silent, her father helped Ellia to her feet and righted her chair. She collapsed into it. But instead of looking at her father or Sang, she looked at the empty cardboard box. Pursing her lips, she knocked it off the table along with a stack of plates.

After the loud crash, her father spoke. "It was Fan's idea."

"And you let her go through with it?" Da had betrayed her.

"It was Fan's idea," her father repeated. "It was the best method she could figure out to keep you from running off again. Obviously I can say nothing to prevent you. Neither of us want to see you hurt. It's for—"

"My own good?" Ellia wailed. Tears streamed down her cheeks. When she tried to dry them, a chain struck her face.

"Fan's trying to do what's best for you," her father insisted. "Please look at me."

"No!"

"Please, little girl," her father said, reaching out a hand for her chin. She let him turn her face, but she sobbed with her eyes tightly shut. He wiped her tears.

"You have no idea how upset Fan became when you disappeared at the fair. She was so worried she had little Della that very night—"

"Blessed with another daughter," Ellia said under her breath.

"You know, little girl, you are old enough to be married."

When Ellia failed to respond to that, her father shook her gently. "Have I ever done anything to hurt you or make you unhappy?" he asked.

Ellia opened her eyes. "What do you call these?" She rattled the chains. She glimpsed Sang's face; she could not remember the last time she had seen him cry. How she hated Fan.

"Have you any idea how much I think of you, Ellia? You have always made me proud, as has your brother. The two of you, as far as I am concerned, are the best children a man could hope to have. But as much as I love you two, I love your cousin Fan also. I cannot explain to you how or why I love her so much."

He sighed. "I would never hurt you intentionally, Ellia, never. But I can't let you hurt yourself. You are a woman, and we can't wish it any other way."

"Ellia, have you noticed anything strange about the amount of time I have spent working recently? You are more than intelligent. Do you think the co-op needs all that to pay taxes and fuel bills? Do you?"

"N-no." Ellia sniffed. "I suppose not."

"I have earned much, working ritual cycle after ritual cycle. I've collected quite a sum, and it's all for you. Since your mother died and you began showing your special qualities, I realized it would be difficult to find you a husband. I have sufficient money saved to buy all the interests in the co-op.

"With the dowry I've collected, we'll have nothing but the best husband for you. He'll let you read and write, or we won't have him. And you will be allowed to travel with him because he will be well off financially. We will have only the very best even if we have to wait many cycles to find a suitable man. Do you understand that?"

Ellia understood. She began to cry again.

Da had betrayed her. She was so angry that she didn't even think of what such a large sum would mean to a young couple starting a family. She didn't even think of Tlezachi. Instead, she began to think how she had been born on the wrong side of the world—and how she could remedy that mistake.

Eleven

Many days passed in frustration. Fan rarely let Ellia out of her sight for more than an hour, except when the household slept. Sang tried to no avail to change his father's mind. Ellia would stay shackled until married.

"Wake up," came a soft, feminine voice. Ellia, in the midst of a dream, decided that the voice belonged to the forest and continued to slumber.

"Wake up." She felt herself shaken. In her dream, a white dog stepped from the forest, causing her horse to rear. She fell.

Ellia sat bolt upright in her bed. She found a hand over her mouth to muffle her. Her Stone Coast reflexes alive, she brought a free arm up and knocked away the restraining arms. She rolled smartly off the bed, away from her attackers.

Her heart pounding, she opened her eyes and by dim kerosene lamplight saw Sang. Marsai kneeled next to him, whimpering, holding her wrist.

Ellia covered her mouth; her chains hit her in the chest. "I'm sorry," she said. "Really I am."

"You hit Marsai with your dogtail chains," Sang whispered harshly, feeling his companion's arm for broken bones.

"We scared her," Marsai said. "You knows she scares easily."

"I don't think anything's broken." He sighed. "Are you all right, El?" Sang asked after a couple of moments. Ellia noticed that Sang, though barefoot, wore heavy travel clothing.

"Except for these chains, I guess so," she said, still trying to calm her breathing.

"We got a present for you today," Marsai said, trying to smile.

Ellia returned to her mattress. "Really? Why so late a delivery?"

"But I don't know how useful it'll be," Sang continued. "I wish I could determine that before I give it to you."

"What is it?" Ellia asked, looking from the red-headed boy to the black-haired girl.

"Tell me, Ellia," Sang said. "What would you do if you could get free?"

Ellia gasped. "You got the key!"

"No," Marsai said. "Sang had a blacksmith make a copy of it. I doubt Fan will know what happened until after you have used it."

"A copy," Ellia said. "Can I see it?"

Sang produced a long, wrought-iron die with about fifteen notches and extensions on the barrel, and placed it in her shaking hand. In seconds she had the shackles off. Sighing, she rubbed at her chafed wrists. Tears in her eyes, she hugged and kissed her brother and her friend.

"But what can you do with your freedom?" Sang asked.

Ellia looked at the long snake of metal laying at her mattress. "There's Tlezachi."

"He really exists?" Sang asked. "I had lost hope."

"He exists."

"But he doesn't seem so attractive anymore?"

"He has to take the Test first, and his family—they give me the creeps. But compared to ours?"

"But you like him."

Ellia was beginning to get a headache. "I do, very much. But getting married?"

"It's not so bad," Marsai said.

"You've not had the taste of what life can be that I have had," Ellia returned. "And having children?"

"Oh, Ellia," Marsai said, putting her arm around Sang's waist. "That's the fun part, or so I'm told." Ellia made a face. "Besides, you get along so well with Shana," Marsai finished.

"We're sisters," Ellia said.

"You are good with children—you can't deny that."

Ellia ran her fingers over one of the shackles. "But having children? I'm barely a woman yet."

"But you are one, and that's what counts."

"I don't know," Ellia said, then recalled her locket. As she pulled it out from under her wrinkled nightshirt and opened it to reveal the stock of pinhead-size tabs, she explained their function.

Marsai obviously didn't like the idea of the contraceptive, but said, "Long as you can have children when you want them, I guess it doesn't matter."

Then, in low tones, Ellia recounted her adventures with Chriz; thinking about the shag still hurt.

"You mean," Marsai asked, "there are really places in the world where women act just like men? And they have children, too?"

"There are—many places. And they certainly have children."

Sang nodded. "Something tells me that is where you belong, not here."

Ellia swallowed hard and gave the final details she

had previously left out in describing her escape from the Open City. "I left Chriz there, and with her extreme form of honor, that would leave me in very poor standing with her."

"But she was trying to free you," Sang pointed out.

"Freeing me or no, I left her in a potentially deadly situation. Her mate threatened the life of a minor for a similar lack of courage."

"But you don't know what happened after you left?"

"Blind priests, Sang! Isn't that obvious? I feel so bad I could almost kill myself!"

"I'd pick Tlezachi, then," Marsai said. "But then, I'm not you," she added, hugging Sang.

Noting that new dimension of intimacy and Sang's tough clothing, Ellia suddenly fit her observations together. "Are you going to take the Test?" Ellia asked Sang.

He cleared his throat. "Yeah. I'm leaving tonight."

"But you're not ready!"

"And how can you judge?" Sang demanded.

"Tlezachi is older than you. Tagii was much older than you when he took it. In fact, all of the boys I knew at the Open City who were planning on taking the Test at the end of the ritual cycle were older than you."

"But I'm ready."

"Sang, it is too dangerous to jump into. Fifty percent don't survive! Our brother Rand is dead."

"Yes, but fifty percent do survive."

"It's dangerous."

"And I've told him so," Marsai said. "But he's going to have to take it sometime. Unlike us, Ellia, he *is* a boy."

"But why now?"

"I am too nice a carrot for him." Marsai sighed.

"Sang," Ellia said in a low voice. "You can wait."

"No, I can't," Sang returned. "This family makes me ill, do you understand?"

"Any more ill than it makes me?"

"What father allowed to happen to you was the final fray in my ties here. He let Fan convince him she was doing the right think shackling you like a horse. He let her! She's a parasite, a tick—but he's a willing host, which is worse."

Ellia could only nod. "But taking the Test because of that? I think cousin Fan hates you almost as much as she does me because Da still loves you. Getting you to take the Test prematurely is another act of revenge on her part."

"Well, it's not going to change my mind, El. I did extremely well at my last shrineschool, and they have offered me schooling and a possible job after I take the test. I want that. Marsai and I will then start our family."

Ellia shook her head as the two teenagers hugged each other. "I think I will try to contact my Pecol friends. They come and go on a ten-day schedule. I'll leave when I can arrive the same day they should appear in the Open City."

Sang nodded approval. "I'll really miss you, but it will be for the best." Sang held his hand out suddenly. "Here's some of the barters I saved for you. You'll need them."

"I will," Ellia said and smiled.

Sang took a deep breath. "I guess I should be going. I don't want anyone to try to stop me tomorrow." He sighed again and took Ellia's hand. She hated to let go, but when he promised to send word immediately after he passed the Test, she let his calloused hand slip away. Sang kissed Marsai's cheek, then he stood.

"That's all?" Ellia said.

"What do you mean?" Marsai asked, beaming from Sang's kiss.

"That's what you are going to leave her to remember you by?"

"I haven't taken the Test yet, Sister."

Kneeling beside Marsai, Ellia whispered something into her ear as Sang waited impatiently.

Marsai gasped. Ellia whispered some more.

"It took you a long time to discover boys," the other girl said, astonished. "You certainly made up for lost time!"

"I certainly did," Ellia admitted, smiling. Marsai giggled once. Then, following Ellia's explicit instructions, she wrapped her arms around Sang and gave him a shaggish kiss.

Later, Ellia sat alone on her bed with the shackles, the copied key, and the coins. Staring at the flickering lamp, she thought about all that had happened this evening. She did not like the fact that Sang was taking the Test.

No, she didn't like that at all.

The sun rose behind a gray veil of clouds, lighting the wet world with an unnatural glow. Ellia stood for hours beside a rain-soaked bench and hitching post, staring at the tracks and worrying that her disappearance would be discovered. When the morning train arrived, she patted Kamakura's nose and hoped someone would return the messenger pony to the co-op. She paid a conductor nine of her eleven barters for passage to the Open City and sat in an upholstered window seat, thinking of Sang doing the same thing just eight days ago. But afterward he would have taken a second train to the Blasted Hills.

Why hadn't they heard from him, or about him, yet? The family had received notification concerning Rand's likely demise twelve days after he had departed. They had learned of Tagii's success by rail post messenger six days after he left home.

Ellia could not imagine Sang leaving Marsai or herself in the dark. So where was he?

As the train rolled out of the mountains and switched to the main eastern coastal line, Ellia grew even more worried. Soon she saw the distant mountains every minor who traveled these rails learned to recognize and dread: the Blasted Hills. Blue and green against the gray sky, they looked like any other mountain range—except that half of the minors who traveled there never returned. Which half would Sang be in?

She tried to shut out the clatter of the wheels as well as her own thoughts by closing her eyes, but it failed. She heard the conductor finish a short conversation with a minor three seats behind her. She took a deep breath and opened her eyes.

"Can I convert my fare for the Blasted Hills?" she asked the conductor. She did not stop to think; if she had, she knew she would not have asked. He took her ticket.

"The Blasted Hills are closer than the Open City, but the difference is nonrefundable. Are you sure this is what you want?"

Ellia held her breath and nodded.

The sign at the platform where she waited for the special train to the Blasted Hills read:

> No Women Allowed Past This Point.

Ellia ignored it. Together with nine other minors, she rode the single passenger car inland. No one talked. Silence and the clatter of the wheels against the rails were her only companion. She had the strangest feeling that she scented death—and that made her think of Sang.

They traveled from forested hills into a small, high valley that was vibrantly green in the sunlight that filtered through the clouds. They rolled into a small station. The town Ellia saw from the train platform was composed entirely of beige and brown buildings the size of warehouses and even larger.

Where was Sang?

"Are you taking the Test?" someone behind her asked. Startled, Ellia whirled to face a red-headed boy she did not recognize.

"N-no, not right now," Ellia answered, barely able to speak.

The boy chuckled nervously. "I know how you feel. I've been here twice already—but this time I have to take it."

"G-good luck."

"Thanks," the boy said and followed a cement path toward the town. Others, mostly adults, milled about, ready to board the train. One person, little older than Sang, caught Ellia's attention. His whole right arm was wrapped in bandages. He looked woozy, perhaps from drugs to fight the pain from his injury. Was he one of the fifty percent who survived?

Whatever had possessed her to come here?

Her curiosity kept her from taking the train back; in any case, her two remaining barters would have only taken her back to the main line where in order to complete her journey to the Open City she would have to hire on mopping floors or doing whatever was needed. Thus she ended up in the town instead, where she saw one of the strange women from the Open City on horseback. A priest walked next to the woman's black stallion as she, swathed in beautiful white lace, laughed and conversed with him. She sounded like a woman. She looked like a woman. Her red mahogany hair fell to her waist. What was she? By the time Ellia saw the fourth such woman, she felt dazed by confusion.

"This way," an old voice said. An emerald-robed priest pointed to a number of minors gathered not ten meters from her under a big laurel tree. Another priest stood watching as a man in a dark blue uniform interviewed the minors. Ellia recognized his voice immediately.

Master Hanssan! She immediately turned around. The priest who had directed her said nothing as she passed him. Only after she had reached the edge of town did she realize she had gone in the wrong direction to return to the train. One more mistake like this—! Then she saw another woman escorted by three priests. Ellia's mouth dropped open. How did those women obtain a status allowing them the independence of men? How?

"Well, hello there!"

Ellia nearly choked. Tlezachi caught her as her knees gave way.

"I'm sorry," he said through clenched teeth. Supporting her with only one arm—his other arm was in a cast—he led her to a seat in a café. He brought her a large mug of steaming, dark tea, then remained silent as she sipped the strong brew.

When she finally smiled at him, he said, "I do like girls with red hair. Lovely."

Ellia grimaced.

"I didn't recognize you until I saw you agape at that woman. Only you could have that expression."

"You passed the Test." Ellia stated the obvious.

Tlezachi smiled. "Quite easily. I was extremely fortunate, or so I've been told," he said, displaying his cast as if it represented something very important. "If it weren't for this, I'd be long gone. But don't ask about the Test, as I can't tell even you about it."

Though no man ever spoke of his Test, Ellia had expected Tlezachi would be an exception. "I wasn't going to ask," Ellia said, sipping from her mug again and warming her nose in the fragrant steam. "What about those women? Can you tell me about them?"

Tlezachi flushed. "They're teachers," he replied. "You wouldn't understand."

She raised an eyebrow. "Teachers?" She could see that Tlezachi had changed. Her Tlee was still underneath, but some sort of shackle bound him, doubtless whatever it was that made a boy into a man. Ellia sighed. How was she going to tell him about her plans to leave for the People's Collective?"

"I *have* passed the Test," Tlezachi said, interrupting her thoughts.

"Yeah?" She looked at him as she drained the last of her tea.

"I, uh, I—we're still friends, aren't we?"

"Yes, I think so."

"I was just wondering—you know I like you a lot, and you know I really don't care if you act like a boy in some respects."

"Yeah?" Ellia repeated, knowing the eventual destination of the conversation.

"I had a lot of problems with my parents when I finally told them about you." His mother had become hysterical when she learned about Ellia, Tlezachi said, then shocked Ellia by telling her how his father tied up his mother when she had attacks like that. And on top of it all, his father forbade any form of friendship with such a "strange creature" as Ellia. The man's bullheaded hypocrisy had bolstered Tlezachi's earlier decision to leave and join his brother Hoshi.

"You've forced me to realize many things, Ellia. In particular, how much I really like you." He hesitated.

"You want to say something?" Ellia reached out to touch his arm.

He looked around to see if anyone was watching before leaning closer. "I like—I—I love you. Would you consider being my wife, El?"

She had been expecting it, hadn't she? Ellia swallowed hard.

"If there is any problem about bride price, or anything like that, my brother Hoshi said he'd loan me anything I need."

That's a laugh, Ellia thought. If she married Tlezachi, Da would present him with her dowry. She clenched her teeth. She could agree. . . .

"Well?" Tlezachi asked after a long silence.

"I'll consider it—but I can't choose now. Oh, don't look crestfallen. I didn't say no, it's just that—that, well, I have another problem. It's my brother Sang—" She confided her worries.

An hour later, Tlezachi walked Ellia around the corner of the big building that housed all the computerized records kept in the Emerald Island. Looking toward the mountains, he said, "They told me it has been seven days since Sang left for the Test, but he hasn't returned yet. That's bad news. They tell us that we should return within five days."

"No!" Ellia cried. Tlezachi faced her again, but she turned to the wall. The day seemed suddenly colder and grayer. He touched her shoulder. She flinched.

"I'm only telling you the truth when I say it looks bad. You know that—"

"That fifty percent don't survive the Test? I know. I've lost one brother already."

"I'm sorry. There's still a chance Sang might survive," Tlezachi shrugged. "The task they give is not easy. It might only be taking Sang a little longer than it did me. Like I said, I was extremely fortunate—"

"What is the Test?" Ellia asked again.

Tlezachi sighed and shook his head. "I can't tell you that, Ellia."

"Why?" she demanded.

"I—" Tlezachi swallowed. He faced the mountains again. "You're a girl," he said angrily. "If you were a boy, you'd be a minor and I couldn't tell you then either."

"But my brother—"

Tlezachi whirled around. "It's his Test, Ellia!"

Ellia turned her back to the young man and walked back toward town, Tlezachi following silently. Suddenly she turned to him. "Have you ever met a Master Hanssan?" she asked.

"Yeah. He talks quite a lot, asking lots of questions."

Ellia hissed. "Only one person other than the master administrator of the Stone Coast shrine can see through my disguise, and that man is Hanssan." Ellia began walking again. "After Hanssan's man failed to follow me home, Mikitsu probably dismissed him from his post. He could always wheedle information from everyone but me. It's no wonder he works here now."

"You make it sound as if it really matters," Tlezachi observed. Abruptly he stepped in front of the girl and stopped her.

"It matters!" Ellia said.

He put his hands on her shoulders and shook her. "You can't take the Test. You're a girl!"

She narrowed her eyes. Growling, she pulled her shoulders free. "That would be foolish," she stated.

His eyes moved back and forth as he scanned her for a second. His intensity broke. "I'm sorry," he said. He took a deep breath. "You are no fool, whatever else you are. I'm sorry."

Ellia said nothing.

"I have another offer for you," Tlezachi added after a moment.

"What?"

"I'll—I'll tell you about the Test if we get married."

"You would tell me?"

"Only if you wanted it. It is a horror you would do better not to know about. You might not wish to have children after you hear, and that would be the most terrible shame in the world." Tlezachi took her right hand and caressed it. Ellia felt nothing. "I have to be going now. I have an appointment with a doctor to see about this cast on my arm. Afterward I have to earn some extra barters. I'll meet you at sunset where I bought you the tea. I'll buy you dinner and a bed in the hostel. All right?"

"Sure," Ellia said, then watched Tlezachi walk away. She took a big breath. Five minutes later she was waiting for the train.

I am a fool, she told herself.

Without barters in her purse, Ellia was at the mercy of the varying needs of the railroad. For hours, Ellia washed dishes for her passage to the Open City. She gave her employers their money's worth, even volunteering to mop floors with disagreeable pine solutions just to keep occupied, but she found it difficult to keep her fears concerning Chriz at bay.

When the train arrived at her destination a couple of hours before midnight, she had no trouble at the fence. She surmised correctly that Mikitsu had been acting unofficially—her pass was accepted without comment. She walked as quickly as she could to the docks.

The ocean lapped idly at the sides of the Star Sailor, and warm yellow light streamed from the main salon window. Ellia felt small and cold as she rang the bell at the gangplank. The staccato rhythm of her heart roared loudly in her ears.

The main door creaked as it opened, and laughter followed a human figure out. "Who's there?" the man asked, framed in the doorway.

Ellia's throat constricted. "It's me, Captain," she said, looking up.

"Greeneyes? Is that you?"

Another voice, much less human, intruded into the night quiet. Ellia gasped. Still alive! "Greeneyes?" Chriz cried, her hands smacking the railing.

"I apologize for leaving you in a bind," Ellia said immediately, leaving enough distance between her and the shag to escape if the situation soured.

"You are alive!"

"Yes," Ellia answered cautiously.

"Lance!" Chriz cried over her shoulder, then looked down again. "Thank the Hunter! You are alive! You should have gotten word to us—you had us terribly worried. Oh, Greeneyes!"

"You—you're not angry that I left you in the middle of the fray?"

"I should be? I committed myself to rescuing you—nothing else matters. I saw you thrown to the cement.

The next time I looked, you were gone! I was worried you might be dead!"

"I'm sorry."

"Come aboard, Greeneyes," the captain said.

"Are you sure you're not mad at me, Chriz?" Ellia asked apprehensively.

"Get aboard here right now, you whelp!"

Shaking with relief, Ellia accepted the embraces of her friends. Once inside and in the light, Ellia actually saw tears in the fur over Chriz's eyes.

"I'm sorry," Ellia said again.

"You can't change the past, so don't try," the shag insisted.

"What happened after I escaped?"

Chriz smiled. "When Master Supervisor Ogawa and company arrived, one of your enemy's warriors surrendered. The other fled."

"No, he didn't," Ellia interrupted. "He followed us, but Tlezachi and I eventually escaped. I thought I had left you fighting alone and at a disadvantage."

"The battle ended too quickly as far as I was concerned—"

"But you were bleeding!"

Chriz shrugged. "In all my seasons as a warrior I never had the opportunity to fight against a human opponent, except in recreational combat. Stone Coast training is quite exceptional. Battle is an exquisite dance—they teach it that way, I deduce. I would have been hard pressed to force those humans to surrender to me."

"Surrender—you mean defeat, don't you?" Ellia clearly remembered Chriz saying, "Humans do not attack skin-faced warriors and expect to live."

"You recall the warning of the Sisterhood?" Chriz asked. "Only humans kill humans these days. Your species continues to project its internecine tendencies—we just profit by them. Enough of that! Do you want to know what happened or not?"

"Yes," Ellia said. "Tell me."

Chriz chuckled. "It was a scandal. It seems that Mikitsu, the former master administrator of the Stone Coast shrine, attacked a pair of minors, one of whom was to be assured a scholarship after taking the Test. He actually scared them from the Open City! This was the same master administrator who whipped an unfortunate girl found in his shrine after she allegedly stole his personal horse. But a review by the Council of the Emerald Island discovered that the horse she rode had been mistakenly issued her. The stablemaster testified so. The theory is that Mikitsu, dismissed from a post that held high honors, became obsessed with finding this girl and attacked the minors in his insanity—but we'll never know for sure..." Chriz went silent and smiled savagely.

"Why not?" Ellia asked.

"It seems that sometime during the fight," Chriz said slowly, "he drew his knife. He had an accident. You see—he fell on it."

"Kantilphanes!" Ellia breathed. Finally she understood what Tlezachi had meant when he said he had hurt the man.

"It is the Huntress's justice, Greeneyes," Chriz explained. "He contemplated killing or, more likely, maiming you. A male does not use training intended to protect his people to hurt them. The Huntress killed him. But on to more important matters." The Pecols questioned Ellia about all that had followed after she had so precipitously left them. She told them of everything—from the shackles and Tlezachi's marriage proposal, to the Test and her fears about Sang.

"If the Test is what you say it is," the captain observed, "there is little you can do about it."

Ellia studied her feet. "I cannot accept that."

"The sensible thing to do would probably be to take Tlezachi's offer," Chriz said. "If you like him as much as you say. On the other hand, we can make you a

second offer now. It was something we worked on
while you still labored for us." The shag took Ellia's
hand in her furry own. "Greeneyes, we have obtained
immigration papers for you to the People's Collective—if you desire them."

Ellia sat with her mouth open. Tears blurred her
vision.

"That must be indecision," the silver-furred shag
said, chuckling.

Ellia shook her head. Helping Sang took priority,
she said. "Tlezachi told me specifically that he 'returned from' his Test. I think it is some sort of quest,
though I can't be sure of that until I am there. If it is
a quest, I just might be able to find him and help him."

"He might not appreciate that."

"I'll worry about that at that point, all right?"

Chriz nodded as Ellia explained her plans. "This
disguise," Chriz finally asked, "what does it entail?"

"Master Hanssan can see through any of my dis-
guises. I need to make sure he won't want to look at
me."

The recorded music sailed up the scale, though the
pulsing bass remained steady. In the main salon, Chriz
began to dance around Ellia who sat in the middle of
the room, tied to her chair.

The white-furred wolf-humanoid pranced, eyeing the
girl with a manic expression, her arms waving like
cherry tree branches blown by a spring breeze. Lance
gazed at the scene with his usual disapproving glare.
The captain stood nearby, holding the tube of specially
tainted plastiflesh.

Ellia tried to relax. The trance into which Chriz was
dancing herself, the shag had claimed, would allow her
to wield her knives with extraordinary accuracy. The
Hunter would control her hand, Chriz believed. Ellia
began to sweat.

Chriz danced around to Ellia's left. The beat doubled suddenly, and Chriz transformed into a wild thing. Her claw knives became a silver gleam. The shag whirled behind Ellia. Something hit Ellia at the base of her neck—

—she became as still as a wooden statue. Chriz jumped in front of Ellia, landing spread-legged, and struck with a precision measurable in microns.

Suddenly Ellia felt the right side of her face give way. Skin separated along parallel gashes just below her eye. Drops of liquid spattered on the plastic apron over her lap. Chris danced off, twirling. The shag's trance snapped when she drew a reddened knife across her line of sight.

The captain rushed to Ellia's side as the stun Chriz had administered started to wear off. Ellia, jerked her head spasmodically, and pain engulfed her.

"*Djo*, Hunter!" Chriz cried, slashing Ellia's bonds.

The captain hurriedly applied the plastiflesh, and immediately the girl felt menthol cold seeping into her tissues. Then it stung like a swarm of wasps. Tears flooded Ellia's eyes while she fought to repress an honest scream. She floated on the edge of consciousness when Lance's voice sliced through the planes of reality. "Chriz!" he yelled. "Huntress, *No!*"

Ellia's eyes focused on the white shag: Chriz had her bloodied clawknife in her mouth, exactly as she had that night she killed the pair of chee.

Chriz stood frozen. It took her a second to realize what she had done. Her hand moved slowly from her mouth as if she could not believe it were part of her, as if it had betrayed her.

Chriz's howl of anguish seared into Ellia's memory.

Ellia did not realize she had blacked out until someone shook her awake. Morning sunshine angled in through the curtains, filling the cabin with rays of floating, slowly moving dust.

"I thought you ought to be awake," the gentle voice of the captain said. "The day has begun."

Ellia's face felt stiff, misshapen. Sparks of pain—

not the agony of the day before—shot from under each eye as she levered herself up. But for all that it hurt, the Pecols had warned that even with the tainted plastiflesh the wound would lose its repulsiveness in about five days.

"Thank you," she got out. "I have far to go today."

"Are you well enough to travel to the Blasted Hills?"

"I have no choice," she answered. "Sang cannot wait for me." That instant she saw Chriz kneeling at the foot of the bed, her hands clasped on her forehead as if praying. Ellia was shocked. "What is wrong with Chriz?"

The captain looked very sad. "She has given a friend the worst insult a shag can give an enemy: I eat you." He sighed and left the cabin.

Looking at the shag, Ellia thought, *I have no time for this, Chris. Not today!* Every minute she wasted was another minute her brother spent suffering, perhaps nearing death. She looked again at the penitent shag, her white fur ablaze with morning sunshine.

Ellia felt ill to see the shag so shamed. She couldn't stand to look at the pitiful heap of fur any longer and pushed herself up from her bed. Determined to ignore her pain, she wobbled into the little lavatory. Leaning against the washbasin, she looked into the mirror.

"Kantilphanes!" she breathed and immediately whirled around. What if it never healed? Chriz had done all Ellia requested and more.

Her friends had been busy during the night. A film of dirt coated her arms and legs. Appalling lines of black lined the insides of her fingernails. She wore a new set of soiled clothes: loose-fitting pants and a ratty flannel shirt. Ellia recognized Chriz's expert stitchery on every patch and on every rend in the faded blue fabric. "You did an excellent job, Chriz," Ellia said aloud.

She received no answer. Ellia growled and returned to the cabin.

"Thank you, Greeneyes," Chriz said distantly.

"My name is Ellia."

The shag cringed but continued to kneel. "Thank you, Ellia."

"Why do you do this to me?"

"Because I have mortally insulted you, and if you were one of the People you would have the right to kill me."

"But I am not one of the People—"

"That is true. Thus you cannot legally kill me."

"Can we just forget it happened, Chriz? We all make mistakes."

The shag stiffened and unfolded her hands. "A reverse insult is unbecoming even to a human. My hand did not move on its own. My mind guided it. I am forfeit."

"But I am not insulted!"

"You are," Chriz insisted, standing, her back to Ellia.

The girl kneaded her throbbing forehead. "I haven't the time for this foolishness!" Ellia snapped. "You are being a burden I cannot carry now, Chriz."

"I must die, then—"

"No!" Ellia rushed forward, but when she twirled the shag about, she found Chriz weaponless. "You mustn't. Whatever you do, you mustn't! I'd never forgive myself if you did that."

"Then I will not," the white-furred shag said emotionlessly. The nonhuman face could have belonged to one of Chriz's stuffed animals, forever frozen expressionless since its creation.

"I don't understand you, Chriz, or what you are feeling. But I forgive you for what has happened. If I thought either of us were perfect, I might not be able to do so, but we aren't. I forgive you."

The shag appeared to think about this a moment, then slumped her shoulders. "You take this lightly," she said and squirmed out of Ellia's hold. "I am ashamed of myself and will always be ashamed of myself. I shall never have a friend again."

"Chriz!"

But the shag walked out of the cabin without looking back. Ellia closed her eyes. Was she going to have to be responsible for this all her life? Her head hurt. She quickly surveyed Peaessa's cabin and found, as she expected, a weapon—a short sword in a belt sheath. As she buckled it on, she noticed under her shirt a second metallic lump attached to an unfamiliar chain.

Tlezachi's locket! Chriz must have picked it up after the fight. She smiled wanly and replaced it between shirt and skin, beside her own locket.

When Ellia entered the main salon, she saw Chriz at a window gazing out at the docks. Lance and the captain stood together, not talking.

The captain spotted the girl. "I've summoned a hack for you," he said. "There is a train down the coast leaving in about an hour from the railroad spur inside the city."

"I don't understand what has happened," she stated as the captain rummaged up a meal for her.

"Chriz has insulted you."

"But I forgave her."

The captain shrugged. "The People do not understand humans very well, I fear. I do not think she believes you, but I am glad you forgave her. I was afraid you would not. I could not force you, or even ask you to do so."

"What can I do?"

"Nothing. Chriz's warrior schooling controls her now and is too powerful. She punishes herself more harshly than any other would do to her. As long as she does not believe herself forgiven, she will continue to punish herself."

"That's not right. I wasn't even insulted. Sickened, maybe, but not insulted."

"You can do nothing more than forgive, Green-eyes."

"My name's Ellia," she said. "What about Lance?"

"He cannot have a wife who says she is going back to being celibate." Ellia's hands formed into fists as she looked at Chriz's solitary form. She already had Sang and the Test to worry about. But she owed the shag her life, regardless of whether they were friends or not. Had the shag not delayed the master administrator as she had, Kantilphanes only knew what horrible things would have happened to Ellia.

After dropping her plate and eating sticks into the sink, she stood silently in the galley, staring at the white-furred shag until Chriz said, "The hack has arrived."

With fifty barters in her purse, Ellia approached the exit to the salon. She saw Chriz's claw knives on a table, encrusted with blood—Ellia's blood. She took a deep breath and placed the silvery weapons in the straw sunhat that accompanied her disguise. Lance and the captain wished her good luck. Ellia thanked them, but as she left, she took hold of Chriz's right hand and led her outside. The shag went without complaint. Ellia had no doubt that at her command Chriz would willingly disembowel herself.

A minute later the two sat in an open couch-and-four. As a cool morning breeze buffeted Ellia's almost girl-length hair, she turned to the glassy-eyed shag. "What is your favorite thing to do?" she asked.

The shag answered without hesitation or emotion. "Having sex."

Ellia's task would be more difficult than she had imagined. The shag had already determined to punish herself in that way. Then Ellia had another idea. "You like the taste of blood, don't you, Chriz?" she asked.

"I do, very much."

Ellia swallowed. "Is that why you tasted the chee's blood that time, because you liked it?" The coachman glanced back, then snapped his whip to quicken the team.

"Yes," Chriz answered.

"Why?"

"Because it is the best part of the hunt."

"Did mine taste good?"

Chriz stiffened and remained silent.

"I asked you a question," Ellia said sternly.

"It tasted particularly good."

"You like to hunt?"

"I do, very much."

"As much as sex?"

"Almost as much. Before my fall from the Sisterhood, it was my favorite activity."

"And the best part of that?"

"To bloody the kill. Few of the People will tell you differently."

"But you like it particularly?" Ellia pressed.

"Yes."

Ellia nodded. They had arrived at the market square where a train waited. Ellia paid the coachman. As she went to the ticket window with the white-furred shag in tow, the crowd opened to let them pass. She purchased a fare out of the city.

Sitting on a bench, she reached into the sunhat she had been carrying and retrieved the pair of claw knives. "Put them on," Ellia ordered.

Chriz did as she was told.

"You like the taste of blood?" Ellia asked again.

"I do."

"And at the sight of it you cannot control yourself enough to keep that which is not yours out of your mouth? Is that your disgusting habit?"

Chriz whimpered. "It is."

"Is that how you insulted she who considered you her best friend?"

"Yes." Chriz whimpered again. Tears began pooling in the shag's facial fur.

"You are still my friend, Chriz, I want you to know that. You made a mistake, but as far as I am concerned, the punishment you deserve should serve a purpose. You must learn to control your urges. You are leaving for the Collective soon?"

"Yes, this evening," Chriz whispered.

"You will return to the Collective without taking off your weapons, not to sleep, not to wash, not for *anything*. When you arrive back in your homeland, you will immediately gather together your friends, relatives, acquaintances—anyone who knows you and is immediately available. You will explain to them how you shamed yourself, then you will go to the wilds and hunt down whatever is your most favorite prey. You'll make the kill, bloody your knives, but you won't taste it. Do you understand?"

"I'll bloody my knives, but won't taste it. Yes."

"Then, without cleaning yourself, you'll take your kill to your friends so they may feast. You'll watch, but you won't eat. You'll watch until the very last scrap is eaten, every last marrow bone is cracked. Then you'll wash your hands so that you won't even taste that. Thus you will learn self-control."

"I'll learn self-control," Chriz repeated. Her voice changed. She nodded and looked in Ellia's direction. "A single kill?"

"No, two. But the next one at the end of a ritual cycle, same procedure. You mustn't burden your friends with your stupid misdemeanors."

"I'm sorry, Ellia," Chriz said suddenly, her voice cracking. "I'm so sorry!" Sobbing, the shag hugged Ellia. "Daughter, oh, daughter," the shag murmured as she cried in Ellia's lap. A lone tear rolled down Ellia's cheek.

Soon the train blew its warning whistle. Chriz stood and bowed to Ellia. "Our offer to you still holds," she said, attempting to smile. The energy with which the shag turned and sprinted away lightened Ellia's heart.

The amazing event of a shag embracing, then bowing to a horribly scarred youth at the market square in the hour past dawn would undoubtedly be the talk of the Open City before evening.

Twelve

By the time Ellia arrived in the Blasted Hills, she had taken on the persona she thought most appropriate to her appearance: dangerous and ugly. She wore her sunhat so that it hid her eyes but emphasized the line of her scars and the droop of half her face. Already she felt her injury healing as the plastiflesh chemicals pressed tissues into accelerated mending. But the disguise gave her the courage to face Hanssan one last time. She actually smiled as she walked.

When she reached the tree at the gathering spot, her appearance drew Hanssan almost as quickly as it chased away the other minors. "I hear a shag bowed to you, Minor," he began. "Impressive." Ellia said nothing. "What is your name, minor?"

"Ghen." She yawned.

"Ghen what?"

"Ghen, period. What is it to you?" Ellia growled, hand on her short sword.

"Nothing, but it might mean something to you. If

something happens to you during the Test, we might need to inform your parents."

"If I die, what does it matter? If I live, they wouldn't care anyway." Ellia managed an exquisite belch. "I have no use for parents. Do you mind?" Ellia said, unsnapping the thong that held her short sword in place. At that sound, Hanssan stiffened. He was unarmed. "I am trying to rest," Ellia finished. "I wish to be rested for the Test."

Hanssan swallowed hard. "Yes. I can understand," he said and retreated a few steps. He shook his head and jotted notes on his clipboard, muttering, "I'd hate to be this one's teacher tonight." As he turned his attention to a newcomer who looked much friendlier, Ellia sighed in relief.

An hour later, a priest arrived to collect weapons from the minors. Then the minors' names were read off in alphabetical order, and each was led into a big building.

When her turn came, Ellia followed a priest into a cool, dark corridor lined with bolted doors, illuminated by the flicker of gaslight. The priest halted before a door.

Ellia allowed herself to be led into the room. Light-footed as a wraith, the priest turned on his heel, and before she could even take note of the contents of the room, the door slammed like a dungeon portal. She spun about only to hear and feel through the heavy slab of stone the concussion of a metal bolt being thrown.

Fear overtook her. But as she pounded on the door, she heard the loud bootfalls of her escort fade down the hallway. She let her arms fall to her sides.

With tears streaming down her cheeks, she turned around slowly to view the room. She saw colors: tans and creams and other soft hues. This was no shrine dungeon. Light streamed in from skylights, capturing the burnt yellow of the late day in a three-story apart-

ment. She saw fine upholstered couches; pleated draperies covered the walls; and on the left side of the room,
the golden parquet floor gave way to tile and a circular
porcelain tub set in the floor. There was a luxurious
bed with four posts and a gauzy beige canopy. The
soapy scent of sandalwood drifted in the cool air.

Ellia froze in amazement. She had never in her life
seen a room more beautiful.

"What is going on here?" she asked aloud. No one
answered, but she did hear a soft padding and spun to
face its source.

Ellia's jaw dropped. Sedately descending a spiral
stair from an upper balcony came a slight but stately
woman wearing robes of the same beige gauze as the
bed's canopy. Her hair shone a rich, earthy jet, the
color of her sparkling almond-shaped eyes. She smiled
with dark ruby lips and rosy cheeks as she set foot off
the stair. She was one of the special women Ellia had
first seen in the Open City!

Smiling a half-smile, reassuring but somehow dangerous, the woman padded forward on bare feet. Ahead
of her drifted a stronger scent of sandalwood. Ellia
finally found the power to back up as the woman offered her right hand. Ellia shivered. Swallowing hard,
she groped behind her to avoid tripping over unseen
furniture. As she sidestepped around a coach, she realized what frightened her about the woman—like the
chee and the great tawny cats Ellia had seen at the zoo
in the Open City, this woman looked her directly in
the eyes and thought nothing of it.

Ellia shivered again. The woman's eyes—such a
clear, cool black! Ellia could not lower her gaze. The
feeling that she would be attacked and eaten over-
powered the girl. Her heart beat so rapidly that she
felt feverish.

Ellia backed into a corner. "Please stop," she
pleaded.

The woman halted and smiled again; she seemed

almost childlike. Tilting her head slightly, entreatingly, she offered her hand once again. The woman was unable to speak, Ellia realized, and was perhaps deaf also. Ellia felt sweat trickle down her neck. She shook her head.

The woman dropped her arm but not her smile. The tilt of her head and arch of her eyebrows asked, "Why?"

Suddenly understanding dawned on Ellia. The room, the tub, the bed, the beauty and promise of the young woman's leopardlike body—Ellia flushed. Someone had to teach the young boys how to be men! She pressed her back flat against the wall. "Oh, no!" she wailed.

By facial movement, the women asked, "What's the matter?"

Tensing again against the wall, Ellia trembled. The woman stepped forward; minty breath puffed lightly on Ellia's face.

"Don't touch me!" Ellia cried.

The woman ignored her and, smiling again, took another step.

For all her fright, Ellia could not budge as the woman's hand brushed her shoulder. Ellia stood in stupid horror. The wildly scented hand pushed off Ellia's cape before nonchalantly traversing the new scar, then Ellia's hair. Her sunhat was knocked away.

"Sang," Ellia breathed aloud, tears running down her cheeks. Caught again, Ellia would be unable to help her twin. But what could she do? She whimpered as the first clasps of her shirt were unfastened.

The woman looked Ellia in the eyes again and smiled reassuringly.

Ellia swallowed hard. "I'm not a boy," she whispered.

The woman's mouth opened.

"I said that I am a girl, not a boy."

The woman's eyes widened in utter surprise. Unexpectedly, her left hand shot out and into Ellia's pants. Ellia yowled in shock. Then the woman retreated a step and looked alternately at her hand and at Ellia as if she could not believe what she had felt.

The woman cleared her throat. When Ellia refused to look up, the woman tilted the girl's head toward her. Ellia gasped. The woman smiled!

Their gazes met, and the woman embraced Ellia.

"You won't tell?" Ellia asked. Her heart pounded so hard she felt faint.

The woman shook her head and mouthed haltingly what looked like: "Why should I?" She smiled.

Ellia's legs became like sand: she found herself on the floor, crying once more. But this time she cried with relief. A hand sought hers and squeezed reassuringly. "Can you let me out of here?" Ellia asked.

The woman shook her head while pointing toward the skylights. She waited until Ellia realized that she was pointing toward the late afternoon sun. Then she traced the path of the past sunset through the night to the dawn horizon. She nodded.

"The whole night?" A sinking feeling formed in Ellia's stomach.

The woman nodded and shrugged. She pointed at a little plaque of etched whale ivory.

"Kiri? That's your name?"

The woman nodded. The name revealed a lot to Ellia: people in the Emerald Island rarely used the "key" or "kay" sound to start a human's name. But the people of the Hamure, the large islands south of the Emerald Island, had different customs. They lived under the shrine system and their men submitted to the Test, but only because the final Emeraline emperor had conquered the Hamure a hundred years before. A wilder people, their features were more Mongoloid than Ellia's own—purer blood, they claimed, whatever that meant. But why Kiri should be here, employed as she was obviously employed, Ellia could not understand. She wished suddenly that she had read more about the Hamure.

Still smiling, the woman pulled Ellia up and led her to the tub. She touched some knobs and threw in a handful of salts as the depression filled with water. Ellia watched the bubbles rise in the tub. "But I'm not a boy," she objected.

Kiri only smiled.

When morning came, Kiri fetched Ellia new clothes, then ascended the stairs to her private quarters to find herself some clothing. Ellia put on the tough, sand-colored pants and snug tunic. She was allowed her old sunhat; it sat on a couch.

After the extravagant supper Kiri had served the night before, Ellia half-expected a similar meal for breakfast. But when she sat at the bar, which served as a table, Kiri provided only a weak citrus drink, orange-lime and very sour. Staring at the offending glass, Ellia pursed her lips and shook her head.

"This gives me a bad feeling suddenly." Shivering in the predawn coolness of the apartment, she added, "I wish you could speak, Kiri, or write. Maybe then I'd understand what is happening here." She put down the glass, its contents barely sampled, and smiled at Kiri.

But the woman did not return the smile. She approached until Ellia scented the sandalwood cloud. Kiri's right cheek ticked once, before she said, "Y—yauh—you really shunt speak weh—wishez"—Kiri struggled—"they ma—mah—may come t—t—true." Kiri's eyes were misty.

Ellia knocked over her glass, spilling it across the bar surface. "You can talk!" she cried as Kiri hurriedly toweled up the mess.

The woman poured another citrus drink, exactly the amount Ellia had spilled, and forced her to drink it before, breathing deeply, she spoke again. "Yah—y—yes. I usushull don't. Y—yah see why," she stuttered. Kiri had needed no language yesterday. The woman explained in few words that "partnership," as she called it, was intended to give initiates a reason to live. At one time in the not-too-distance past, less than twenty percent of those attempting the Test survived. Kiri herself had never seen any of the returnees immediately after the Test, but other teachers had accidentally seen. "Walking dead," were Kiri's exact words, unstuttered and quite clear.

"And Sang is out there now." Ellia moaned.

"Sang?" Kiri asked. Ellia explained about her twin brother and her fears. Kiri shook her head. Ellia fought back tears.

"If tha—thaat's your on—un—only reason to be here, the—then you ha—had better let me tur—t—t—turn you in as a girl." Kiri sat beside Ellia, placing a reassuring hand upon the girl's shoulder.

"If even the slightest chance exists—"

Kiri turned Ellia's face with her hand. The woman's black eyes locked on Ellia's; she shook her head.

"No!" Ellia cried and bolted from her stool.

"Ni—i—i—ine days n—n—now," Kiri insisted, following Ellia as she paced around the room. "T—t—too long."

"No!"

"Yah—y—you want t—t—die?" Kiri asked shrilly.

"That is a stupid question!" Ellia turned and glared at the woman.

"Then go back to y—your home. Your br—bru—Sang is dead, consider th—that."

"How would you know!"

"Nine!" Kiri yelled back, her voice cracking.

Ellia turned to face a wall and found the four-poster bed. She turned again. In a very low voice, she said, "I can't go home. Fan would have the shackles welded on this time."

Kiri heard Ellia's words and gasped. She walked up to Ellia, but when she tried to touch the girl, Ellia said simply, "Don't touch me." She gave a short synopsis of her life since the day her mother had died and Sang dressed her as a boy. She explained the shackles and why being identified as a girl was unacceptable.

Kiri was silent for a while. "All boys must take the Test," she said finally.

"But I'm a girl!" Ellia wailed. The Hamure woman merely raised an eyebrow. "Well, I'm not a boy either!"

Kiri shook her head. "We ha—haf an int—ta—in-tahresting custom." Kiri haltingly explained how before the Emeralines had conquered the Hamure, the Hamure had given more freedom to their women. Those few woman who were determined to be warriors, merchants, or priestesses were allowed to do so—but were not allowed to raise any children they might have subsequently. Some took this option, and a few at the time of the final war actually held great power as matriarchal warlords. But the Emeralines had possessed a navy, better supply lines, and the Stone Coast warriors. To prevent a massacre, the Hamure warlords had surrendered and submitted to the conqueror's way of life.

With the advent of the Test and the new shrines, a Hamure woman's option had changed. Though a boy could take on a woman's role by simply refusing to take the Test, to take on the role of a male, a woman *had* to take the Test—without the knowledge of the Emeraline priesthood. Ellia listened, amazed.

"Why wasn't I born a Hamure?" Ellia asked after Kiri finished.

"I thought ye—you were unt—t—til just momen—its ago. Yo—oo are brave."

Ellia half-smiled. "Thanks."

"I'm not s—s—so brave, Ellia," Kiri continued. "I am Hamure. I—I can—na—not have children, but I—I c—c—c—didn't take the Test and they—"

"They caught you. I'm sorry."

"Don't be sorry for m—me!" Kiri snapped. "I'm a t—teacher now. I can go anywhere I want, and p—

people respect me. I'm a good friend an—and the lover to m—m—many an important councillor in the C—c—counsss . . . that city."

Ellia wondered what Kiri had wished to be before taking the Test, wondered what dreams had been shattered by ill fortune or failing courage, but she knew better than to ask.

"I think I understand now," Ellia said quietly. "A reason, you said? If Sang is there, I will find him, but if he is not, I will take the Test for myself." Now Kiri smiled.

"For yourself first?" Kiri asked without a stutter.

"If I die, it will be for myself," Ellia returned.

"You are b—brave," Kiri said and gathered Ellia into a tearful embrace.

"I love you, Kiri," Ellia said.

Kiri chuckled. "You'll la—huve men better," she returned. "Those I've t—taught, especially." They embraced until the tears ended.

"And for yourself first—when Kiri?" Ellia asked, holding the woman at arm's length.

Kiri dropped her eyes. "I—I'm not brave," she repeated, then coughed. For about a minute, she said nothing. "Me f—first, one day, yes." She nodded.

A priest led Ellia and five other minors through a kilometer of dank underground catacombs that must have dated back to the time of the Recolonization after the Reversal. They emerged in a forest glade where, when seventy minors were finally gathered together, a choice of starting places for the Test was presented: the mountains, the desert, or the forest. Recalling Sang's many cycles at the Karta Deep shrine, Ellia chose the forest.

Ellia's group loaded into a truck which followed an asphalt road through woodland and green rolling hills. Dread grew inside Ellia as they descended finally toward the western coast. A huge wall of blue-gray clouds appeared ahead, then hove over like the immense wave claimed by the old stories to have ended the era of the Ancients. The sun seemed to dissolve in the haze.

The road straightened, and a line of azure appeared in the distance. An hour and a half after dawn, the truck stopped beside a sandy beach smelling of kelp and salt. The minors disembarked and watched the priests unload supplies, the surf roaring gently behind them.

"Sit down," the senior priest commanded finally. His voice was gravelly to the extreme. He smiled, showing yellowed teeth. "Look at your neighbor. Chances are he will be dead five days from now. Face it. Face it, now. Everyone of you, large or small, Stone Coast trained or pacifist, has one chance in two—of dying." No one said a word. Ellia doubted that anyone breathed; she didn't.

"Did I scare you? Well, I intended to. Death in any philosophy is an imperfect substitute for a long life. I hope all of you are ready to give your fullest effort in the next few days. Those of you who aren't will die. All right, enough scare." The man began strolling in a circle around the gathered youngsters, nodding.

"I heard many of you grumbling in the truck. You are right, we haven't said anything about the Test yet, and there is a simple reason." As the priest paused for emphasis, Ellia smelled smoke and noted one of the attendant priests tending a small brazier. Ellia gulped and looked away when she recognized brands like those she had seen utilized at the Stone Coast to mark cattle. "There is a chance a girl sits amongst you." The senior priest was looking in her direction.

Somehow Ellia managed not to freeze.

The priest continued. "Every year the Hamure send a number of girls to take the Test. From these, a few pass through partnerships, for many of our teachers are Hamure themselves. Others just have warped tastes. The Hamure think we don't know but, oh, we do. If you are a girl, you have three options: one, keeping your silence; two, returning to your islands; or, three, becoming a teacher. There is no dishonor in becoming a teacher."

No, just failure, Ellia thought.

"And in payment, you receive privileges no other women in the world enjoy.

"Look at me, all of you. Do you hear my voice?" he asked, pointing to his throat. "After years of painful operations and reconstructive surgeries, I can speak again, though not as well as I could before I took the Test. I am one of the unlucky ones; though I survived the Test, I did not escape the cancers.

"Women are more prone to such illness than men. All right, is anyone going to speak up now?"

Ellia shivered but said nothing. The slap of the senior priest's sandals, as he walked around the minors was the only sound besides that of the surf.

"You have one more chance. It is our opinion that no woman has ever passed the Test. No female has the vigor needed to survive the hardships ahead."

Ellia took a deep breath.

The senior priest sighed and signaled to one of his juniors. Tan fabric haversacks were issued to each minor. Ellia's contained a thin, silver thermal blanket, a long sharp knife in a scabbard, one kilogram of jerked meat, a similar package of dried fish, a brick of hard yellow cheese, a large canteen, and two vials.

"Now the Test begins," the senior priest announced. "These are all the supplies you will receive and stretched, they should last the five days *at most* it should take you to accomplish your Test. I see most of you are looking at the vials, and I will get to them in a minute.

"The primary rule is that you must fulfill the Test in the next few days. Each of you will be branded as outlaws—anywhere outside the Blasted Hills, you may be hunted and killed by any and all persons."

Ellia gasped, then covered her mouth when everyone looked at her. She remembered that second day after her mother had died; she remembered the outlaw and his diseased hand.

The priest nodded as if he had heard her thoughts. "Outlaws do exist, and in horrible misery. But should you contemplate that alternative, let me warn you that the periphery of the Blasted Hills is well patrolled. I'll guarantee you a rifle bullet in your skull should you flee."

Silence, except for the crash of the surf.

"All right. Your task is to trek inland until you find an emerald—you will know it when you find one—then bring it back to the coast. You all start equally, with no tools except the knives we have provided you. All that matters is that you return with an emerald. Clear?"

Ellia was too stunned to even nod.

"No, it is not that easy. You are entering the harshest and most deadly lands in all the world. You must eat nothing you discover, however edible it appears. If it doesn't poison you outright, it will kill you in three or four years if you otherwise survive the Test. Every sort of wasting disease can be contracted here. And if you should think about teaming up with someone, don't. You will find that *no* rules of normal society apply here. Teaming up with someone will probably earn you a knife in the back, or a slit throat. I saw it happen when I took the Test, so believe it.

"One other rule: at all times you must carry your emerald in your hands where it can be seen—to rescue you, a priest must clearly identify you as one who has passed the Test. Use only one hand if you can, for that hand will quickly become useless for anything else. And never, never let that hand or the emerald itself touch any other part of your body. Though not strictly true in a technical sense, consider that you are retrieving the most lethal poison known. Consider it well. Breathing emerald dust can bring lingering death. Even so, merely touching an emerald will probably kill upward of thirty percent of you. Whatever happens to you—bring your emerald back. That is your only admission to adult society and to the medical care you will require after the Test.

"All of you will suffer the same pain and sights your ancient forefathers lived through during their lives; your resistance to radiation and the most fearsome diseases of the past is your legacy. Emeralds nullify this strength, though, so bring us your emerald and we will restore you to health. Stay alert and chances are you will survive. All those who have survived have used their heads. Am I understood? Any questions?"

No further questions were asked.

"Good. In the vials is a medication that prevents the absorption of the toxic agents to which you will be exposed. Without it, you will probably die. With it, well, you have a better chance. You have two vials. One you will take in a minute, the next you will take in five days, should you still be out there alive.

"All right, unscrew your first vial and drink the entire contents without stopping."

Ellia sniffed the solution; it smelled heavily of lime. She took a deep breath before drinking, but found that the liquid went down like a fine liquor, menthol cool. Others around her began coughing. A few boys were holding their throats, but the priests did nothing. Ellia shrugged. Not about to be surprised at anything she saw that day, she screwed the top back on the empty vial and began repacking her haversack.

Occupied, at first she did not notice the menthol cold creeping out from her stomach. Then living ice spread outward amoebalike, oozing into and around her lungs. All of a sudden Ellia could not breathe. As her hands went for her throat, ice flashed through her heart and toward her head and abdomen.

Poison! With that thought in her head, she pitched over and lay drooling, unable to move except for occasional spasms. A junior priest took a red-hot brand from his brazier and unclenched Ellia's right hand. A second later, her flesh sizzled and stank as the triangular mark of the outlaw was branded into her palm. She did not even feel it.

Two hours later Ellia woke to find herself and one other minor alone with the priests. The others had departed on their quests. When she righted herself, her head spun and dry heaves kept her hunched over. Her right hand hurt so badly she could not open it so she supported herself with her fist as the spasms racked her. Eventually, though, she was able to stand. When she did, the senior priest strolled over.

"Yes," Ellia said, knowing intuitively what the priest was going to ask.

He asked anyway. "You are a girl?"

Ellia nodded.

"You are branded an outlaw now; you cannot be a teacher or return to a normal life until you return an emerald to us. Do you understand, girl?"

"I understand very well, thank you."

"Good. Now you must give me your most solemn oath, on whatever protector gods you worship, that you will *never* repeat to *anyone* what you have learned today and all that you experience until released from the Test—on penalty of outlawry. If you plan to give your oath and not comply, you will be sorry. I know not whether you are truly religiously enlightened or not, so if you are not, realize that if you tell anyone what you have learned, you will be reported to the shrine authority. Fathers have been known to report sons, and remember, you are a girl. This is all assuming you pass, which you won't."

"Thank you," Ellia said. One of the junior priests supplied a paper and a stylus to the senior.

"It says—"

"I can read," Ellia said, rudely snatching the paper from the senior priest. She signed the oath left-handed. "Now what?" Ellia asked.

The man shook his head. "I've never before met a girl who could read or write. What shrines have you attended? I assume you have attended some."

Ellia named the most impressive: "The Stone Coast, the Open City."

Suddenly the priest smiled. "You're her! You're the one who caused the Mikitsu to lose face and his post. Kenjii, protect me! Elthen? Is that your name?"

"Read the oath," Ellia returned, stony-faced. "I signed my real name."

"Ellia Kellzi? We'll need this to contact your family should you return. Kellzi. Kellzi? You have a brother who just left on the Test a few days back?"

Ellia gasped. "My twin brother! He left from here?"

"Yes, but he should be back by now, if he survived. Given two of you, at least one ought to survive," the priest said. Ellia was not reassured.

With the priest looking on, Ellia kneeled toward Ji and prayed to her protector god. Then, after checking her supplies, she struck out inland. She crossed the road, then entered the forest. The sound of surf faded quickly.

For Ellia, the Test had begun.

Thirteen

Ellia's boots crunched on the dense mat of dry pine needles as she walked. All about her grew rough-barked conifers, fragrant pine and tall, scraggly fir. Rectangular-leafed fare trees grew in gray-green profusion, low and bushlike. So much green, the color of life, the color of deadly emeralds. The forest was quiet—there were no birds or insects there. Ellia quickened her pace.

As she strolled into the afternoon, the cloud cover refused to burn off, and she feared the muggy scent in the air meant impending rain. A cool breeze blew upland and left her shivering. She thought about Sang—nine days in the wilderness when the priest said a successful Test ought to take five days or less. What had gone wrong?

A drizzly mist filled the air moments later, chilling the back of her neck. The drizzle lasted less than an hour, but by the time it ended, the land she walked through had changed. The pines grew more ugly, and the meadows between them sported broad swaths of dried, yellow growth. As Ellia approached the hill country, rocks began to poke up from the ground, but lichens covered the gray surfaces with yellowed green and she feared to sit on any of them to rest. Then she encountered her first sign that humans had ever traversed this land: sections of lead pipe breached the grass-cover and ran inland. Did people actually live in this forsaken land? If not, who needed the methane or propane the pipe transported?

She followed the pipe until a dense stand of fir gave way to a tall, barbed wire fence. Astonished, she walked toward the fence, but stopped when she scented something rotting. Looking to her right and left, she saw nothing. Finally detecting a loud buzzing on the other side of the fence, she approached until she saw the remains of an animal no larger than a cat. She looked away after she saw the misshapen paw touching one wire of the fence.

"Kantilphanes!" she breathed. About three fence posts away she spotted a sign that proclaimed: DANGER—ELECTRIFIED. Ellia fought nausea as she ran from the fly-ridden corpse. She had almost touched the fence! Her body shook. An illiterate girl coming this way would certainly have died.

A few minutes later, she noticed familiar sounds: the chugging of a propane engine and the whine of a generator. She pushed through the trees to see a squat, log cabin surrounded by three fences of electrified barbed wire.

The fence continued on past the generating station, and Ellia began to think she had made a mistake in following the pipe. Finally she reached a gate. Ellia stared at it for a moment. Did the fence actually surround the entire Blasted Hills? Ellia felt sure that she had found the only way through the fence within many kilometers—the chances of meeting another minor there would be greatly increased. Uneasy, she assured herself she was a good two hours behind the rest. She gathered her courage and approached the gate.

She saw another sign emblazoned with big red letters on one line, followed by smaller letters in black:

DANGER—ELECTRIFIED
NO EMERALDS can be found outside this fence.
To operate gate, push button until a click sounds.
You then have half a minute to climb through the gate until power is restored. The timing is exact.

Ellia swallowed hard. No pictures—nothing! No unschooled girl could ever hope to pass the Test. How many had died over the ages, she wondered as she looked at the aluminum ladder leading up to the gate. Ellia shuddered.

With her left hand, she pressed the red plastic button and heard the click. She rushed up, then down, sweating. Turning her back to the fence, she trudged on. The path she followed was worn by centuries of adolescent feet, and she realized how visible she was. She cut off the path to her left. *Think*, you must *think*! She mentally needled herself with the fact that fifty percent of the *males* who passed this point never returned.

"*Gheek*!" an animal called suddenly. Ellia gasped. She ran for the closest tree, her heart pounding. "*Gheek, gheek*!" the creature cried again, much farther away. Ellia waited a couple of tense minutes before moving on.

Soon she came to the first of the many truly crippled trees she would see. Isolated in the middle of a dead yellow meadow stood what looked like a wind-blown cypress. A few bits of green tipped the extreme tips of the clawed, gnarled branches of the otherwise gray and dead tree. In the next meadow, Ellia found a similar tree with higher branches. To see nature so wronged hurt Ellia's sensibilities.

Suddenly she froze as she glimpsed out of the corner of her eye—something big with a long, straight tail. A wild councillorcarry!

Ellia bolted for the misshappen tree. Behind her, something crashed. Wood splintered explosively, then all she heard was a heavy thump, thump.

Ellia lost her haversack before she reached the trunk of the tree. One kick sent her flying into the branches. She scrambled higher and higher.

The tree began to shake. Ellia hugged her branch with all her strength to maintain her perch. She looked down.

Horse-sized, shaped like the swift, docile animals that carried the councillors around the Emerald Island, the monster was covered with a light tiger-striped down, except in spots where great oozing sores ruined its hide. Beady eyes hungrily peered up at Ellia. Frustrated, it shook the tree again with its two small arms.

For many heartbeats, Ellia was too frightened to do anything but hold on for dear life. Finally realizing it could not shake Ellia out of the branches, the tigerstripe paced around the tree. For a moment it halted to scratch at one of the sores on its sides. Blood and yellow liquid oozed.

The tigerstripe's black eyes blinked back to its prey, and using its huge rear claws, it began to climb the tree. Ellia gasped and tried to climb higher—but there were no more branches to climb. The tigerstripe hooked its little hands into the bark, and in a moment it was halfway up the trunk. Slavering jaws snapped within decimeters of Ellia's boots. It scratched away hunks of gray bark to get its next handhold.

Ellia screamed and hurled her knife.

The tigerstripe coughed loudly. Losing its grip on the tree to claw at the knife plunged hilt-deep through its nose, it fell backward with a crash. When it regained its feet, hissing in rage, it also discovered a dried branch stabbed between its ribs. It shook its head furiously. The knife flew out. Mad with pain, the tigerstripe clawed at the branch, then ran away downwind. Too jittery to climb down yet, Ellia chose to rest there a while. She sighed and shut her eyes.

Then without warning, an explosive *crack* resounded through the woods. Those few birds gathered in the crippled trees fluttered skyward.

Ellia climbed down from the tree and retrieved her weapon. After cleaning the gore off, she sheathed the knife, then hefted her haversack and followed the path of the tigerstripe. She soon sighted the fence, and ten meters away she saw something large laying obscured in the grass. She froze. The thing moved and jerked, but seemed to make no effort to right itself. Ellia creeped slowly toward the form. When she came close enough, she saw the orange tinge to the creature's fur.

It was her tigerstripe!

Her fear evaporated, and she strode through the grass right up to the creature. Looking down at the monster lizard, she saw a bloody gaping wound where the branch had been. Then she gasped. The creature's eyes opened, showing whites in pain—it was still alive! An expertly placed rifle shot had hit the creature in the neck behind its skull, snapping its spine; its head curved sideways at a peculiar angle.

But it was alive. Regardless of the fact that the creature had tried to attack her only minutes ago, Ellia was horrified. She looked past the fence toward the woods in the distance. The dark line of the tree canopy hid the rifleman, no doubt. Why hadn't he used a second shot and put the tigerstripe out of its misery?

Ellia looked down again at the creature. Its ribcage heaved rhythmically. With proper training and its teeth filed, the animal might have been a respectable mount, albeit one with weird markings. Ellia grabbed her knife and did something she had never before contemplated.

In one defiantly swift stroke, she dispatched the creature.

She took extra care to clean the blood off her knife, stabbing the ground many times until the blood shone silver. She resheathed her weapon.

"Gheek!"

Ellia jumped, whirling in the direction of the sound, her knife flashing.

"Gheek!" a second animal called. Her heart pounding, Ellia raced from the approaching wicked sounds, upland and away from the fence. As she reached the woods, she caught a glimpse of brown shapes loping into the meadow clearing.

They looked like speckled dogs with jaws massive enough to crack steel girders. Running along the path, she put as much distance as possible between herself and the scavengers of the Blasted Hills. She knew that if she suffered a major injury, those creatures would be pounding the soil to get at her flesh. She understood then that the fence had been erected to keep the creatures in, not to keep people out. But she realized also that the only way to exit the Blasted Hills was by one of the gates. And if a minor had no emerald. . . .

Ellia shuddered. She must find an emerald and her brother—and quickly!

Early in the afternoon, Ellia began to see other minors, but only in the extreme distance. As she gained altitude, the trees became thinner, weaker, and more twisted. More and more often she saw solitary dead trees isolated in huge swaths of yellow grass. Where green did exist, it existed in islands of growth, pocket-sized woods small enough to traverse in about a minute. The recent rain caused the hills to smell like alfalfa gone bad.

When the sun finally peeked out, the extra light merely washed out what little vitality remained, making even the healthy trees seem blighted. Mountains reared up far ahead, blue toothy ridges ready to eat the sun as it drifted toward its nightly rest. And as the sun sank, Ellia's spirits sank also. The comfortable bed she had shared with Kiri seemed far away.

She had yet to find a suitable spot to spend the night. Nearby hills appeared leprous, cut with treacherous gullies, providing no cover.

Suddenly indistinct muttering reached Ellia's ears. She hid immediately behind an outcropping of crumbly diorite, scuffing away loose pebbles as she tried to look small.

"No one's going to get this one away from me, I tell you, no one!"

Ellia swore, realizing that she should have run. The owner of the voice would pass this way. She thought about climbing over the rocks, but it was too late.

"Let him try this time! He won't be able to do it, he won't. Let him—" The minor stopped just outside Ellia's field of vision. She did not know if she had been seen. Then she heard pebbles sliding and bouncing down the hill.

"You can't have it!" His voice cracked and wheezed as if he had asthma.

Ellia hugged the ground and remained quiet.

"I know you're there! You can't have it, you hear? You can't have mine!"

Ellia gulped. The diseased voice reminded Ellia too vividly of the dead and poisoned trees she had seen all day. She took a deep breath. "I don't want your—"

"You do and you can't have it! I've had to go back once already to get this one because of you, and I'm not going back again!"

The boy was mad. Ellia shivered as she recalled the mad dog that attacked her a cycle ago, then shivered again. Anything unpredictable was dangerous; she couldn't predict the course of madness.

"I don't want your—"

"I can't see you! Get where I can see you! You can't have my emerald!"

Ellia looked up. The top of the hill was a decameter above her, the slope barely climbable.

"I know you want it!" the boy screamed. Chills ran down the girl's spine.

"Please, go around the other side—" she tried.

"And walk into your ambush! You come out from your hidey-hole, you scummy rooster, or I'll come and get you. I'll face you—I will—this time. You'll not get mine easy, let me tell you."

Sweat beaded on her forehead. Her foot slipped as she tried to reposition herself, causing pebbles to skip a couple of meters down.

"I have my knife out. You won't cut me this time! I'll have you in ribbons the right size for a little girl!"

Ellia put her hands out and let herself slide down to level ground. She saw the minor. His shirt clung to him in tatters, slashed, Ellia surmised from the long brown lines of scabs across the boy's chest and shoulders. Yellow sores, similar to those on the tigerstripe, oozed in patches. His hair was as red as her own. For a second Ellia feared she had found her brother—but no.

The boy clutched something in his blackened, seemingly charred hand. Even in the dark recesses of his grip the stone was totally visible, glowing with its own energy, glassy and yellowish green.

"You see my emerald, eh? Well, you won't get it if you try for it, you hear? You hear?" His knife hand, too, was charred to his elbow where puffy, rotted skin showed under his rags.

"I don't want your emerald," Ellia said. "I am going to climb this hill and stand there. You can see I am not following you then. I am going up the hill now."

"You can't have my emerald!" The moment she inched back toward the hill, the minor lunged, knife first.

Adrenalin pumping, Ellia scrambled uphill, scraping her hands raw. When she looked back, she saw that the minor had halted his pursuit the moment he realized he had to use his hands to climb. He watched her progress all the way to the very crest of the hill. Then he nodded.

"You can't have it!" he taunted.

Shivering, Ellia watched the boy trot away. Was that what happened when you found an emerald? she wondered. Did it poison the mind as well as the body? If the boy's body displayed the ravages of a few days in the Blasted Hills, what would she find if she found her brother alive?

She slid down into the gully where she ran from the greasy black hand marks on the stone. The tigerstripe had scared her, but this scared her worse. Every time she thought of the funguslike black stuff, her stomach twitched. Were the mental scars of the Test so awful that they kept men from speaking of them afterward? In all her travels, Ellia had never seen pestilence; Emeralines rarely contracted disease. Obviously doctors were able to erase the outlaw brand, which throbbed in her right palm, therefore they ought to be able to remove the ravages of the Blasted Hills disease. Did a man mortgage his soul for the removal of all signs of the Test? Was silence the payment for health?

Ellia felt ill. Staggering with exhaustion, she finally reached a copse of healthy trees after traveling another kilometer. Night fell suddenly. Through the trees she felt the cool sea breeze return. Remembering her Stone Coast paramilitary training, she forced herself to survey her surroundings before darkness became total. Finally satisfied that no animals or minors were near, she searched out a tree whose strong, sturdy branches she could climb. High in the tree she took out her thermal blanket and made her bed.

"Sang!" she screamed, and bolted straight up. Instantly she remembered where she was and lunged for the tree trunk in panic. Her silver blanket fell to the ground, but she slid only a meter before finding a footing. Breathing spasmodically, she hugged the tree and peered downward, belatedly realizing it must be morning. A snatch of her dream came back to her before it evaporated completely: animals chasing her, tiger-stripes and gheek-dogs with emerald eyes. Ellia felt as if she had not slept at all.

She shimmied down the tree. Immediately, her nose warned her of a pungent effluvium. Brown pine needles crunched under her boots as she examined the tree. She saw the splash of urine—so the gheek-dogs weren't only in her dreams. She was glad she had slept in the tree.

After only a sip of much needed water, Ellia put kilometers between herself and her night's resting place. She must complete the Test as soon as possible and then find Sang if she could. Trudging through the cloudy dawn gloom, she lifted her collar against the wind that blew from the coast.

Sometime about noon, Ellia's foot caught on something in her path, and she fell forward. In that instant she realized that what had tripped her was not natural—recalling that the mad minor had spoken of an ambush, Ellia dropped her haversack and hit the ground rolling. When she came up in a crouch with a boulder at her back, she had to give credit to her Stone Coast instructors. Days of drills and exercises, even during cattle drives, had added a whole new set of reflexes to her innate set.

Knife in hand, she surveyed her surroundings. Over the sounds of her heartbeat and breathing, she listened. To either side of her were hills dotted with boulders, gray scree, and leafless bushes.

She waited five minutes.

She heard only a bird hoot. Had she overreacted? Cautiously she walked over and hefted her haversack, scanning every possible ambush point.

She approached the object that had caused her fall. The angular object jutting from the ground wasn't a rock. Brushing away dirt and leaves, she noted that it was nonferrous metal. She dug away more debris. The hunk of metal was the butt of a twisted I-girder. Had men ever made this land home?

She adjusted her haversack on her shoulder and with renewed caution continued her trek. The mountains ahead seemed closer, and the hills she traveled were growing bigger and steeper. She hiked through valleys and ragged gorges and over hogback ridges. Lone skeletal trees dotted land clothed in waist-high golden grass. She occasionally saw scavenger birds circling distant targets, but otherwise the land seemed devoid of life. After a piece of cheese and a short rest, Ellia pushed on toward the mountains.

Presently she discovered more debris from a lost age. A heap of twisted junk lay at the lower end of a little valley. The rusted steel girders neatly bent over like pieces of taffy scared her. Chunks of masonry lay crumbling amongst cement blocks, and in the middle of it all sat one lone golden train wheel, sheared neatly in half. The strength of the force that had crushed and carried pieces of buildings must have been enormous. Ellia shuddered. The land had experienced extreme violence eons ago—were the emeralds a symptom of that? Ellia tried to lift the wheel, but though it looked light, it weighed almost as much as she. In the process, she scraped her hand against glittering pebbles of green and sapphire strewn about the base of the artifact.

She looked at her left hand and found delicate slivers of glass stuck into her knuckles. They were easily pulled out, leaving behind beads of red. After that she put a bridle on her curiosity, and only examined things by sight. On a few of the objects, she saw stamped pictographs simulating brush strokes in Ancient Emeraline, attesting to the antiquity of her find. Gradually, though, a gnawing fear grew in Ellia. Elsewhere on the Emerald Island such a find would have been catalogued and stocked in a museum. In the Blasted Hills, the evidence of the great violence just moldered.

What a waste, Ellia thought as she climbed to the ridge and rapidly put the "junk heap" valley behind her. The world had belonged to the Ancients long before it belonged to the Emeralines, the Pecols, and the Dron. The Ancients had built and prospered all over the planet, supposedly even taming the monsoons and the power of the sun. If the Ancients were that powerful, could it be that the unbelievable legends of their demise were true?

Considering that question, Ellia recalled an old story that she had heard when she and Sang were toddlers and their mother had been reasonably healthy. Tagii was to be taking the Test a few days later, and he had wanted to know what the Test meant. Da told them the story of its origin.

Many, many generations ago the Ancients had lived on a mountain called Fujiyama, whose remnants formed two peaks, the largest of which was volcanic Ji. In those days, though, the mountains were covered with snow and ice, and only the very best people lived there, such as councillors and merchants. Why such rich people would choose so poor a place to live, no one understood, but these very best people traveled from all over the world to live on the slopes, and they had been there the day the sky fell into the ocean and dronfire blighted the Blasted Hills. The destruction was apocalyptic. Fire engulfed the entire Emeraline coastline, outshining the sun, producing tornadoes and thunderstorms composed completely of ash and flame. But the gods would not allow this travesty of nature to continue and sent the Great Wave to cleanse the world. Tall enough to wet the clouds with spray, the wave broke over the coastline and ate fire, flesh, everything in its path. Thus the world of the Ancients ended in infernal flame and water.

And so the world had been reborn. The very best people made due with what little they could eke out of the high valleys which had been spared. Few living things survived. Livestock existed in numbers that could be counted on one hand, and a few grains and seed were scrounged by luck. Edible fare trees, which thrived even in the worst brackish conditions, nourished the survivors. But the troubles were not over. One day the compasses stopped working, and years of disease and further hardships arrived. And just as the people made progress replanting the barren lowlands, nature began eating people alive—as the emeralds seemed to do, Ellia thought. The people could no longer afford to support the weak.

Then the compasses began working again, albeit pointing to reversed poles. The very best of the very best carried on the species. And after the Reversal, they invented the Test. What was the Test for? Da said the Test ensured that only the very best people, like those who lived on the slopes of ancient Fujiyama, survived.

That was before Rand failed the Test. Experiencing it for herself, Ellia wondered if the Test was just a little bit arbitrary and perhaps cruel: luck seemed as important as shrineschool training, at least so far.

The story explained the refuse of an earlier millenium. Wherever water could have collected as it ran down the slopes of the mountains, Ellia found heaps of wreckage. In one pile she found the remains of a railroad passenger car, crushed flat so the roof touched the floor, and all the paint was scoured from the golden metal frame. And in other places, the wreckage—the steel, aluminum, and titanium skeleton of a civilization—jutted from the soil like a burnt-out forest.

In Da's story, a city had completely encircled the coast of the Emerald Island: Ellia could hardly imagine so great a city. She could not comprehend its destruction, even when she found another forest of peculiar metal trees. The ragged pillars climbed for three meters, exactly the height of the ridge surrounding the tiny valley, then bent, all in the same direction, across the valley. Some fantastic, infernal wind had done the job, Ellia concluded, noting that many of the girders had begun to flow and drip before solidifying again. Next to such forces, Ellia felt like little more than dust in the wind.

Intuition told her that she would find what she sought if she went toward the source of that which had flattened the metal trees of the valley. She changed course to the east, toward the late afternoon sun.

Presently Ellia approached high basalt palisades. Massive pedestals of metal and cement supported the remnants of a gigantic ramp that rose until it merged with the wall at the caved-in entrance to a cavernous tunnel. As she threaded her way through the debris and once-melted bits of metal, she imagined ten trains traveling abreast into and out of the mountain.

Ellia's chosen route became treacherous. Boulders the size of houses barred her path as if some huge concussion had slammed them out of the very bowels of the mountain itself. She climbed them, ignoring the pains in her legs and arms, and the hunger in her stomach. She had few hours left before dark: she did not relish the prospect of spending the night in that ghostly land.

Finally, she climbed to the ridge around the valley of the ramp. Looking down gave her vertigo. She drank the few swallows of water she rationed herself and wiped her forehead. Recapping her canteen, she pushed it back into her pack and continued on. Soon the ridge shrank to a ledge with a long drop-off into another valley. Occasional boulders blocked her path, forcing her to climb around or over them. She noted with particular relief that there were no signs that large animals or humans had ever been that way.

Soon the ledge curved into the mountains, ascending into a pass with steep walls on either side. Curious as to where it might lead, Ellia chose that course, keeping to the right of the rust-tainted stream that flowed

down the center of the trail. Soon the pass angled east-
ward; the setting sun warmed her. Except for one or
two scraggly bushes, the path was as barren as the face
of Slen.

When the pass widened into a upwardly sloping canyon, Ellia saw more of the bones of the Ancient civilization. Enough steel and titanium was littered here,
smashed against the black rock walls, to have rebuilt
the entire Open City. The heap soared thirty to fifty
meters skyward. She scented the bland sting of oxides
in the air. Rusty water from the rain days before still
dripped loudly from girders, parts of bridges, the gutted
hull of a tanker ship, lengths of rail, and entire sections
of what appeared to be incredibly tall buildings molded
of metaloid plastic. All Ellia could think about was the
tremendous loss of life the debris represented. The
sight terrified her. She had not realized how much she
believed in spirits—she shook as she trotted to the
eastern entrance of the canyon and quickly put the
technological graveyard out of sight.

The pass threaded farther into the mountains, ascending endlessly until finally it widened into a plateau
littered with small boulders and a few hearty, wind-
blown plants. Holding onto her sunhat, Ellia felt the
strength of the wind that had sculpted the plants.

The pass continued on to the southeast, but Ellia
followed the plateau, which extended east about fifty
'meters before it abruptly vanished. *Another valley*, she
thought and approached the jagged, snaking edge, her
boots crunching on a gravelly, fractured surface. She
gazed down into another valley, peculiarly round, in
which once-melted hunks of metal like those she had
seen earlier radiated from a central point. There stood
an astonishing single building, structurally intact.

But her eyes didn't linger long on the building. A
patch of color, like a patch of flowers in bloom, sparkled in the distance and attracted her gaze.

But flowers never sparkled! And no flowers Ellia

knew had this particular yellowish-green glint.

Emeralds!

Ellia's breath caught in her throat as she understood what had created the emeralds. The blast of heat from above that leveled this part of the city had vitrified soil, sand, bits of plastic and metals from buildings, and perhaps the bones of the unlucky people who had been there at the end. No wonder the emerald glass produced such a potent poison—the fire of technological hell had given it birth. Ellia shivered and retreated from the crater's edge.

Then the ground shook.

At first it felt like a minor earth tremor, something experienced once every dogday or so on the Emerald Island and never thought about. She should have run. The vibration increased until Ellia heard a roar. Suddenly the world rumbled and twitched. The land went into convulsions as the whole side of the crater began to slump off. The land seemed to liquify under Ellia.

Ellia screamed as she tried to run. The world refused to stay vertical. A sudden blast threw a spray of pebbles. She lost her footing. The land sighed. Ellia found herself on a toboggan of rock as the crater around her flowed like so much mud, streaming and splashing beside her, crunching and exploding with every collision. Pebbles stung the girl on the side of the face—then something larger struck.

Ellia woke at twilight and found herself buried to her hips in black and red-gray jagged gravel. She quickly dug herself out. By some miracle, she had suffered nothing but scratches over her face and hands. Her clothes were intact, as was her haversack; her left hand hurt from clutching it in a deathlike grip.

She looked toward the sunset, toward the mountains that obscured her view of the colorful dusk. The crater wall rose decimeters higher than she could hope to climb, and bits of gravel continued to fall in her direction, bouncing and clattering by with deadly velocity. Ellia crawled toward the single building in the center of the crater. She could barely get her footing. It took a while before she slid off the last hill of shifting pebbles onto the smooth, boulder-strewn crater floor. The wind whistled above like an insane owl, but stayed out of the depression, leaving the air still, stagnant, and very cold. The empty windows of the central building seemed to follow her silent progress. The brightest stars sparkled forth in the dark blue sky as she put the building behind her. But as she walked, she had the uncanny feeling that the building—or something within it— watched her. She found herself running.

When she reached the opposite side of the crater, her fear faded, and soon she thought about finding herself one of the emeralds. But darkness had descended fully, blanketing the crater in black. Ellia thought that perhaps she would just have to spread out her blanket and await the morning—when suddenly her eyes chanced on a faintly green phosphorescent patch not very far up the crater wall.

With the help of a ten-kilogram scrap of metal, she struck a fist-sized hunk of glass from the mountain. Then she stared dumbly at the luminous rock, which pulsated as if its internal energies gave it life; Ellia decided it was just her eyes trying to adjust to the dark. She made no effort to touch the stone. She gulped as she studied her passport out of the Blasted Hills, knowing she had to pick it up. But each time she reached out, her hand began to shake. She closed her eyes and fell to her knees. She clenched her teeth and shot out her branded right hand.

The emerald felt like a chunk of obsidian and was as cold as the rest of the crater. Then a strong, almost electrical tingle pulled and ate at her palm and bones. She wanted to drop the rock, but her hand had clamped around it and would not let go.

Ellia opened her eyes. She had her emerald. And

she knew it would kill her if she gave it a chance. Through the darkness, she searched the horizon for the lowest edge to the crater and began scrambling up the loose rubble. At times the gravel gave way and began to flow, but she slid only a short distance down the slight incline.

By the time she scratched her way to the crest of the crater, almost an hour had passed. Dirt coated her. She smelled of soil and rock and something metallic, something grossly wrong to her senses. She thought for a moment and decided to keep the sea breeze at her back so she would breathe no emerald dust. As she walked along the crest of the crater, careful of her step, she noticed a brightening on the horizon. Slen was rising. Though impatient, she sat and waited until these was enough blue-white light to see by.

Slenlight illuminated another valley sloping downward in the general direction of the sea. Whatever had caused the crater had blasted away the head of the valley and the settlement that had thrived there. Ellia wanted to be as far away from the ancient death as she could get. She picked her way downhill, skirting fans of rubble and dirt and large shreds of metal.

Slen had risen to its zenith before she found anything living. A lone fare tree with just five leaves to rustle in the breeze clung tenaciously to a rocky ledge. Ellia smiled. The ledge looked like a safe place to rest. She got her hand to release the emerald behind a large rock. She barely got her thermal blanket spread before she fell unconscious.

She woke after a dreamless night to find a rash covering the entire lower part of her right arm. It itched insanely. She scratched the palm of her hand on a rock, but that didn't help much. Her palm had become a dry, parched white and felt as tight as a drum head. Ellia swallowed hard. Her hand was dying.

Ellia shook as she opened her haversack and prepared herself a meal. She had little appetite, but forced herself to eat anyway, gauging the amount of strength she would need to return to the sea as quickly as possible. Her stomach went sour immediately, and she had to skip a ration of water to avoid throwing up. The sun peeked over the mountains just as she finished repacking her haversack.

When she picked up her emerald, she experienced again the drawing sensation in her bones. Unhappy but ready to move, she climbed from her ledge to make her way downhill toward safety. By noon she had most of the mountains behind her, and she could look outward toward a distant haze which hid the sea. Her hand itched even more and felt half-roasted. She had to hurry.

She began to hear animal sounds. Though the whistles and jibbers were unfamiliar and sounded dangerous, they lifted her spirits and lengthened her stride. Trees became more numerous, at first only windsculpted skeletons, then living pines in pocket woods. Her spirits would have been lifted further if she had not begun to see and hear other minors. She fled for cover often. Another problem was her hand. The skin of her palm split in midafternoon. A smelly yellowish fluid seeped out, and velvety blue-black began to form under her nails.

Except for a sip of water to fight dehydration, she skipped an afternoon meal completely, trying to keep her pace up. She planned to be on the other side of the fence before midnight. Perhaps then she would have enough energy to continue to the sea. But the cadaverous smell of her hand proved a better spur than fear. The mountains sank on the horizon behind her. As the sun fell toward dusk, Ellia figured the fence was about five kilometers away.

Then a scream shattered the silence. Ellia searched for a place to hide, but she had chosen to travel along the gravel banks of a river, and the closest hills with any tree cover were a couple hundred meters away.

Ellia ran until her breath left her throat raw. She knew quickly she was being followed, but her pursuer took advantage of the hills, rocks, the golden color of his clothes, and the noise Ellia made running.

She could only run so long.

She had passed many dead trees today and many stands that appeared to be failing, but ahead she saw living wood that looked like the woods near the co-op. She began to stumble. *Laurel trees*, she thought, and gave it her last gram of effort.

Breaking through the hanging branches, she plowed a few meters in, then climbed. From a high branch, her mouth over her pack to muffle her breathing, she watched for her pursuer.

She saw movement near a stand of trees on the next hill over. A rot-scarred minor with black hair searched there for her, but when he did not find her, he screamed his frustration and scanned the other hills. Ellia's skin crawled. She hugged her perch harder and slowly drew her knife from her sheath.

Suddenly the minor froze and looked to Ellia's right. Then, haltingly at first, he began running back toward the riverbed!

Ellia had no idea what had attracted him away from her, but when she could barely see him anymore, she moaned. Had the world gone insane? She would have killed the minor if he had come near! Tears filled her eyes, and suddenly she yelled her rage, hitting her emerald against the branch she rested on, again and again. Finally she just cried.

When she calmed down, she smelled something pungent. She groaned, feeling warm liquid seep down one leg. Her head throbbed as she slid out of the tree. She decided to cut through the woods, hoping to find a fare tree: surely spreading the cinnamony sap over her moist clothes and the emerald sores would mask the unpleasant scents. The detour would also put time and distance between herself and the other minor. She walked on, her eyes generally on the ground.

"Stay away from me."

Ellia gasped, but reacted by learned reflex. She shucked her haversack and drew her knife. Had the minor circled back? She searched the darkness between the laurel and pine trunks for movement. Something rustled up ahead.

"Stay away from me," the voice said again, moaning. "I don't have an emerald. You'll profit little from killing me."

Ellia's mouth fell open. "Sang? Sang? Is that you?"

"Who's there? No, stay away. I have a knife—"

"Sang, do you hear me?" The voice originated behind a big pine tree ahead. Ellia saw no movement. She looked up. Nothing moved on the branches overhead. More silence.

"Sang, it's Ellia!" she tried again, stepping forward.

"Stop! I am Stone Coast trained. You want my knife in your throat?"

Stone Coast trained? Sang had always obeyed Da's prohibitions. "You've never been to the Stone Coast."

Silence.

"Sang!"

Somebody sobbed faintly. "Get away from here. I'll kill even you!"

Ellia gasped. Was she wrong? She took a few more steps.

"I'll kill you!" he cried.

"You won't kill your sister, Sang." Her boots snapped a dried twig. An unstable form, unable to stand, scrambled from a tree right next to the central pine, tripped, and landed behind some other trees. "You're hurt!"

"Hurt?" the voice echoed. "I'm dying. I should kill myself, but I can't. Can't pass the Test. Can't even die like a man—" Ellia took a couple more steps forward. Another twig cracked.

"Stay away! Do yourself a favor and stay away. The

living do not belong around the dead. Ellia, please go.
I—I don't want you to see me this way! Grant me this
one last favor."

She took two more steps. "You're giving up, Sang."

"Giving up! If the gods counted effort, I'd have
passed the Test the first day! Never more than fifty
percent pass the Test, Ellia, never more. You know
why? Do you know why? They crack. Emeralds ex-
plode the mind. Minors wander the Blasted Hills with
their brains running out their ears, killing people. Effort
means nothing—*stay away from me!*"

Ellia halted. "You're hiding here. That sounds like
giving up to me. What about Marsai? What about her?
You must try until you die trying."

"Look who's talking."

"What do you mean by that?"

"Don't you understand? I haven't got an emerald.
You try attacking me and I'll kill you, sister or no
sister. I won't die at the hands of a raver—"

"Raver? *What?*"

"I heard you screaming moments ago. Think you
are going to get an emerald from me?"

"But I have my own emerald!"

"Then you're truly mad. At least I'll die sane."

"Oh, *Sang!*" Tears burned in her eyes. "The world
is what is mad! I was beating my frustration out on the
tree, that's all. A 'raver' chased me here."

"And you expect me to believe that? Come on,
chance my defenses. Even the living dead have teeth."

"Sang, look at me."

"And have a knife thrown at me? I may hurt, I may
be rotting away, but my mind is not gone, sister!"

To turn around and leave the woods would be easy.
In two hours, maybe three, she would be outside the
fence. Before morning she could actually be sleeping
in a bed—with sure knowledge that her brother was
dead? Ellia moaned as she dried her tears with her
knife hand. He was her brother, her friend. He was

the one person in the world most responsible for the person she had become.

"Sang!" she cried.

"Leave me. I promise, I'll kill you!"

"If you try, I'll let you!" she said in a quaver. With that, she threw her knife. The boy jumped. Her knife buzzed metallically as it hit wood and stuck in the tree above Sang's position. "I have no weapon now, Sang." She took a deep breath before stepping forward.

"Stay away!"

Ellia walked on, disregarding his warning.

"I'll kill you anyway!"

"Go ahead. I'll let you."

"You're insane!"

"Maybe I am. Maybe I'm sane. I just hope you are."

Without warning, a pale form appeared in her path. It had a human shape; tattered clothes clung to it. Ellia's heart beat madly as she walked with her palms out, her emerald easily visible. Sang supported himself with his right hand. His left hand held an object that extended past his fist a quarter meter. In the gloom of the woods, the weapon did not sparkle or shine, but she could not be certain of what she saw. Had she miscalculated? Would he actually kill her?

"Come no farther!" Sang yelled.

"Or you'll kill me? I have no weapon—"

"Except your hands. At the Stone Coast they teach you how to kill with your hands, I know!"

"'Cause Da told you? I went there. They teach knife dance and defense only. Killing is only taught to adults who wish to fight the dron."

"Surrre—"

"I am telling you the truth."

"Stay away! I am warning you."

Ellia continued until Sang was within striking distance. She held out her emerald. "It's yours if you want it," she said. For a moment they stood as if frozen.

"You smell terrible," Sang said suddenly.

Ellia's heart fluttered, but she didn't move a muscle.

"What just scared you?"

"A raver. He must have seen my emerald. He ran after me with a knife."

"Tracking you like a chee? You know, Ellia, I can almost believe you." He chuckled, shuddered, then collapsed into a heap.

She was at his side instantly.

"Please don't touch me," Sang moaned. Ignoring him, she tried to right him. Her grip faltered on sulfurous-smelling slime; his hand slipped right out of her grasp. Ellia had to crawl away. She retched until she brought up bile. She pried her hand open and put down her emerald.

"I warned you," Sang said weakly. When Ellia looked up, she found that her brother had managed to pull himself up against the tree.

She wiped her mouth on her shoulder. "It's awful."

"You get used to the smell quickly. When the skin splits, the pus eases the itching. I'm dying, can't you see? Why do you think I chose this spot? The laurels remind me of home, but it is also particularly dark here."

Ellia felt the ground and found the long stick that Sang had brandished as a knife. Feeling wood instead of metal came as a shock. "What happened?" she asked.

"What happened? I almost got to the fence with an emerald. And what an emerald! It weighed half a kilo. It took me three days to find it. I tried breaking it into smaller pieces, but it would not crack so I carried the whole thing. It was particularly visible, I guess. Someone who had just started his Test saw me. He obviously took seriously the warning that "no rules of normal society apply.' He attacked me, sliced open my arm before he managed to knock me silly. I woke the next morning with a headache instead of an emerald and was covered with rot. It was my sixth day in the Blasted

Hills. I was determined to pass, but a monsoon struck that evening. The gullies in the foothills flooded almost instantaneously. I lost my pack, saving only, of all blind things, my canteen. My medicine, my food, my blanket—gone. And here I am.

"No strength. How can I go anywhere? Each time I stand, I begin retching. Ellia, you really should have left me. I'm an insult to the living."

"Don't say that."

"It's true. Look, you're wiping your hands clean of me. Tell me I'm not sickening. Ellia? Ellia, give me your knife. It'll take only a moment, then you can take it back."

"Huh? No! I couldn't!"

"Sure—let me die in five days after my hands have rotted off. The bone in one of my fingers is already exposed. Would you rather see me die that way?"

"I don't want to see you dead at all!"

"Gagging again, Ellia? What a beautiful sound. There is nothing you could do to save me now."

"Stop it."

"Give me your knife, Ellia."

"I can't do that!"

"You really do make me ill," Sang said. Suddenly he wobbled to his feet.

Ellia's eyes fell on her faintly glowing emerald. She was still healthy. She could make the trip to the crater again easily!

"Sang!" she yelled as he sprang for her knife. She was not fast enough. Sang fell. Her knife gone, Ellia scrambled to her brother's side. "Oh, *Sang!*"

"Stay *away!*" The blade whizzed within a decimeter of her nose.

"You're alive!"

"Please, Ellia. I have one last thing to ask you. Leave the woods for a minute, then you'll be able to get your knife. When you return home, do this one thing. Tell Marsai I love her."

She took a deep breath. "Sang, give me the knife."

"One centimeter closer and you'll see me die before your eyes. Please, just leave me."

"Sang, you don't understand. You can still pass the Test," she said quickly. "All you have to do is give the priests an emerald! That's the only real rule of the Test! You return an emerald, they'll fix you up, make you healthy again! Sang, you can have my—"

El!" Sang screamed. "You say that again, and I *will* kill you. Whatever you think, you are still a girl. I'm a boy. I have more pride than to pass a manhood test through the agency of a girl."

"Pride and no sense," Ellia spat.

"You can't understand." Ellia watched Sang shimmy away from her and lean against a tree.

"I can too. You're being stupid, just as Chriz was being stupid about her stupid honor." Rapidly, Ellia related the incident that had occurred because of Chriz's taste for blood. "Stupid, stupid, stupid!"

"Chriz isn't human, even if she is female. They think differently. And I'm male. I think differently than you, even if we are twins. It's not stupid, my pride. It's my pride. How could I live knowing that my sister did my work for me to allow me to pass the Test, sacrificing her life to do so? Slen-blinded, starry-headed priests, Ellia! Talk about stupid! What is your honor, if not self-destructive?"

"It's my honor."

"It's my pride. I think you understand now."

"No, I really don't," she returned. "But what can I do? You have the knife."

"Right, now you *do* understand."

"Anything but death can be repaired, Sang. Death is permanent."

"It's hard," he said, his voice cracking. "Don't make it harder."

"If you won't take my emerald, can I at least give you something instead?"

"I won't take anything of yours, Ellia, nothing!"

"Please! Sang, you're my brother. Try to underst— just, just answer a question, please."

"What?"

"When you took the vial of medicine at the shore, how did you react?"

"Why? It half-burnt my stomach out. I thought I was going to die, but I didn't."

"How ill did you become? Did you become unconscious?"

"No, nothing like that. You—you mean, you had problems? I saw one minor go into convulsions. The priests did nothing for him."

Ellia jumped at her brother's change in temperament. In the faint light she saw the hand holding her knife begin to shake. "The problem is that I am a girl, as you so aptly pointed out. The stuff nearly killed me. I was out for hours."

"What you're trying to tell me is that you would like me to watch you while you take the medicine? I— I—yes, I guess I could do that, if I would promise that you'll do my job for me if I become incoher—"

"No, Sang, that's not it."

"No? What are you getting at? No! I won't take your medicine either. You're female, every gram!"

"Then I should just spill it out?"

"I won't let you!"

"Try and stop me then. I don't know about you, but I have no intention of dying, no intention at all. That medicine will kill me if I take it once more. Death, Sang. Do you really want to die?"

"I—"

"Aren't you the least bit interested in making love to Marsai. She's your carrot, Sang. And thanks to the teachers we both know why. Marsai needs you—you, Sang. Do you really want to die?"

"I—" Sang began, then started sobbing loudly. "I don't want to die! Really, I—"

"If you were able to find yourself another emerald, you would, wouldn't you?"

"If I could, I'd search until I died trying!" he cried and choked on his tears.

Ellia rose and walked to her pack. Worried that Sang might kill himself, she calmly said a prayer to the protector god they both honored and hefted her haversack over her shoulder.

But when she stood at his side again, he didn't move or say anything. Ellia's throat constricted. She fell to her hands and knees as dry spasms wracked her. Finally she collapsed on the ground in exhaustion. Sang was still. Ellia turned her head to see her emerald, yellow-green and pulsing with malevolence not a meter from her face. "One day I am going to make sure no children have to submit to a test by atrocity to prove their adulthood!"

"And one day you are going to walk on the mountains of Slen, sure Ellia—"

The girl shrieked and rolled away, putting the glowing gem between her and Sang. "You're, you're—"

"Alive?" he whispered weakly. "Give me your vial. At least if I die, maybe it won't be by rotting away."

Ellia cried as Sang traded her knife for the vial.

Ellia waited hours for fitful sleep to overtake her brother. When he finally began to toss and groan with dreams, Ellia returned to the search that had so fortunately brought her to the center of the woods. To her relief she found a number of fare trees that appeared unaffected by the poisons of the Blasted Hills. She picked a couple of rectangular leaves and cracked their fleshy integuments to produce a dewy, cinnamony sap which she spread over her rotting hand. Sulfur, urine, and cinnamon—at least the last scent was strongest.

By the light of Slen, Ellia removed her clothing to rub it clean using a mixture of sandy soil and fare tree sap. She sat naked in the blue-white light, her knife exposed on the ground beside her.

Eventually she put her noisome clothes back on and returned to Sang's side. She made sure he was as well as could be expected. After burying her emerald in the leaf mold within easy reach, she too went to sleep.

When she awoke, morning sunlight filtering through the trees flashed directly into Ellia's face. *Such a short night*, she thought as she recalled the mood—but none of the substance—of a good dream. Her good mood didn't last long, though. One look at her right hand, blackened all the way to the wrist, made her shudder. The black looked like charred meat, but its velvet texture reminded her of the blue fungus that formed on old cheese.

Yet, as Sang had described, with much of the skin cracked open and weeping, the itching was gone.

Sang snored lightly. When he grunted and rolled over, Ellia thought that he was already largely recovered. The priest had said that the medicine fought the poison. Doubtless it fought the charring disease also.

Maybe, just maybe, Sang would be able to pass the Test. Ellia faced Ji and kneeled, touching her head to the ground, and prayed to her protector god. Kantilphanes had done much for her in the past nine ritual cycles. She thanked him, and asked favors for her brother.

She dug up her emerald and looked at it. In the sunlight the stone looked like a piece of opaque, greenish glass—nothing more. How could something be so deadly? Belatedly a thought came to her mind. She walked away from her sleeping brother, then struck the gem against a rock. It clacked dully. She groaned, then proceeded to strike again, putting all her strength into the effort.

Ellia sighed. What had to be done, had to be done. About ten minutes later she had repacked her kit, then hefted her haversack. She put on her sunhat so it hung on her back by its strap and looked at Sang again.

Could he make it? She hoped so, for she knew he would accept no more help. He had to find an emerald, then take it all the way back to the shore. Ellia nodded.

She tossed some sticks. They landed on his chest, catching him mid-snore.

"What? Huh?"

"It's me, Sang," she said, retreating to the perimeter of the woods.

"Oh," he said, groggy. "What's the matter?"

"How are you feeling?"

"Where are you?"

"That doesn't matter. How are you feeling?"

"Well—" Sang stretched. "Weak, and I hurt, but much better altogether than yesterday. Say, the sores have stopped weeping!"

"That's good," she said, pausing to feel the slime in her right palm. "I'm leaving now. You are going to search for an emerald to replace the one stolen from you, right?"

"Most assuredly!" He actually sounded happy.

Her eyes began to burn. She stood outside the woods. Quickly she scanned the hills to be sure no one else was around. She called, "Sang, can you hear me?"

"Yes. Where are you?"

"Don't let your pride waste it, Sang! Please! I hid my emerald in the woods not fifteen meters from where you are lying. It's well-hidden, but with work you'll find it."

"*Ellia!* You soft-headed girl! Come back!" Ellia shut out his voice by singing loudly as she ran. By evening she ought to reach the crater again. As she ran, silvery gems of a purer sort than the one she had left behind rolled down her cheeks. Somehow she feared she would never make it to the crater to get another emerald. She had cheated death her due.

Fourteen

The trek inland wasn't quite as bad as the first had been two days before. Without the clouds, the sun beat down on her, and she sweat away precious moisture she could ill afford to waste, but she made better time following the river. She neither saw nor heard minors or dangerous animals. By later afternoon, though, her luck changed. Twice she heard the crunching of boots against the gravel river bank, and mutterings. She struck out across the hills. It occurred to her that the minors she was hearing were probably members of her group returning. When she finally sighted a boy, he was carrying an emerald.

Around sunset, another minor happened on her path. Ellia heard him just in time to scramble around a hill— where she almost ran into a second minor! Ellia dove for some bushes and rolled into cover.

When the minors saw each other, they froze like

251

pillars of marble. Ellia noticed almost immediately that one minor had an emerald while the other did not. She had a sudden, sick feeling. The boy with the emerald waved in a friendly way, keeping one hand hidden.

"Good hunting?" the other minor hailed. He was big. His hair was black as midnight, and his eyes were as green as the emeralds for which the island had been named.

"Quite!" the other returned. He may have been seventeen ritual cycles old. His brown hair appeared muddy; his cheek ticked.

Ellia's heart fluttered when the young boy allowed the other to approach unimpeded. Ellia wanted to cry out, but could not.

The black-haired youth walked within a couple of meters of the other, then lunged. But the boy wasn't about to be taken that easily. Ellia smiled as a knife appeared in his hand with practiced ease. He slashed back, dancing out of reach, weaving a pattern of silver swirls before his antagonist's face. His finesse extended to his use of the arena as he defined it, keeping the attacker always on his guard. Unfortunately, the black-haired youth's hands were healthy and unmarred by char; his victim held an emerald in one black and rotting hand.

Suddenly a slash connected with the boy's arm. Fumbling the emerald, he lost his guard for an instant. The attacker brought his blade across his opponent's face. The boy warded his eyes, but the blade entered his neck.

Ellia hid her eyes, but not quickly enough to prevent glimpsing red liquid shoot through the air. A scream branded the event into her brain. She shivered and tried not to think. "Take the emerald and go," she mouthed silently, holding her face almost to the ground, fighting stomach spasms. Why hadn't she acted, she who saved the world? Why hadn't she cried out? What had she allowed to happen?

A laugh shocked Ellia to her senses. "Ha! So easy! They said no rules apply here, didn't you listen?" he said to his victim. "You killed yourself." He laughed again, then Ellia heard a meaty slugging sound as he made certain three times that his victim was dead. "And I thought the Test wasn't going to be any fun!"

Ellia lifted her head as irrepressible rage took over. She stood and pushed aside the brush. A dry branch snapped.

Startled at first, the victor grinned when he saw Ellia. He tossed his knife from his right hand to his left and back. He chuckled as he motioned with his free hand.

Ellia swallowed the lump in her throat, knowing she had witnessed what had almost happened to Sang. She stood her ground and returned the victor's stare. Everything about the Emerald Island offended her—not the least of which was the presence of the boy grinning at her. She reached to her hip and very deliberately slid her knife from its scabbard.

She circled right until the orange rays of the setting sun were out of her eyes. Quickly she felt out the safe boundaries of the arena and the irregularities of the ground. A stone, trees that could distract there, brush and uneven ground—and the body of the loser.

"What's the matter with you?" the victor said suddenly, breaking the silence.

A different sort of grin formed on Ellia's face. Without unlocking their gazes, she removed her sunhat with her damaged hand and tossed it behind her. She heard the straw cap impale itself in some branches as a cool breeze started blowing strands of her hair. Her opponent's expression became unsure. She gestured for the boy to approach, knowing the revulsion the loose, blackened skin on her right hand would produce.

"Where's your emerald?" the boy asked, ignoring her challenge. He tried circling around her, but Ellia had forced him to a position where he must either walk into the trees or attack. A branch poked him in the side. "Did someone steal it from you? Huh?"

Ellia let her expression go bland. He squinted at her, into the sun. Her instructors at the Stone Coast shrine had taught her how to let her opponent win the battle for her. She watched the minor swallow repeatedly. She let fear brew strong.

"Are you a mute?"

Ellia licked her lips slowly, like a chee hungry for the kill. The minor lunged and sidestepped to her left.

Expecting the move, she jumped left also and brought her knife around. She missed the other's face by centimeters. His unready parry missed by half a meter. His boots scuffed a rock. He had to retreat back to the trees to keep from falling. Ellia's shadow overlapped him.

"So you think you're good, don't you, eh?" he said too loud. "You've one small victory—I have a rather large one."

Ellia pretended not to hear his voice while she figured out what moves she would make. The next moment, he faked a lunge, checking her reactions, feeling out her defenses. He breathed heavily and began to sweat. With her ruined hand, Ellia gestured for him to come closer. When she gestured the third time, he attacked, lunging, slashing down and across—ineffectively. Ellia gave ground. She smiled and gestured again.

Again he slashed, up, left, back, and across. His knife cut air, whistled. He feinted, then came around and stabbed down over his head. Ellia dodged and kept her meager distance, careful not to show any emotion or give any clues to her proficency. Having neglected her practice exercises since the trouble with Comos, she felt rusty; thus when she attacked, she knew the result would have to be sure.

"Come on!" the boy growled. "Are you *afraid*?" He lunged more accurately. The bloody silver streak flashed by like a swooping bird.

Ellia's reflexes betrayed her. She warded with her ruined hand, but without wrap or shield to protect it, skin and muscles ripped. Though nerves were already deadened, she felt a red shock of pain as her hand clenched uncontrollably.

Ellia caught her breath and held it. She retreated a few steps and stared as if unaffected. Her heart beat like a mad drum; she barely controlled an urge to break and run.

"You're a freak!" the boy cried, retreating until the trees stopped him. "You've lost your emerald, and now you're trying to steal mine!"

"I did not *lose* mine," Ellia said in a breathy whisper.

"Oh, yeah? Then where is it? Did you eat it?"

Ellia smiled, though her injury ached so badly she felt lightheaded. "No. I gave it to my brother."

"G—gave?" he said, shocked. His knife stood once in his hand before he remembered himself.

"Some piece of trash like you stole his," Ellia replied. "His Test will be to survive to find and return with the emerald I dug up. There is no rule against giving away an emerald, is there?"

"Or killing for one!" the boy cried and lunged again.

His knife flashed dangerously within her defense. He grabbed for her knife arm, at the same time slashing for her jugular as he had with the dead minor. In momentary terror, Ellia warded off another knife blow. As she struck away his knife, the boy stepped in, bringing up his knee to strike a sledgehammer blow to her groin. He twisted her left arm, ready to break it at the elbow.

But she was not as incapacitated as he expected. She spun from under his grip and stumbled away, unable to breathe, feeling as if her viscera had been rearranged. Yet when her opponent stepped in for the kill, he discovered she wasn't doubled over as he had expected.

He was fast, striking within her defense again. Ellia

whirled away, barely in time. She stumbled farther back, but remained in the arena as she defined it. The setting sun shone in her right eye.

The boy instantly understood the significance of her mysterious recovery. "Blind priests! A girl! A dogtail girl!"

"Yes," Ellia returned, her voice diminished by the pain in her side and groin. "A girl, but this one was trained at the Stone Coast!" She lunged.

As they collided, grunting, she grabbed his knife hand; he hers. But he had a decimeter on her height, kilos on her weight, and her slippery, shaking right hand could barely grip his. Gradually he bent her knife back toward her neck. Ellia brought up her knee. He blocked her with his knee.

The minor was well-trained. Out of her left eye, Ellia saw his knife and her trembling, rotted hand. Her strength was failing quickly. Had she really thought she would ever actually pass the Test? How could she have expected to do what no woman had ever done?

She had done what she could to save Sang. She could do no more, even for herself. Tears streaming down her cheeks, she did something she had never considered before—she gave in. In complete resignation, Ellia let her knees buckle under her opponent's weight.

She went limp.

But she collapsed so quickly that the minor's knife only nicked her temple, cut her scalp, then slashed off-balance into space. An instant later, he fell on her, and lost his grip on her left wrist. Ellia gasped. She shot upward like a skyrocket, crashing her forehead into her opponent's nose. His face cracked. She twisted her knife inward; as he dropped on her again, she embraced him.

"Blind," he hissed.

She extracted her knife from his back. Giving an asthmatic cough, the boy spasmed and withdrew too late from the fatal hug. As Ellia dropped to the ground, he stood, blinked, took a step away with eyes held wide—then tumbled backward. His left hand jerked as if searching for the knife he lost, but after a few heartbeats he was still.

Panting, Ellia examined her ruined right hand and found a useless claw. A bloody slash traveled from her wrist to her elbow. Blood oozed into her eye. She checked her scalp with her ruined hand. She hurt. *What a collection of scars I'm going to have!* she thought.

Then she gazed at her left hand which still grasped the knife. Her hand was covered with blood, all the way to the elbow! Her jaw dropped. She looked down. She screamed and crawled away, retching.

This was a test of manhood? She would pass now, she had her emerald, but how could she live amongst people controlled by a priesthood that condoned the murder of sons by their brothers and the unforgivable treatment of its daughters? Ellia screamed in pain. What had they made her do! She beat the ground until, exhausted, she just lay on the ground and cried.

Eventually the pain in her head dulled, and she regained some control. She could not blame the marionettes manipulated by the puppetmasters, after all. They did not understand or see the disease—they just died because of it, or killed.

She shuddered and levered herself up. Using her knife, she tore the fabric of her opponent's shirt into strips. She wiped the blood from her wounds, then bandaged her head and arm. As an afterthought, she reached out with her ruined hand to close the corpse's surprised eyes.

Her hand wavered. "No," she whispered. "You had free will."

Standing, she walked to where the small brown-haired boy lay face heavenward like his murderer. Ellia bent down and shut his eyes, then clasped his ruined hands together over his chest in a peaceful attitude.

She hoped it would bring his soul some peace. She sighed and dried her tears on her shoulder. She could think of no appropriate prayer for the dead and hoped her tears would do. Then she stood and walked to the hunk of glass that glowed eerily in the waning light.

"Two lives for that?" About the size of an egg and the same shape, the emerald glowed with the same ancient malevolence that had killed ten billion people nearly a millenium ago. With her left hand, the hand she had protected so diligently, she picked up the deadly gem. Refusing to look at it, she walked into the night, forgetting her knife, her pack, and her sunhat. She hoped the emerald's radiation would burn away all traces of stickiness from her fingers.

For the first time since she had entered the Blasted Hills, Ellia knew she must travel on through the dark hours without stopping. Slen rose in a gibbous phase, shimmering as in a fever dream, its face alternately veiled and revealed by filmy clouds which drifted at high speed across the stars. By the time the white-faced moon reached its zenith, Ellia's head whirled each time she gazed upward. She stumbled frequently and had to fight to focus on the gray shapes she passed. Her whole body throbbed with pain. As sure as she held death clasped in her hand, she knew she would die if she stopped. Her wounds still bled, sapping what strength she had left. She craved water.

Her conscious world faded over the hours into a delirium, yet she continued to put one foot ahead of another, unaware that she moved at all. Animal sounds filled the night with song and horror; partially soothed, Ellia heard all of the chitters, squeaks, or jibbers. She knew she could no longer defend herself, but she was past caring. She stumbled and righted herself while she tried to recall what was so dangerous about the fence ahead.

The wind wafted the scent of something cadaverous to her nose. She was smelling herself.

"Gheek!"

Poor tigerstripe, Ellia thought, ignoring the forms loping toward her in her peripheral vision. A tree appeared directly in front of Ellia's nose. The spiteful plant walked into the girl, bounced off her forehead, and left her stumbling about, moaning and swearing. Suddenly her sight was not so blurred. She spotted metal wires about a hundred meters away and changed her course. Things, moving faster than her eyes could track them, trotted circles about her. She swatted out at them, but the annoying flies refused to leave her alone.

"Gheek!" they said.

"Gheek," Ellia coughed back at them. One fly lunged at Ellia's hand. She hit it in the eye with her emerald. She found the usefulness of the sickening thing supremely humorous and began to giggle.

The insects tried again to bother her. Grinding her teeth, she kicked out. She kicked again. The third time she hit. The insect buzzed away, yelping in pain.

As she stumbled closer to the fence, putting one foot before the other became harder and harder. Then, without warning, her right foot went sideways, her left forward.

The gheek-dogs rearranged their hunting formation into a wedge. The lead animal, an old mange-ridden female, attacked.

An instant later, Ellia clearly heard a loud *crack*! Then another, and a third. Fire blossomed in her hip. The world spun, shapes flying and diving and skewing through a phantasm of marching skeletal trees and a flowing sky full of mud. Something inside her snapped and collapsed.

Crack!

Lying on her back, her left leg folded crazily under her, lucidity returned, induced by shock. She had been shot! More shots rang out, and she screamed.

Blood splattered across Ellia's face, hitting her eyes

and almost blinding her. Through the red mist, she stared into the dawn sky between walls of peacefully waving, tall grass.

The soft whistle of the sea breeze rustled the grass as the furious animal sounds diminished, then dissipated altogether into the dawn air. Peace fell like a hammer stroke, oppressive and lonely. She lay shivering for a long, long time, cold and unable to move. Tears pooled in her eyes, eventually flowing down her cheeks. Had she been left to die?

She didn't want to die!

Sometime later, Ellia sensed a large, broad cloud eclipsing her view of the sky, and then something stinging her throat. A soft touch followed. Darkness, cold and complete, descended gently. A spark inside the girl balked when she realized what the cloud really was—a priest.

Fifteen

When the murk began to dissipate, Ellia remembered nothing. Slowly she became aware of her breathing, of warmth, of attention, of being cared for. Weak, she fought to open her eyes. She saw only a little orange light, like a distant campfire, to her right. She focused on it. As she blinked her leaden eyes to moisten them and clear her vision, she saw widely spaced, extremely straight trees which marched down the horizon in the direction of her navel.

She lay where she had fallen! Ellia moaned and allowed the great darkness to engulf her again.

Much, much later, she sensed herself afloat. Her skin felt flush with fever. She became aware of the rough texture of a blanket against her chin. She was laying on a firm platform with something soft and dry under her head. She blinked, and the row of trees resolved into vertical, metal bars supporting a long bar of wood. In the distance she saw an indicator light mounted in the wall. A vine wound across her vision out of her sight: it was a tube feeding into a needle in her arm.

"Kantilphanes! A hospital!"

Excited, Ellia searched her room to see if she was alone. Her head whirled. On a nightstand lay a small wooden box sitting on a roll of parchment, some potted flowers, and a large card propped so that she could hardly miss seeing it. The orange light provided sufficient illumination to make out the words when she squinted:

"I didn't waste it—Sang."

Many more days passed before Ellia became coherent, though she knew she was being tended, and even ate solid food. Eventually she realized that her euphoria had vanished. She felt pain, dull and throbbing, mostly in her right arm and hip. Pain meant she was alive. And Sang was alive too!

At that thought, she opened her eyes and found herself in a whitewashed room with a high ceiling. Late afternoon sunlight angled through open draperies. The intravenous was gone. She looked to her right, saw the orange light and the nightstand. She spotted Sang's card first, then her music box and the parchment roll. She recognized on the inner surface of the roll part of a blue zigzag border—it was her calendar of rituals. So Da knew and had provided her with the two most important items she possessed. Ellia sighed. So what if he knew? By definition of the Test, she was an adult— neither he nor Fan had any power over her any longer.

That was a heady realization, Ellia thought. She was *alive*! Though weak, she managed to kick off the overly warm blanket so that it lay in a heap at her feet.

She saw that a cast encased her right arm, but otherwise she was whole again. All evidence of the emerald sickness had been eradicated. She saw only healthy golden skin where her arms stuck out of her sleeveless hospital smock.

She was alive!

Regardless of all the pain she felt, she felt absolutely, impossibly good. Kantilphanes had given her a second chance at life, and she could not be more grateful.

She broke out in a fit of giggles. She was alive, and they had said she wouldn't survive!

Ellia sighed loudly. Though she barely had the energy to do it, she leaned over, reaching to the night table to swat the switch on the musicbox. She hit the brass button, and one of the never-to-be-repeated, tinkling concertos began, filling the room with a beautiful, sweet sound. Ellia smiled and reached for the card. She nearly pushed it onto the floor, but managed to snatch it from the air. She rolled over onto her back.

She found a paper taped to the inside. She snapped the cellophane, then unfolded the letter and began to read her twin brother's scribble.

Well, Ellia, congratulations.

I always knew you could do anything you wanted to do, and against that the Test was nothing. Nothing? You've been in a coma for two dogdays as I write this, but your doctors are optimistic, and so I am. As you can see, Father came here the moment he got word that I returned and that you had attempted the Test. He sent for your music box in the hope that it might cheer you up. He has told me that he loves you, but—and this is difficult—he says he can never see you again. He says his elder daughter has died and it is none of his business to meddle in the affairs of another woman. I think he had a fight with Fan, and she won. I don't know, I really don't know. He's changed.

Well, on the lighter side, I have contacted Marsai and her parents, and they have agreed to the marriage—as if there was any doubt! I think you approve of Marsai as a sister, don't you?

And guess what? I have met this mythical personage you have talked of in such glowing terms. Tlezachi is definitely nice—and intelligent—he has twice as much as me on the second floor, I can tell you. He'll succeed at whatever he does. And he has good taste too, picking you.

"Sang," she said, shaking her head. She laughed, and continued reading.

I'd better get to the point.

You see, Tlezachi's brother Hoshi lives in the same town I was going to move to with Marsai! Anyway, with the money Father is giving Marsai and me as a wedding present, the four of us— Marsai says she wants to learn to read and I figure that I'll try to teach her, so that makes four—the four of us are going to form a trading company. Sound interesting? Well, I'd like to offer you a part in it with us.

But there is one thing I want to say first, and that is that for once you must do what you really want to do. You have sacrificed for everyone through the cycles. The wagonmaster, Terra, Shana, even this Chriz you have told me about, not to mention Tlezachi himself. Now you have sacrificed for me—and I forgive you for forcing your emerald on me as I understand you could do nothing else. Forgive you? I owe you! You're my sister, and I want you to remember I will always love you, whatever you choose.

This time, *this time*, do for yourself. Understand, girl?

The music box had stopped tinkling. Ellia faintly remembered hearing a door open while she read, but the fact that she was no longer alone did not register until a voice said, "You are awake!"

Startled, Ellia sat up suddenly, pulling her knees up to her chest. Pain like knife strokes flared in her hips and side. She whimpered, barely able to breathe. Shaking, she looked up to see an emerald-robed priest smiling at her. Ellia recognized him as the senior priest who had started the minors from the coast.

The priest walked around to the left side of the bed. "That position certainly looks uncomfortable."

"It is," Ellia whispered, unable to unfold herself. The priest chuckled as he stretched her out. Ellia lay shivering.

The priest shook his head. "Who do you think washed, cleaned, and took care of you these last few days? Your mother? You think you are hiding something other women don't have or I haven't seen?" He threw the blanket over her. Ellia relaxed, feeling immediately warmer.

The priest gazed out the window to Ellia's left, hands clasped behind his back. "You looked like a five-day-old corpse when we found you, almost dead from blood loss. We pumped you full of a blood substitute until we could find your blood type, which turns out to be rare. Your right arm looked like you barbecued it." He turned to smile at Ellia. "We replaced some bones; your right hand from the wrist is entirely regrown flesh, as is part of your hip. I shan't bore you with the other grisly details, but the fact is, once the bandages are taken off you will be as good as new."

"Nobody likes scars," Ellia commented, trying to sound unworried.

The priest looked away toward the door. "Yes, that's why our medical sciences worked so hard to perfect reconstructive surgery. You'll see no man, unless he so desires, with scars in the Emerald Island. We even work on special cases from the People's Collective; we are highly regarded in our art. You've heard of the People's Collective? Yes? Well, keep in mind the perfection we have achieved in your case.

"You see, once we remove your bandages, there will be no physical evidence that you have taken the Test. Any man finding you running about the island will be obliged to find your husband, brother, or guardian and return you to his custody, as is provided in the *Codex of the Unification*."

Ellia sat up, her mouth agape, forgetting her pain. *All for nothing?*

"It's as if you didn't take the Test at all," he continued. "Unless you'd like to go to the Hamure. I understand they sterilize their special women there, though. You could also be a teacher, but somehow that role seems wrong for you."

"It—it can't be. My emerald?"

"It's our official opinion that no woman has ever passed the Test. Who would believe you anyway?"

Ellia sunk back into her pillows. It just wasn't fair. But she understood all right. Unlike the Collective, Emeraline society was not structured to deal with thinking, independent women, and could only deal with them as deviants. Ellia began to feel ill all over again.

"On the other hand," the priest continued, "you could get married. Seventy percent of the male survivors from the Test are married before the end of the first ritual cycle of adulthood. A good man might allow you to get away with a lot, but I don't know. Ten girls have survived the Test in all the years I've been here. Nine were Hamure, the tenth was something like you, but we haven't heard from her since she left the Blasted Hills. It is a shame you did not speak up when we asked you to confess you were a girl. I would have been glad to tell you how much of a waste it would be for you to take the Test."

"I had to find my brother!"

"And did you find him?"

"As a matter of fact, yes! And we both survived the Test."

The priest just shrugged. "You'll notify us if anything works out for you as a result of the Test, I trust? I swear we'll pass on faithfully whatever information you give us. We understand the hardship of the Test and have no wish to waste the experience of any girl."

Ellia stared out the window at the blue sky beyond. Her head hurt.

"And remember your oath. You can't even tell your sons. Be warned, the *Codex* does allow for punishment of women for such a crime." With that, the door whooshed closed behind him.

"Bastard!" Ellia whispered, and balled her free hand into a fist. Tears streamed down her cheeks. "Bastard."

Epilogue

Ellia packed her belongings in a white drawstring bag she found in the closet. She took special care with the music box, but made a point not to listen to it. She sighed and looked about the bland hospital room. After a while, she went to the window and threw open the drapes to let in the hazy afternoon sunshine. The world outside looked hot and unfriendly.

"You can't stay here forever," she said aloud. She drew up her shoulders, suddenly feeling tired. She could stay as long as the bandages were needed and her right hand continued to throb.

In sudden decision, she shucked the smock they had given her and opened the closet. Beside the garments of her disguise—the cape, the dark shirt, and the rust pants—hung three plain sarongs. Ellia selected the rust fabric and wrapped it on. She found no footgear, but she had not really expected any. She cursed loudly, then examined her sheathed short sword and the utility knife. She buckled the weapon belt over her sarong. Finally she gazed at her image in the small mirror hung on the closet door. Doctors had neatly removed the scars on her cheek. Her hair had grown long.

Her one and only souvenir of the Test was on her head. After the knife fight, she had checked out her head wound with her emerald-rotted hand—in that spot her hair sported a silver-white streak in bizarre contrast to the dark red everywhere else. She smiled as she buttoned her shirt.

Minutes later she squinted into the sun. As she stood on the walkway to the hospital, surveying her surroundings, she felt as if everyone who passed stared at her, evaluating the oddity of the weapons she wore and especially the bandages on her right arm. Ellia subconsciously drew herself up to her greatest stature.

She still had to make her decision.

Under her breath she said, "If either Sang or Tlezachi appear to stop me, I will do as they say." She swallowed and turned to see shadowed eyes following her progress. She recognized no one. The heat caused her to sweat as she followed the directions on a signpost to the railroad spur.

As she approached the little ticket building, the line of men in front of the window parted for her, as had the line in the Open City six dogdays ago. The dangerous beauty of the most recent woman to pass the Test caused all to hush. Ellia's lips tightened as she stepped up the window.

The clerk looked up. "May I—" he began, then his words vaporized. No women except the teachers were allowed in this part of the Emerald Island; no doubt he knew all the teachers by sight. "What are you doing here?" he asked, anger roughening his voice.

"Buying a ticket." She laid her bandaged arm on the window ledge and pointed up at the orange schedule board behind the man. The man gulped audibly. "I want a luxury fare for train 248," she finished.

The man stared at the bandages, then gulped again. He appeared hypnotized.

"I said—" Ellia began again, but the man blinked and complied.

"Sure, yes, I'm sorry." She had her ticket in seconds. As a new adult just having passed her Test, her ticket was free. She snatched the piece of orange cardboard rudely. All eyes were again on her as she strode down the brick path to the platform. The wood was cool to her bare feet. Again as in the Open City, a long bench was vacated for her. She dusted off the dirty soles of her feet, then relaxed into the comfortable seat.

In a little while, she rose and purchased a newsheet for a fractional barter. But as she noted first the date, then scanned articles on the intrigues in the Council City, her mind was really elsewhere. Though she did not look up, she listened for any familiar voice. If Tlezachi or Sang were to appear . . . She periodically closed her eyes but stopped short of wishing.

No one came to claim her free will. Soon her train rolled down the three rails. She folded the newsheet and walked for the silvery passenger car, ignoring the blank stares of her companion travelers. With the polite assistance of the conductor, she stepped up into the carriage. She quickly found a seat, and a window through which to stare—as she would for hours, first on that train, then on another.

Sunset had arrived in all its fiery glory as she arrived at the Open City fence. Her pass was honored without question. She didn't even recognize the black-uniformed guard until he asked her if she was still friendly with shags. When she looked at him blankly, he asked her about her strange costume. She told him that she was a woman. His mouth dropped open and stayed open as she walked through the gate.

She folded the pass back into her silver pendant and

let it fall back under her shirt. But as she walked along the asphalt lane into town, she took out Tlezachi's locket. She stared at it, at the engraved flowery pattern darkened with oxidation.

Tlezachi hadn't stopped her. He hadn't even visited her! Her fist tightened over the disk, and she drew it up on the chain to snap it off her neck.

But only her anger snapped. Tlezachi loved her enough to let her do as she wished. Tears pooling in her eyes, she strode on, letting the locket fall against her cheek to lie outside her shirt. She would treasure that single piece of jewelry forever.

Somehow she reached the bay, where she became conscious of the creak of old docks and the oily scent of water lapping against them. Someone walked toward her. She could not mistake that quiet, padding step with its accompanying claw clicks; she turned and fell into a furry embrace. Presently the white shag held the girl away from her and with her fingers collected the tears from Ellia's reddened eyes. The moisture around the shag's own eyes glistened in the light of a street-lamp.

"Chriz," Ellia said, and felt more tears roll down her face. She sniffled.

"You're my daughter now," Chriz whispered, wiping away the new tears. As Ellia smiled a little, Chriz asked, "How fares your brother?"

Ellia looked down. "He's alive and well," she said. "He'll be married soon and probably be very success-ful."

"And Tlezachi?"

Ellia smiled and displayed the locket that lay against her shirt. "He let me go," she replied, "when he could have possessed me by merely asking."

For a long moment the shag remained silent. Then she put her other hand on Ellia's shoulder and spoke in a voice so motherly it almost hurt. "Perhaps such a love ought to be pursued. You may never find it again."

Ellia swallowed but still didn't look up. "Tlezachi trusts me to do what is right for myself."

"But do you trust yourself, little daughter?"

Ellia didn't know.

But she had made her choice. The next day, at the stern of the hydrofoil freighter, she looked back at dark blue smudge fading along a brighter blue horizon. As the wind blew through her hair and ruffled the pages of her notepad, she put pen to paper and wrote: "Forgive me, Kantilphanes, but the *Codex of the Unification* is not honored everywhere. I cannot hold my tongue. Protect me."

END OF FILE

CROSS
REFERENCES: Emerald Island, the Anthropology of,
Changes in, "Emeralds" of, Females of,
Intelligence collection in, Males of, Male
domination of, Population control in, Pre-
adult education in, View of the People's
Collective in,
(INTERRUPT KEY FOR MORE...)

INTERRUPT

PERSONAL NOTE: (Ellia Kellzi)
ADDENDUM TO FILE 2110sea/4031

Here in the Collective, the Emerald Island is shrouded in
mystery, even to those adventurous souls who are in constant
trade with the merchants of my homeland. I sense that I am
considered strange and exotic for the shape of my eyes, my skin's

golden color, and my accent (which fades with time). I hope now people can understand the Emeralines better, understand and learn to abhor the horror they perpetrate on their own seed.

I am an outlaw, I guess, but it makes little difference here. Sang, Kiri, Marsai, and especially little sister Shana—I apologize if ever you read or hear of this account. Please try to understand that I wrote this because the Test is an atrocity. One day maybe somebody will bring an end to it. It is also true that I was able to submit this account in lieu of two years and one season of government service to win Pecol citizenship, and for that I am grateful.

(signed) Ellia, daughter of Della, and in the protection of Kantilphanes—may his name be forever honored—this the 2110th season of the Onnakine Treaty.

---->> SELECTED FILE (2110sea/4031) EXHAUSTED /

About the Author

Born during 1958 in Detroit, Robert Steven Blum has lived in Chicago, St. Louis, and currently resides in Los Angeles. He has hazel eyes, red hair, and likes to wear brown and black.

Interested in science from childhood, he began reading SF when his Uncle Jerry gave him a copy of Andre Norton's *Breed to Come*. He attended UCLA, where he began a major in biology, then switched to Ethnic Arts, specializing in Folklore and Mythology. Robert studied the arts and culture of many nonwestern societies, and he swears to all disbelievers that the strange degree he holds made it possible for him to write believably about alien civilizations. In 1982 he traveled to Bali, Indonesia, the only place left in the world where the arts are essential to society—as he feels it should be.

Robert shares space with Isis, a Siamese cat. He keeps aquariums, programs computers, and is a hacker from way back. Like one of his characters, he also collects plush animal toys.

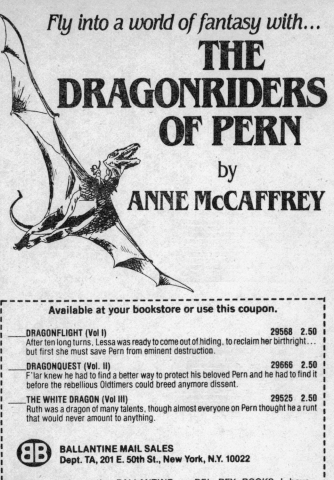